W9-AJM-280

The Pages

The Pages

HUGO HAMILTON

Alfred A. Knopf

NEW YORK   2022

THIS IS A BORZOI BOOK
PUBLISHED BY ALFRED A. KNOPF

Published in the United States by Alfred A. Knopf,
a division of Penguin Random House LLC, New York,
and distributed in Canada by Penguin Random House Canada
Limited, Toronto. Originally published in Great Britain by 4th Estate,
an imprint of HarperCollins Publishers, London, in 2021.

www.aaknopf.com

Knopf, Borzoi Books, and the colophon are registered
trademarks of Penguin Random House LLC.

Library of Congress Cataloging-in-Publication Data
Names: Hamilton, Hugo, author. | Roth, Joseph, 1894–1939. Rebellion.
Title: The pages / Hugo Hamilton.
Description: First edition. | New York : Alfred A. Knopf, 2022. |
"This is a Borzoi Book"
Identifiers: LCCN 2021014700 (print) | LCCN 2021014701 (ebook) |
ISBN 9780593320662 (hardcover) | ISBN 9780593320679 (ebook)
Classification: LCC PR6058.A5526 P34 2022 (print) | LCC PR6058.A5526 (ebook)
| DDC 823/.914—dc23
LC record available at https://lccn.loc.gov/2021014700
LC ebook record available at https://lccn.loc.gov/2021014701

Front-of-jacket photograph © Mary Ellen Bartley
Back-of-jacket photograph by PhotoTodos / Shutterstock
Jacket design by John Gall

Manufactured in the United States of America
First American Edition

The Pages

HERE I AM, STORED INSIDE A PIECE OF HAND LUGGAGE, being carried through the departure lounge at JFK airport. The owner of the bag is a young woman by the name of Lena Knecht. She is getting on a flight to Europe. Bringing me home, so to speak. Back to Berlin, the city in which I was written. Where I was first printed by a small publishing house almost a hundred years ago, in 1924. Where I was rescued from the fire on the night of the book burning in May 1933. The city from which my author fled the day Hitler came to power.

My homeless author. My restless, refugee, itinerant, stateless writer on the run. Living out of a suitcase. Fleeing for his life.

His name—Joseph Roth.

The title—*Rebellion*.

I was born—

I came to life—between the wars. During the Weimar Republic—what they call the waiting room between the First World War and the Second World War. Between what was first thought to be the fields of honor and later became the fields of shame. A time of orphans and child poverty. Women running the cities while men were left behind on the battlefield. Defeated men who came back missing limbs and needed help to bring beer to their lips. Men with nightmares of decomposing hands emerging from the trenches. Cold winters they called God's fist sweeping across from the East. And hunger in the blank expression of a tram conductor munching on a box of chocolates left behind by a passenger after the cinema.

A time of hardship and glamour. A time of revolution. Emancipation, cabaret—love and art without rules.

Everybody was in a club. Everybody wanted to belong to groups and social federations—chess clubs, dancing clubs, dog-breeding clubs, stamp-collecting clubs, orchid-growing clubs. Women's fraternities. Gentlemen's fraternities. Hunting clubs. Drinking clubs. Laughing clubs. Prankster clubs in which members challenged each other to look stupid and eat too much, or reward a passing pedestrian for permission to pour a bottle of wine into the pocket of his trousers.

Everybody was in a league or a trade union. The League of Blinded Warriors. The Association of Newspaper Vendors. The Central Association of German Watchmakers. The League of German Butchers. The League of German Brewers. The League of German Canteen Leaseholders.

Everybody was against something. Everybody had a manifesto. Right and Left. A time of envy and grievance and clubs with closed membership. When a book was no longer safe. When Hitler was already busy plotting to eliminate me and my author, and his people.

What does time mean to a book?

A book has all the time in the world. My shelf life is infinite. My secondhand value is modest. Some devoted collector might pick me up for a few dollars on eBay and keep me like a species gone into extinction. *Rebellion*—I have been reprinted many times. Translated into many languages. Scholars can find me in most libraries. Twice I was turned into a movie.

But here I am in person, first edition, slightly bashed up and faded. Readable as ever. A short novel about a barrel organ player who lost his leg in the First World War. The cover image shows the silhouette figure of a man with a wooden leg raising his crutch in anger at his own shadow.

Lena, my present owner, has the habit of throwing things into her bag in a congested heap—passport, purse, mobile phone, makeup, medical things, a frayed toy duck she's had since childhood, along with a partially eaten pastry. Here I am, living in a dark sack with these fellow travelers, all hoping to be brought into the light of day when her blind hand comes diving down.

Mostly it's her phone she picks out. How can a book compete with such an intelligent piece of equipment? It contains her whole life. All her private details, her photographs, her passwords, her intimate messages. It knows her mind and shapes her decisions. It does everything a book used to do. It behaves like an unfinished novel, constantly in progress, guessing her worst fears and her wildest dreams.

Her father was German, but he didn't speak the language to her. He was a baker from East Germany who arrived in the United States after the Berlin Wall came down and, denied his mother tongue, didn't want to be known as German. His eyebrows were often covered in flour. He came home from work with white eyelashes. And white floury hands that gave him the appearance of a ghost, alive and moving, his inner being left behind in a country that no longer existed. Her parents became uncoupled when she was around twelve. Her mother went back to live in Ireland and Lena stayed with her father in a two-room apartment in a suburb of Philadelphia that smelled of yeast. Where I was kept in a bookcase by the door, unread, unborrowed, until I was handed over to

Lena one evening when her father was dying of cancer. In a slow voice that held on to the accent of a lost country, he made her promise to take care of me.

Look after this book like a little brother, he said.

Is the past more childish than the present? Does history need to be kept safe like part of the family?

I have been defaced a little. Some annotations were written into the margins by my original owner, a Jewish professor of German literature at the Humboldt University in Berlin. His name was David Glückstein. He drew a map on a blank page at the back. It's more like a diagram—half map, half illustration. No specific location given. It shows a bridge crossing a stream. A path with an oak tree and a bench underneath. There is a forest to one side of the path and some farm buildings on the other. The shadows cast by the farm buildings have been sketched in as though you'd have to arrive there at the same time of day to recognize the place. It's a private memory, drawn to remember a day on which the professor stood in the company of the woman he loved, and buried something precious under a sundial to keep it from falling into the wrong hands.

Needless to say, the map has nothing to do with me. It's not part of the original publication. The sole purpose of a book is to live another day and tell the story ascribed to it by the author. In my case, the story of a man with a barrel organ who is down on his luck.

It could be said that I am lucky to be alive. On the night of the fire in Berlin, with a large crowd of spectators gathered on the opera house square to watch books being burned to death, I somehow managed to escape. While all those human stories were being disfigured by the flames and dispatched as smoke and charred remnants into the night sky above the State Library, the professor looked into the future and handed me over to a young student for safekeeping. The student was Lena Knecht's grandfather. He kept me hidden inside his coat. That's how I was rescued and passed down through the family into Lena's possession, why she is now on a flight back to Berlin to find out where that map leads to.

2

FOR WEEKS I LAY ON THE BEDSIDE TABLE, SILENT AND inconspicuous. Nothing more than a lifeless object in the room. I was quietly present at night while they lay stretched out, staring at the ceiling, getting their breath back. How can a book match the living? All a book can hope to do is imagine things in words that have once been true in life.

They are not long married—Lena Knecht and Michael Ostowar. Their wedding took place in Ireland. In a small hotel in Kilkenny, they held hands cutting the cake and smudged each other's faces with a tiny dollop of chocolate as the bride and groom are sometimes expected to do. Their honeymoon kicked off on the west coast, where they stayed a few nights in a lighthouse on Clare Island, waking up to the waves crashing on the rocks below.

They have set up home in the Chelsea neighborhood of Manhattan. Lena is an artist and Michael works in cybersecurity. They talk about starting a family.

Let's have a baby.

As if their lives, their happiness, their sense of belonging to the world, will always remain incomplete without some enduring family context going forward. A baby would give purpose to their emotions. It would turn the intensity of their joy into material evidence.

They've had all those ethical discussions about whether it's right to have a baby at this time. What kind of world would they be sending their child into? What are things going to look like fifty years from now? They can be heard talking about the carrying capacity of the earth. They are fully aware—though he refuses to repeat it even as a joke—of the carbon footprint of a human child being compared to that of twenty-four new cars. They have read the book by Margaret Atwood and seen the TV series about the handmaids being confined as baby machines. They're big fans of *The Matrix*. They love anything to do with space travel. Their favorite movie is called *Annihilation,* about a couple who need to fight through a translucent wall in order to find a way of getting back to each other again. They talk of having a child that might live for two hundred years, maybe longer, an eternal child that would never grow old.

A shout from the future.

On their honeymoon they went to visit art galleries in London and Madrid. It was Lena's wish to stand in front of Picasso's masterpiece—*Guernica*. At the Prado Museum they came across a disturbing painting of Adam and Eve prominently hanging in the main hall. It shows the Garden of Eden with the serpent in the apple tree turning into a smiling baby. What a thought! A human snake-child bringing an end to paradise. Neither of them would have much time for faith-based narratives. To Lena, these biblical tales are no more than a grain of truth turned into art. But she saw in this painting at the Prado some kind of premonition, as though they had been found out. The snake-child was calling time. It's a cruel fact of life that ecstasy can only exist in the moment it comes to an end. Standing side by side, looking at the snake with the face of an infant grinning at them, they experienced those acute expulsion fears that all lovers go through. There was nothing they could do but talk about having a baby of their own. They would love it to bits and turn themselves into the most devoted parents.

Whenever these conversations take place, she tells Mike he will make a wonderful dad. She wants their baby to be a boy, just like him. But first, she needs to be herself. Her instinct as an artist is to convert everything into a visual story. The presence of a child right now might distract her from that goal.

He fears that her creative pursuits might take away those maternal instincts. He usually rounds off the argument by saying, with a touch of irony—if you want to save the planet, Lena, if that's your main concern, to make a contribution to this earth, then you better get pregnant right now, don't waste another minute, because our baby is going to be the next Einstein, or the next Rosalind Franklin, it's going to be so cute and so clever, it will fix everything.

To which Lena replies with a laugh, tapping her belly—let's wait a bit. All right with you there, Einstein?

One night, while they lay uncovered on the bed, she became aware of me on the bedside table.

The book, she said, as though there was somebody else in the room. It made her self-conscious, seeing me right beside her like a human presence listening in. An intruder. A watcher. The snake-child.

She picked me up and looked at the image of the shadow man on the cover with his crutch raised in the air. Pulling the duvet around her legs, she sat up and ran the flat of her hand over my face. She read out the title printed in Gothic font, more like handwriting. *Die Rebellion*—Joseph Roth. The edges scuffed and worn. Faint thumbprints left behind by readers long disappeared from the world. She was unable to read the text of the book in German, but she had already managed to find a translation in the library and read the story of the barrel organ player in English. As she began leafing through the pages, she came across the speck of a mosquito printed like a capital letter in a top right-hand corner. A summer's day begging to be remembered. The scribbled annotations in the margins made no sense to her. She was more intrigued by the hand-drawn map at the back and allowed her finger to cross the landscape as though she'd entered a fairy tale.

Look, she said, this must be a forest of pine trees. She pointed to a wooden shrine with a pitched roof to shelter the icon from the weather. She found an oak tree and a bench. And here, she wondered—is that a monument of some sort. A sundial, maybe?

Mike became a little irritated by the fact that her mind was elsewhere now, as if a book could have the power to come between them.

There's something in it, she said.

As she continued studying the map, she was aware of the duty imposed on her by her father. She made up her mind, there and then, to go to Berlin. She had an uncle living in Germany, in the city of Magdeburg. Her father's brother. He might be in a position to shed some light on that map.

Mike didn't like the idea of her going. His protest came in the form of praise, reminding her how well her career was going. New York was the place for a young artist like her. It was a mistake to move out of that circle. She told him she needed new energy, new raw materials. This would give her a vision to follow—the life story of a book.

I'll miss you, Mike said.

In artistic terms, Lena Knecht would describe herself as a thief. Her work makes use of images selected at random from other media. She has been inspired by the famous final frame of a Truffaut film in which a boy runs away from a detention center. When he reaches the sea and turns around, his static face in that long final shot captures an entire life, all his optimism and all his pain. She looks for those lived expressions online. Her break-out came with a collection called *Misfortune*—a series of images sampled from minor domestic calamities posted on YouTube. Funny scenes of dogs running into doors, people falling off bikes, children crashing into each other. She picks out the expressions of surprise. By slowing these private moments down into stationary images, she removes the comic element, creating something that is both endearing and grotesque at the same time, what some art commentators have described as the inner despair of a world laughing at its own misfortune.

On the day before her flight to Berlin, she managed to find time to visit MoMA. She stood before a painting by Rothko as if she needed to say goodbye. When they say a piece of art speaks to you, it is understood that some visual energy has been transferred from the work to the viewer. And in reverse, a tiny part of the viewer is transposed into the painting. That Rothko painting must have soaked up a million hearts by now. Just as I have accumulated the inner lives of my readers. Their thoughts have been added in layers underneath the text, turning me into a living thing, with human faculties. I have the ability to remember. I can tell when history is in danger of repeating itself.

3

THE MOOD ON THE FLIGHT IS FULL OF OPTIMISM. THE catering cart is on its way. Lena's voice can be heard over the hum of the aircraft. She has fallen into one of those random in-flight conversations with a passenger sitting next to her. They have strayed onto the subject of insects. Driving up from Princeton, the woman beside her says, she arrived at the airport parking facility and was surprised to find there were no insects on the windshield. She can remember driving home at night with her father and the headlights shining through a cloud of insects. As a child, the woman says, she loved the job of cleaning the car, hosing off the dried flies and moths. Often you had to scrape them off with a stick.

To reciprocate, Lena tells the woman about a time she was on vacation in Ireland, when she left the bedroom window of the cottage in Cork open and woke up in the middle of the night with the room covered in bugs. She had left the light on and by the time she awoke the whole room was moving. All kinds of bugs on the walls, swirling around the lightbulb.

Oh my God, the woman beside her says. Did you have to go and sleep somewhere else?

Lena gives a short laugh. An affectionate laugh, turned inward.

No, she says. She couldn't move. She could not even walk across the room through the cloud of flying things to reach the door. She was too scared. Or maybe too embarrassed. All she could do was cover up and hide until she fell asleep again.

In the morning, Lena says, most of them were gone.

At this point, I have the urge to contribute. A book wants to get out there and speak up. I want to tell them that I spent two years on the shelf right next to a small book on insects. It was written by a French author who went out into his garden one day and had the idea of recording all the different species he found there. He named them. Made drawings of them and collected them in his journal as if they were part of his family. It was full of warmth, that book. We became great friends. It was the happiest time of my life, living with all that buzzing, like a constant summer.

But this is absurd.

I cannot speak directly to Lena. I remain a silent passenger. I am nothing until my story is set in motion by a reader. What is it they say about reading—it's like thinking with somebody else's brain? Stepping inside the mind of the other.

And how I crave a reader. Somebody to breathe life back into my pages.

We (us books) tend to stay out of live situations. We talk among ourselves in libraries at night. You think public libraries are quiet places. You should hear the racket, the debates, the sheer volume of opinions going back and forth along the shelves until dawn. Everyone talking at once. It's like an enormous thought-fight. Like an ongoing trial in which each book throws in its own piece of evidence without any conclusive verdict ever being reached. Some books are louder than others. Some downright overbearing and full of self-regard. Some droning on like endless lectures, grinding out warnings. Some brightly feel-good, well dressed, trapped inside their own plot. Some just being themselves, speaking only when they have something to say. At times it's hard to get a word in—the sound of voices rises to a humming din, all cutting across each other like a parliament in session, until the librarian returns in the morning and the hush is restored.

When the food trays arrive, Lena's fellow passenger returns to the subject of insects. In Africa, she says, she once tasted a burger made of flies. You won't believe this, she says. Huge swarms of flies drifting over Lake Victoria. The children catch them so their parents can make black burgers that contain five times as much protein as beef burgers.

Lena smiles.

After dinner, the woman decides to watch a movie with a story set in outer space. Lena is going to listen to some music. She puts the earbuds in and closes her eyes. With her foot, she gently pushes the bag in which I lie awake on my back under the seat in front of her.

For a while, everyone is asleep.

And when the plane lands, when the passengers get ready to disembark and start looking at their phones, when they gather their belongings and avoid things falling out that might injure other passengers, it seems for a moment that they have all been turned into books like me. Each one of them a novel, standing in a crowded aisle, ready to be set in motion. Full of thought. Full of self-fabrication. Eyes loaded with possibility. Like a passenger manifest of alternative plots, waiting for the doors of the aircraft to be opened.

Lena stands up and finds herself being watched from behind, a man trying to guess her story. She is wearing a green leather jacket that has become scuffed at the elbows. Her jeans are torn. There is a tattoo, a gecko, emerging from the shoulder onto her neck. She throws a wave of hair across the top of her head.

Her eyes are instantly engaging, shaking off the observer with a smile. Her smile could be said to be prominent. She grew up with a mouth full of overcrowded teeth. She likes to describe the marriage between her mother and father as a random, ill-fitting assembly of German-Irish teeth, like a three-dimensional print-out of their incompatibility. A mixture of her father's pragmatism and her mother's devotion to dramatic climax. It took years to straighten them out. Now she smiles easily, with an expression that will remind some people of photos taken of Bianca Jagger at late-night parties, seen with Andy Warhol and other celebrities who lived it up long before Lena was born.

She reaches into her bag and takes out her phone—a message to Mike to let him know that she's arrived. The passengers slowly begin to move toward the door. All these narratives glancing around to make sure nothing is left behind before they walk away along corridors following the signs for exit and baggage, holding out their passports when they reach border control.

| 4 |

IT MUST BE THE AIR. THE LANGUAGE. THE UNMISTAKABLE
acoustics of Berlin. That timeless echo of voices reverberating
along the buildings. Lena appears to have strayed into a crowd
of protesters. People moving at a steady pace, calling out their
slogans, with drums beating. They want change. There is no time
to waste—it's our future.

Like a swimmer, she throws herself into the crowd and
becomes a temporary participant in the demonstration, taken
upstream in the strong current. She ends up on the far bank, some
distance down from the starting point. Leaving the human river
behind, she comes into a quiet street and enters an interior space.

It's a café bar. There is music playing. A man's voice singing
about seven days to live your life and seven ways to die. Lena is
swept up into an embrace by another woman. The woman's name
is Julia. Julia Fernreich, the owner of an art gallery in Berlin.

They sit down, they order coffee.

Julia wants to know how things are in New York—tell me
everything. They list off the names of people they both know in
the art world. Julia is preparing for a new exhibition at her gallery.

The room Lena will be taking up at Julia's apartment nearby is all ready for her, but the living room, she warns, is still full of stuff right now, mostly packaging.

By the sound of it, Julia is a big woman, in her late forties. Her voice is husky and confident. She has a large laugh. Her choice of words is full of fight and irony, giving advice, pointing out all the places where she has gone wrong in her own life. She goes right to the heart of the matter and begins to talk about happiness. Wrong goal, she says. I've never heard so much shit being talked about happiness, she says, and the world is out of control with anxiety. We are humming with optimism in a time of doom, she says with a broad laugh. Living in the moment, they might as well go back to religion. Have you ever known so many people talking things up, using positive words like great, fantastic, amazing, awesome, epic?

Beautiful. Tremendous. Terrific. All liar words. It's a triumph of lies. They're running out of superlatives.

In the middle of this, Julia asks Lena if she's hungry—would you like to eat something?

No thanks, Lena says, I'm good.

Happiness does not make people happy.

Look at me, Julia says. Not very lucky in love. My latest partner has just moved out. It's my default situation, getting left behind. Crazy bitch. I still love her. You see her going around on a motorbike.

I have a son from a previous relationship, Julia says. Matt—you'll meet him later. He's a lucky boy. He's got two mothers. He's not entirely without a father either, you know, a male father. I try to make sure we go on vacations as a family once a year, all four of us. Matt has got himself into some bad company, a bit of trouble with drugs. Might have to send him up to his other mother in Hamburg.

I hope he'll be okay, Lena says.

I'm sorry, Julia says. You didn't come to Berlin to hear me complaining.

Then it's Lena's turn to talk about her life. She speaks with a younger voice. The words come up in a wave of enthusiasm. Her body leans forward as she tells Julia that she's hoping to do something new. My work, she says. I hope that being here in Berlin will take it in a new direction. I'm gathering material, let's put it that way.

Go for it, Julia says.

Lena is slow to say this about herself, but her *Misfortune* collection has won her quite a bit of acclaim. Julia already knows about that exhibition at a small Lower East Side gallery in Manhattan and wants her gallery to do Lena's next show. She gives Lena a bit of straight advice. As a curator, she has seen a lot of artists come and go into oblivion. It's not about fame and success. It's about being outrageous. Aggressive. Ruthless. You have all that, Lena. Trust yourself. Tear up the clichés. Allow yourself to do something completely crazy.

Thanks, Lena says.

Take a shit, Julia says, right in the middle of the floor, for yourself.

Lena laughs.

On the back of her success, Lena has managed to get a research grant to help tide her over while she's in Berlin. All she needs is a small studio space.

Let me nose around, Julia says. Maybe we can find someplace. I'll put out the feelers.

The music in the café seems to have become louder. Now it's the screaming voice of a man asking a woman where she slept last night and she replies that she slept among the pine trees, where the sun never shines, and she shivered the whole night through. The singer's voice seems infected with great sorrow.

Julia says—I love Cobain. I mourn him every day. He took a

shot of heroin, he masturbated to a picture of his wife, then he shot himself, in that order.

A shout rises above the roar of the singer. It's the voice of a customer inside the café, sitting at the bar, turning to say—ladies, mind your handbags. A piece of delayed wisdom drifting across the room, which might have been confused initially with the voice of the singer belting it out from the back of his raw throat. The man at the bar repeats his warning—handbag—but it takes time for the word to reach the table where Julia and Lena are sitting.

Julia stands up. The chair howls.

Hey, she shouts. Is that your bag, Lena?

Oh my God.

The bag in which I have been happily recalling my early years in this city is now being hoisted onto the shoulder of a thief making his way out of the café. How come it doesn't surprise me? This used to be the capital of book thieves and disappearing bags. The city of opportunists. Where people were constantly offered the chance to buy back their own possessions at a knock-down price.

I was content inside that bag. Dreaming about my newly printed days, when I was first published. I was well received, if not exactly celebrated outright, a newcomer on the literary scene. I was overshadowed by a bigger, weightier book, with many more pages than mine, a masterpiece about a sanatorium that came out in the same year. It's a book I envied very much. I sometimes wished my author had thought of it. But then, I have to say, I've always been happy with the brevity of my own story about a man who gave up one of his legs in defense of his country and is then betrayed by his own people, forced in the end to rebel against them all.

There is no time for that kind of reflection. I am being rushed out the door onto the street.

My first night home and I get stolen.

You were meant to keep me safe, Lena. I'm supposed to be your little brother, right?

I become conscious of sudden acceleration. I feel myself running along the street. I hear Julia's sharp voice coming after me, as if the shivering singer on the sound system in the café has been brought back to life and has run outside with his burned-out throat roaring along the doorways. A shout like a piece of vocal graffiti. The person carrying the bag is fast, a young man, light on his feet in soundless shoes. Julia cannot keep up with him. By the sound of it, she hurls a beer glass, swiped off the bar counter at the last minute, with extraordinary accuracy, striking my assailant, my wrongful inheritor, somewhere in the back of the head with a solid knock before it crashes in shards on the ground.

Glass in the street. Not something I can forget.

My thief is cursing. He checks for blood. He holds on to his plunder and continues his escape. Julia's shouts fade away and I want to call back like they do in movies—I will find you—but I am taken out of earshot into a nearby park. In darkness, next to an overfilled rubbish bin, my thief calmly turns the bag out. He takes what is valuable to him—passport, phone, money. He throws the bag on top of the bin. He leaves me rejected on the ground. I lie abandoned in the city of my birth, a witness to my own robbery, next to the remains of a Vietnamese takeaway. It begins to rain. A warm, late-summer rain that is nonetheless cold and has the potential to chill me to the core. I feel the dampness under my skin. My pages are beginning to warp.

| 5 |

IT WAS RAINING ON THE NIGHT OF THE FIRE IN MAY 1933. A last-minute downpour threatened to ruin the event. It was too late to postpone plans that had been under way for weeks. A specialist pyrotechnic company had been hired to oversee the spectacle. On the opera house square, they had set up a dovetailed structure of wooden logs doused with fuel. Underneath, a layer of sand to protect the surface from scorch marks.

At the State Library, next to the site of the proposed fire, students were heard entering with their slogans echoing around corridors, carrying with them a list of unwanted books. The list had been drawn up by a disgruntled former librarian who found you could hate books as much as you could love them. My author was on the list. He had already fled to France by then.

A sense of fear ran through the shelves as the titles were called out. Books saying quick goodbyes to each other as they were being tied up in bundles with twine, ready to be carried outside. The students worked diligently, using their considerable learning skills to search the catalog for titles to be torn from the canon like bad teeth, passing them along in a human chain to the site of the fire outside on the square.

Incompatible with the national interest.

The students had an air of triumph. This was their moment. Their revenge on learning. All those years spent sitting at desks, forced to love books they detested. Their hearts and minds were no longer dedicated to books but to new infrastructure, the auto-bahn. This was their chance to step outside received wisdom and take part in a glorious act of self-vandalism. Returning to a time before knowledge. The right not to know.

Unlearning everything but the spirit of the nation.

As it happened, I was not in the library myself that evening. My author's books were part of the catalog at the State Library, but I belonged to a professor of German literature by the name of David Glückstein. He had brought me with him in his briefcase to Humboldt University on the other side of the square because he was unsure how far this cleansing action would go, whether the students would also be going into people's homes, which they later did. In his office, the professor had arranged a meeting with one of his trusted students, where I was quietly handed over for safekeeping.

The student's name was Dieter Knecht—Lena's grandfather. A tall young man with a soft voice, given to reading more than to athletic pursuits. He was about to finish his undergraduate degree in German literature. He took me in his hands and they spoke about my author for a little while with some fondness.

By accepting this contraband novel, by rescuing this single volume from the fire that evening, Lena's grandfather set in motion a quiet wave of resistance that has continued to this day. It was a small but significant event taking place behind closed doors, away from the catastrophe outside. It changed the course of people's lives. It had an impact on decisions made later under entirely different circumstances, long after the book burners disappeared.

Hearing the chants and slogans in the corridor, Lena's grandfather swiftly tucked me inside his coat, next to his heart. He held me in place with a stiff arm across his chest and made his way out, down a wide set of stone stairs.

Outside on the opera house square, the fire was going strong. Students had already raided the offices of the Hirschfeld Institute for Sexual Science. They railed against filth in literature, against sexual freedom, capitalism, Jewish dominance, as they called it. The human chain leading from the library to the site of the fire continued delivering the hated books. Each author was denounced in a summary trial, the name called out, giving a reason why they no longer fitted into the national vision, before their books were committed to the fire. All this was being broadcast by radio around the nation.

My author belonged to what was called asphalt literature, the new writing of multicultural cities.

The first books to be thrown into the flames were written by Karl Marx. Followed by many more Jewish authors. An author who was mistaken for being Jewish by the sound of his name and later protested vigorously at being maligned in this way. A woman whose female characters showed too much self-assertion and didn't fit in with the Nazi ideals of motherhood. *The Magic Mountain* was spared from the fire but his brother *The Blue Angel* was not. A playwright who wrote about a man who has his genitals blown away in battle. And the more famous playwright, whose *Threepenny Opera* had won huge acclaim in Berlin and who later wrote a poem to express how glad he was not to be left out—burn me, please don't leave me unburned.

Among the spectators gathered around the fire, a woman's voice was heard saying—beautiful time, beautiful time. What did she mean? Rejoicing at this new anti-intellectual age in which you could stop thinking, when you no longer had to find out anything you didn't already agree with?

More and more books were being added to the flames. A man in a white shirt recoiled from the slap of heat when he got too close. Fire brigade attendants stood by. An author whose books were being burned in front of his own eyes had to leave suddenly when his name was called out.

Many of the books burned alive that night had something to do with war. Books that refused to glorify death. Non-heroic accounts of men with missing limbs and severed spines and lung trouble. Men with half faces. Berlin was full of shivering men sitting in rooms with their families unable to make sense of them. All those descriptions of casualties were to be taken out of the public domain because they were deemed bad for morale and they put people off war, encouraging a poor attitude toward death and suffering.

As a journalist, my author reported on his visit to a hospital where two thousand five hundred men lay recovering, all born healthy and remodeled on the battlefield. A soldier went out to the front and came back a fragment of a man. Living war memorials, he called them. One of the men he met in that hospital was missing his lips. A grenade had struck him in such a way that he was otherwise completely unhurt, only his lips were gone—unable to kiss.

The main character in *Rebellion* is based on these damaged men. A war veteran by the name of Andreas Pum who finds himself in a military hospital full of broken bodies. He has lost a leg in action and received a medal. Like the other invalided soldiers, he envies the shivering man because he will be looked after by the state. When Andreas finally goes before a commission in charge of handing out livelihoods, he drops his crutch in a panic and falls into a fit of shivering. A moment of luck. His shivering is the making of him. It draws the empathy of the officials watching him fall and he is instantly rewarded with a license to play the barrel organ. A secure future as an artist opens up for him, playing a rotating selection of eight tunes around city streets. He takes up lodgings in a house with a sausage thief named Willi and his lover, Klara. She works as a cashier and earns money on the side. Andreas watches her undressing. He hears them kissing and falls asleep dreaming of love.

The story of this decorated veteran, with no intention of harming state laws or doing any more than earn a living, was now classified as unworthy of life in literature.

Lena's grandfather stood watching the fire with me tucked inside his coat. The faces of the onlookers were lit up in the warm glow of the flames. Their eyes turned jet black. Their lips were green. Their nostrils inhaled the pungent paper-smoke that came from those books, like the smell of burning hair.

It was a bonfire of life stories. The pages were curling and flying in black scraps over the rooftops. These imagined lives, these human thought-roads, were being turned into worthless heat. The words were no longer bound together in sentences. They had been discharged of all meaning. From inside the flames came the sound of voices rising in a collective stream of consciousness, extracted like free prose from the text, a ghostly recital of absurd phrases and detached bits of dialogue. Expressions of love. Men calling their mothers. Crying children being removed from their parents. Homes turned to ash and family histories dissolving into vapors in one long, silent scream of pity that could be heard right around the city.

Just before midnight, Joseph Goebbels came to make a speech. Microphones had been set up for him away from the fire. Some bottles of water on a small table in case he got thirsty. Wearing a beige coat and speaking in a voice that overestimated his stature, he praised the students for their cleansing action. He said it was the end of Jewish supremacy in literature. No more asphalt writing. Time to regain proper admiration for death.

He spoke about the will of the people.

| 6 |

THE DEALERS STAND AROUND IN THE PARK ADDRESSING their customers with soft voices in the dark—everything okay? Need anything? They pick up their stash from under a bush and do their deals by the overfilled rubbish bin. What do they care for a book about an invalid? They come from countries where they've had enough war and missing limbs. Countries where boys step on land mines and play football without the kicking leg.

Beside me, the Vietnamese takeaway has little more to offer the world. Its contents have already been digested and converted into clubbing energy, followed by sexual energy, followed by sleep, followed by more clubbing energy in a wonderful sea of bodies before it is eventually turned back into soil.

A rat comes running across my face. The tip of his rubbery tail lies on my author's name—Joseph Roth. His pink illiterate eyes are on the Vietnamese takeaway as he urinates and sniffs, prevented from getting at the remains inside the single-use plastic container. The rat shows signs of pulmonary dysfunction. Some poison, perhaps. Blood thinners. What is good for humans can be bad for rats.

A man, a bottle collector, forces the rat to retreat into the shadows while he roots through the overfilled bin. He takes an interest in Lena's discarded shoulder bag and tries it on. It has the stolen look, so he puts it aside and takes out two bottles of Beck's Gold, which he adds to his expanding nightly collection of clinking glass.

Would he not be interested in taking a discarded book back to his shelter for the night? A seller of antique books would give him a couple of euros. But he has other priorities and walks away with his blue IKEA bag full of spent fun.

Hey—his story is not unlike that of the man working the streets with his barrel organ. Joseph Roth was a champion of the homeless. As a reporter, he wrote about men sleeping rough. That homeless shelter in Berlin where they ran a cinema for the guests every morning at nine thirty. He wrote about the women on the streets, the prostitute with the golden smile, the woman accused in court of giving poison to her men to steal from them. He stood by the beggars, the unemployed, the missing, the murdered. Dead faces with no names. A dead man released from prison after serving a sentence of fifty years, staring in wonder at the traffic on Potsdamer Platz.

He wrote about a man collecting cigarette butts. How the weekend yielded a better crop. He asked his name and invited him back to the hotel where he was staying, but the cigarette butt collector never came. He got into the habit from that point on of throwing away his cigarettes with a longer butt, in the hope that everybody else would feel generous too and leave something for others to find after dark.

And the disabled war veteran who found a nail file on the street. What use could that instrument be to a man so badly damaged? Filing his nails as though that's all he needed to restore him.

He wrote about the migrants. Women arriving in Berlin carrying children like sacks of laundry on their backs. Followed by a child crawling on crooked legs, nibbling on a crust of bread. A young man with his hands in his pockets dreaming about getting away on a ship from Hamburg to New York. And the family arriving with scissors, ruler, a needle and a spool of thread, ready to set up in business.

In public discourse they became known as the Threat from the East. Which is where my itinerant author was from. He understood the need to keep moving. He never had a birth certificate. Never had a father. His place of origin in Galicia (now Ukraine) was twenty percent Jewish, a community that would soon disappear from the map.

The rain has stopped, but the night is cold.

A book doesn't want pity. Literature is a long game. There is no shame in living among the discarded. Obscurity can have its vivifying air, one of my author's successors liked to say.

My patience finally wins out. A young man wipes the rain from my face with his sleeve. I am held up to the light coming from the street. And you know what, it becomes instantly clear that this man is a reader. Some intuitive affection spreads to my damp heart as he begins leafing through the pages. It's an emotional thing. A refugee book in the hands of a person who gulps in the first sentences before he places me into the pocket of his jacket for later.

What luck!

We reach an apartment. We enter a kitchen where there is music playing. A female voice singing about walking on water. My new custodian is greeted by two men and a woman who invite him to drink whiskey with them and I hear his name for the first time—Armin. They offer him a joint, but he decides to go to his room.

He lies on his bed and enters the story.

Andreas Pum, the invalided soldier. The dampness in the air causes pain in the stump. His missing leg continues to send messages of distress from a desolate landscape where it lies buried among thousands of other severed body parts calling for their owners to come back and bring them home. Whenever the clouds build up and the rain comes in, the missing leg feels the pain and the stump begins to mourn.

On a good day, playing his barrel organ in one of the court-yards, a woman asks him to play his saddest tune for her. She has just lost her husband. He gives her the song of the sirens luring men to their death along the Rhine. A sorrowful melody which he renders with great feeling while she stands leaning out of the open window listening. Katharina Blumich is her name. The woman of his dreams. She invites him inside when it rains and gives him food to eat. They fall in love. They get married. She provides him a warm home and buys him a donkey so that he no longer needs to carry the barrel organ on his back. People love his music and the money comes raining down from the windows.

| 7 |

A SMALL CREATURE CRAWLS ACROSS THE SHEETS. A PAS-
senger brought from the park. Armin sits up and positions his
hand in the path of the earwig. It climbs on but soon walks to
the edge and falls off. He tries a second time. Once more the earwig falls off. On the next attempt the earwig seems reluctant and
turns back, so Armin stands up and carries the lost insect to the
open window. It has no sense of gravity.

Armin goes back to reading.

From the kitchen, the sound of talking can be heard coming
along the corridor. A burst of female laughter from a head thrown
back. They stop laughing abruptly, as though they have been
reminded of something serious that cannot be laughed at. After
a short pause, they set off again and the joke seems even more
funny the second time around.

Somebody has begun to knock on the wall. The night is full of
noise and counter-noise. Next door, or maybe in one of the apartments above or below, somebody feels offended, or excluded, by
these sudden explosions of laughter. The knocking, wherever it's
coming from, has a lonely quality, like something people do in

prisons, the signals of a solitary person trying to communicate with the world. It's hard not to imagine the complainant standing on a bed, or a table, jabbing at the ceiling with the handle of a broom, desperate to know what's so funny.

And then it appears the knocking is coming from another source entirely, from a couple fucking somewhere in the building. The beat is rhythmic and methodical, possibly the sound of a headboard banging against the wall, or a chair being whipped back and forth on the floor. It could be any one of many possibilities. We cannot be absolutely sure, of course, that what we're hearing is love. It could be that somebody has decided to hang a picture late at night without any consideration whatsoever for the neighbors, hammering a nail into the wall and then placing the picture up, standing back for a moment only to discover it's too high, the nail needs to be taken out and a new one hammered in just slightly below. But then the hammering gathers pace. Too much urgency to belong to any spontaneous, late-night redecoration plans. Better to go back to the chair theory. The chair, if it is a chair, seems to be moving steadily from one side of the room to the other, speeding up like the sound of a horse galloping across the bare floorboards and turning around when it reaches the wall.

By now, the counter-knocking has come back. The person complaining downstairs has become so worked up that the broom handle poking at the ceiling sounds like encouragement. The knocking downstairs has become an assistant to the knocking upstairs, urging the couple on the chair to hurry up, for God's sake, get this over with—the happiness of others can be so infuriating. The entire house has become connected, participants in this magnificent sexual act. The couple getting carried away in one room, a misanthropic individual responding with furious indignation down below, people in a kitchen laughing their hearts out, while in a room nearby, somebody is trying to read a book.

One of the men in the kitchen comes to Armin's room and

opens the door. He wants to know why Armin hasn't joined them for a drink—the night is only beginning.

Maybe later, Armin says.

He continues reading the story of Andreas Pum making his way around the city with his barrel organ strapped to his donkey. Business is good and he's thinking of buying a parrot to enhance his act. He knows which courtyards to avoid. Where they have signs erected saying—no begging, no peddling. He sticks to the places where his tunes are welcome. Where children come to stare in fascination at the fairy-tale scenes painted on the side panels of the barrel organ. Where coins come floating down from the windows wrapped in tissue paper, so as not to injure the donkey.

He plays the national anthem when requested. It makes people feel good in these times after the First World War when they have lost so much. He can vary the tempo and the emotion of the melody by altering the speed at which the handle is turned. Sometimes he plays it as a waltz. Sometimes he plays it to the pace of a stirring march. Sometimes he plays it as a requiem to reflect the plight of a nation in defeat. And sometimes he plays it as a lullaby, comforting all those who cannot sleep at night because of the agitation and the resentment that has taken over the streets. Angry invalids with no money in their pockets have begun to march with placards calling for the government to be brought down. The shivering men with nothing more to lose, all protesting against the state.

Andreas Pum is a law-abiding citizen with no grievance against authority. Proud to pull out his busking license whenever a policeman asks. His luck revolves around that crucial document issued by the state. It gives him a place in society. It validates him as an individual. It allows him to eat and be hungry. It gives him the right to live, to love, to be happy.

At the time, the barrel organ represented a considerable

investment, somewhere between two and three thousand marks. According to my author's newspaper reports, the number of musicians working the streets of Berlin was estimated to be up to twelve thousand. Licenses were awarded exclusively to war invalids. They did best in the open with passing trade, not so well in the courtyards. Blind organ grinders had it tough because they could not tell a theft from a donation. Working the barrel organ involved no skill apart from the minimum requirement of one arm to turn the handle. There was something exciting and artificial about the mechanical sound of this machine, a little fake like all new technology, soon to be overtaken by the radio, which could deliver an entire orchestra right into the living room. Andreas Pum was fortunate to have acquired the most up-to-date barrel organ. With manufacturing improvements, the old barrel organs whose tunes were worn down and which played only an intermittent handful of wheezing notes were thankfully being phased out.

Sadly, the story of the organ grinder inevitably enters a downward spiral. He is vulnerable to the favors of the community. Having left the donkey and his musical equipment at home one evening, he goes into the city for the first time on a recreational outing. Celebrating his luck and his reasons for being alive. His marriage, his home, his family—his place in society is assured. Now it's his turn to be generous and give some busker a coin.

On the way home he rewards himself by taking the tram and runs into a businessman of good standing who swiftly brings about his downfall.

The businessman runs a successful haberdashery firm. He is married with a family, but he sees nothing wrong with desiring and eventually attacking his young secretarial assistant in the office. It's a classic case of sexual harassment in the workplace, an abuse of power in which the man in a position of authority subjects the young woman to a violent assault. At the top of her voice she lets him know that she is engaged to be married and finally escapes. Next day her boyfriend, a gifted bird imitator, arrives at the haberdashery firm to accuse her employer of attempted rape. He announces his intention to sue for damages and refuses to be paid off. He wants her honor to be restored and turns the office into an aviary with a spontaneous performance of his best bird calls. He continues delivering his shrill repertoire of ornithologically verifiable hits until the haberdashery owner is driven into a rage.

On the tram that evening, the businessman takes it out on Andreas Pum. With the deafening bird imitations still piercing his head, he refuses to move aside for the organ grinder. He accuses this decorated war veteran of simulating his invalid status. The wooden leg is a fiction, he claims. Easy to let on that a real leg is prosthetic. Andreas Pum is used to people standing up and offering him their seat. Now he's been called a faker. The city is full of fakers, the businessman says. They have been out demonstrating with placards all day, these revolutionary cripples, trying to disable the state. The businessman assumes Andreas is one of them. Another passenger concurs, saying the man with the crutch is probably a Jew into the bargain. At which point the offended organ grinder, who fought bravely and lost his leg on their behalf, raises his crutch in anger. A policeman is called. The law sides with the businessman. Andreas Pum has his license removed.

He becomes undocumented.

| 8 |

BEFORE I FORGET.

On the day of the book burning, Joseph Roth's work had already been quarantined in a restricted section inside the Berlin State Library. Right next to the site of the fire on the opera house square, his books were stored in a place set apart for toxic literature. Available only with special permission. Shielded from the general public, even from students who wished to burn them. This special status inadvertently protected many of them from the fire, at least in Berlin if not elsewhere around Germany. As he continued publishing in exile, each new title was added to this collection. Whenever Nazi troops entered a new country on their march across Europe, they would come upon copies of his work and ship them straight back to Berlin to be stored in this chamber of contaminated books.

When the bombing of the capital city started, most of the precious stock of ancient books was taken from the library to be housed in a safe place outside the city. Ironically, the special category of illegal books was rescued along with the more cherished volumes. While the Berlin State Library was destroyed during the war, these banned items were kept safe in a remote mansion near Köslin, now part of Poland. Years later, after the Berlin Wall came down, two of Roth's books from that reserved collection turned up in a Polish library. Originally printed in Holland and shipped by special courier back to Berlin, they received the Berlin State Library stamp, then they were taken away to safety in a country mansion and eventually made their way to the university library of Łódź, where they are now, once again, available to the public.

The day after the book burning in Berlin, Lena's grandfather brought his copy of *Rebellion* with him to his hometown of Magdeburg for safekeeping. He passed by the site of a similar fire which had been lit on the main square of his own city, then he went straight home and stored me away in his small, growing library.

This time, I was placed beside Goethe. Schiller. Fontane. Büchner. Safe books, so to speak. Reliable masters that kept me company in relative peace. They tolerated me, perhaps even got to like me a little.

I remained safe on those shelves for some years. My keeper took up a position as a schoolteacher in Magdeburg. Professor Glückstein disappeared from the teaching staff at Humboldt University, so it was hard for Lena's grandfather to return me safely to my original owner. What intrigued him was the curious map at the back. He wanted to know if there were any further instructions, what the map depicted, where it was located, and whether there was something he should know about or do when all this trouble with book burning was over. He waited for the professor to contact him, but there was no word.

As a student, he had once been invited to the professor's home for a literary evening at which a number of people had gathered to celebrate the launch of a new collection of poetry. A woman read a selection of poems while about twenty people sat in the library on chairs on a summer evening with the doors onto the terrace open, and the words were carried off across the calm surface of the lake. At the reception on the terrace afterward, he was introduced to the professor's fiancée, Angela Kaufmann, who also worked at the university in the philosophy department. Among the distinguished guests at the gathering that evening was an author Lena's grandfather had admired from an early age, the writer of a book called *Emil and the Detectives,* the same writer who stood watching his own books being burned in the fire when a woman turned to point at him—look, that's him, there he is.

Lena's grandfather still had Professor Glückstein's address in Wannsee. Knowing that any mention of a banned book would place them both in danger, he wrote to ask the professor if he had time to meet and talk about some of the latest books being published.

There was no reply.

One Saturday morning, not long after the day of glass in the streets, he took me down from the shelf and placed me on the table. He then pulled out a well-known novel by Theodor Fontane and placed it beside me. A classic called *Effi Briest.* The story of a woman who falls in love with her husband's friend, an army officer by the name of Crampas.

We lay side by side on the table, like some comparative exercise.

A knife normally used for cutting meat was brought in from the kitchen. Lena's grandfather sharpened the knife and began to carry out a piece of urgent surgery that changed my life. He cut out the pages of the Fontane novel. The slicing of paper produced an agonizing squeak, like a stale crust of bread. I was surprised there was no blood. Once the vacant space had been hollowed out, he placed me inside the covers of the Fontane book as though I were being measured for a coffin. I was given a new title. A new author. I had become a stowaway. Like a duplicate key hidden inside a book to be brought to a prisoner in jail.

I am Effi Briest, I said to myself.

From that moment on, I saw the world from her point of view. I watched her getting ready to go and meet the army officer named Crampas.

My author would have studied this book at university. Some part of the Fontane story had already become transposed into mine. Books have a way of dwelling like parasites, carried forth in the minds of readers, turning up by force of succession in later works of art. I was part of that living chain of ideas reaching into the future.

Under Fontane covers, I entered a double life. Hiding underneath Effi's winter cloak as she leaves the house on the day of the fateful sleigh ride with Major Crampas.

After Christmas dinner, her story goes, the guests depart on a recreational outing into the snow. On sleighs pulled by horses, they travel through the winter landscape by the sea and come to a hidden river. The horses know it's too dangerous to cross. The party must seek an alternative route, and while the rest of the guests return to the house by carriage, Effi follows her husband on a daring route back through the forest. At the last minute she is joined by Major Crampas, who jumps onto her sleigh, saying he cannot let her travel alone.

This is the point when they become lovers. She falls under a spell from which she has no wish to escape. In the movie version, they are placed inside a carriage, stopping for a brief minute in a clearing. A deep silence that feels like the interior of a white room.

Here is the love scene described by Fontane—

Crampas speaks her name softly in her ear. He prises apart the fingers of her tightly clasped hand and showers them with kisses. She is about to faint. When she opens her eyes, they are out of the woods again.

After that, her world falls apart. Her husband discovers the affair in her letters and she is ousted from the marriage. The child she gives birth to is taken from her. She descends into a deep depression.

Once I had been implanted into the folds of this tragic story of a woman's quest for freedom, Lena's grandfather brought me with him on a journey back to Berlin. It was winter, not unlike the day of the treacherous sleigh ride. There was no point in going to the university, so he made his way out to Lake Wannsee. The lake was frozen over. People were skating on the ice, making designs like handwriting on the surface.

He found the house where Professor Glückstein lived and rang the doorbell. There was no answer. He waited for a while, then he began looking in the windows. The rooms seemed empty. He walked around to the back of the house to see if everything was all right. On the terrace overlooking the water, he placed his face up to the glass, but it was hard to see inside with the bright reflection of the lake. He discovered the back door onto the terrace had been left open, so he entered the library in which he had once been honored to belong to a literary salon. The room was abandoned, with books strewn all over the floor.

What are we doing here? Don't stay in a place that has been so desecrated by haters of books.

We heard voices in the hallway and were forced to hide behind one of the bookcases. My heart, Effi's heart, was pounding inside my chest. She was out of breath. A tiny cry emerged from the back of her throat and I thought for a moment that her sense of guilt and adventure might give us all away. Two men came into the library carrying boxes of letters and other documentation. They began searching through this material and when they found what they were looking for they went back through the hall into another room. At the first opportune moment, we made our way back out onto the terrace and slipped away through the gardens onto a lakeside walk.

| 9 |

BACK IN MAGDEBURG, IN THE HOUSE WHERE LENA'S grandfather lived with his aging mother, there was a knock on the door one morning. It was the same two men who had gone through Professor Glückstein's documents at the house by the lake. They now came into the library and began searching through the shelves where I was kept undercover inside *Effi Briest*. I felt the security of her cloak around me as well as the respect of other classics. I was placed right next to *Woyzeck,* that great figure of human jealousy and natural destruction, the unfinished drama about a soldier who kills his lover after she sleeps with a drum major. Perhaps the barrel organ player should have done the same when his wife, Katharina, called him a useless cripple and began to seek the affections of a police officer with two legs, but he merely turns his sorrow like a knife on himself.

As the men were searching through the shelves, book by book, they asked Lena's grandfather why he had written to his old professor in Berlin. He no longer had any connection with Humboldt University. Lena's grandfather said it was a courtesy, nothing more, just to see how his former literature professor was doing. They accused him of belonging to a degenerate group of academics who were conspiring against the state. They sat him down and began to question him more thoroughly. One of them took his wristwatch off and placed it on the table to show they had all the time in the world.

My author would have described the chief interrogator as a man with a beige-colored face like unrisen dough, thin lips that hardly covered his teeth and yellow ears that were translucent against the light coming from the window.

We know you have it.

What?

You were his favorite student.

He's a brilliant lecturer.

You became friends.

It was the classic interrogation scene in which each party gives away as little as possible. The person under questioning pretends to know nothing. The interrogator pretends to know everything.

Lena's grandfather responded to their questions by saying he had no idea what they were talking about.

All this time, I was worried that Effi might open her cloak and let out the faintest sound of the barrel organ.

Nobody mentioned the title, but it was clear as daylight that they were looking for the book with a map at the back. The map led to untold rewards. Everyone was aware that David Glückstein was the sole heir of a paper industrialist and that, like many family traits that skip a generation, he had little interest in the wealth that had fallen into his hands, preferring to devote himself to the pursuit of literature and art. The father produced raw paper—the son became the end user. He was more interested in what could be printed on it, particularly those books written by new revolutionary authors like mine who defended characters with no wealth.

The chief interrogator told him not to waste their time. It was another one of those well-worn interrogation strategies in which the person under questioning is reminded that there is a limit to politeness. It led to a moment of confusion in which Lena's grandfather said he had no idea what book they were referring to.

The interrogator smiled.

What makes you think we're looking for a book?

Why else would you be searching the bookshelves?

The innocence of that answer displeased them. Still refusing to mention the title, the interrogator simply said in a voice that was now depleted of all patience—you know the book I'm talking about.

Tell the truth, the other man shouted.

At that point, Lena's grandfather became aware of how little the truth mattered to them as long as they got what they wanted. He could avoid a lot of trouble by handing over what they were looking for. He decided there was no way out but to be perfectly honest with them, even going so far as to mention the book in question.

You mean—*Rebellion,* by Joseph Roth.

Exactly, the chief interrogator said.

Lena's grandfather began to explain how the book had come into his possession. On the night of the book burning, he told them, a copy of that banned book had been given to him for safekeeping by the professor. He had wrestled with his conscience, he explained, not knowing what he should do with it. He didn't want to be seen with the book he carried under his coat out of the university. As he emerged onto the opera house square and saw the crowd standing around the fire, he told himself to do what every good German would do under the circumstances.

Of course, the interrogator said eagerly.

I had to do the right thing.

What's that?

I threw it into the fire.

It was one of those moments in police questioning when the lie sounds just right. Not only plausible but politically fitting. The interrogator clearly found the words hard to disbelieve. It was impossible to argue with a double bluff.

The interview was brought to a conclusion. Perhaps the men were already thinking of other ways in which the information could be attained. The interrogator picked up his watch and put it back on his wrist in a feigned gesture of satisfaction. Just to be certain, they carried out another search through the bookshelves, and for one moment they picked *Effi Briest* out as a suspect. But they were not readers. They failed to see what she was hiding and left empty-handed.

THERE IS NO WIND. IT'S LIKE A FUNERAL MORNING. THE mist in the streets of Berlin seems to bring the city to a standstill, even while everything is moving. The people Joseph Roth described a century ago are back in their starting positions. Same lives down the road in history. The little girl pouring sand on a balcony. An old man reading a book in his room. The young man in a parallel room putting on some music, sending out a fragment of sound into the city.

A fragment of a fragment, he called it.

Inside Armin's bag feels like being in the back of an ambulance. You follow the imagined street map in your head. Another five hundred meters straight ahead, then left. We have now reached the market stalls on Hermannplatz. Where the shopping center once stood like a giant anniversary cake with two towers, before the bombing took it away and it was replaced by, what, a shopping center with no towers and no swimming pool on top.

All around, the flow of people passing by like a library in motion. Books gathered in clusters around fruit and vegetable stalls. A melodic book shouting special offers on avocados. A steady stream of books going down the escalator, joining the books already waiting on the platform. Books getting off and books getting on. A last-minute book, rushing to jump in before the doors close.

That musical gift for hearing what cannot be seen—it was something the organ grinder had. The ability to distinguish the tiniest sounds. His ears became sighted. He knew the difference between the hoofs of a carriage horse and those of a dray horse. Between the old and the young. Between the weak and the strong.

My fellow travelers this time—a notepad, a measuring tape, and a laser distance meter. Armin's livelihood involves measuring empty spaces. As part of a research project, he has been tasked with surveying sites around the city such as gas stations and parking facilities which have been given over to private motorized transport. In his notebook, he has recorded the details of a single-story corner site, once a beer store, then a Starbucks outlet, now an Italian restaurant. The aim of the project is to calculate the available vertical space, how many housing units could be provided once the capital has been turned into a green zone.

I have now become a measurer's assistant.

Only one thing troubles me. I am carrying a cargo of cash. Inserted between two pages right in the middle, there is a bundle of banknotes. This calculable world of money gives me a bloated sensation. Have I now been turned into a wallet? I want to renounce this wealth. I want to be a book that carries only its own literary content, a vehicle of storytelling, not for transporting money.

On a street of twenty languages, Armin steps into a barbershop. He sits on the waiting bench. In front of him there are two men draped in black sheets, buried up to the neck, it seems. On a TV screen a woman is seen walking along a beach, singing with the sunset behind her.

The men in the barber chairs show implausible levels of masculinity. The man on the left is getting a buzz cut, leaving a full black beard untouched. His eyes are fierce and self-hostile—that's how I imagine it, ready for a fight with his own reflection. The other man has a pointed beard and a tattoo of what looks like a chainsaw on his neck. He's getting a skin fade, but again, the beard stays. The space underneath their barber robes is spring-loaded with musculature, as though they are both armed.

Are men always going to war or returning from war? Either defeated or going off to fight in a conflict that is already lost? Are these men getting ready for some unknown enemy? Maybe a big fight with nature. A battle with water. Without water. With fires spreading.

This sacred cutting room where men face themselves in the mirror with great intensity while the barber works on their external appearance. It's a day of reckoning. A place to reflect and fess up and collect the latest news. Joseph Roth wrote a newspaper piece a hundred years ago about a man who walked into a barbershop and started talking without any introduction, giving a stream of political developments to the silent men in their chairs.

A large fly has entered the room, taunting the men, making their strength appear ludicrously overstated. One of the barbers tries to chase it out from behind bottles of spray with the use of the hair dryer. The fly is blown away in a hurricane, lifted vertically like a helicopter.

The overwhelming masculinity of the two bearded men, along with the barber's deep voice and the scent of aftershave, makes Armin feel androgynous. He will tell this story about himself later. A memory of childhood in which he was once turned into a girl at school. For a minor misdemeanor, he was dragged out from his desk. The master decided to bring him over to the girls' section of the school, where he was dressed up with a veil over his head and made to sit at the back of a classroom full of girls. They kept turning around to giggle at him as if there were something funny about being female. He sat there wearing his veil for a full day, inside the life of a young girl, waiting to escape back into his own body as a young boy. He tries to forget that memory of the time when being a woman was a form of punishment.

The barber picks up a magazine with a woman in a swimsuit on the cover. He slaps it down on the counter with lightning speed. The big fly is dead. Twice dead. Once in life and once in the mirror. His black corpse is carried over to a bin, where it becomes part of a vast collection of cut hair. The fur of a dozen men has become his grave.

A new customer enters the barbershop and sits down on the waiting bench beside Armin. He is in his forties. His leather jacket makes a squeaking noise as he grabs me out of Armin's hands and begins leafing through the pages. He takes the money I've been storing and counts it, then he puts it away in the inside pocket of his jacket.

What's a Muslim doing reading a book in German?

I'm not Muslim, Armin replies.

You were born Muslim, the man says. Chechnya, right? You can't just take it off like a coat. You can't just leave it behind on the bus and say it's not mine. You're a Muslim until you die, my friend.

I grew up here, Armin says.

It's in your shit.

The man is clearly not a reader himself. He doesn't even want to know what the story is about. The life of a barrel organ player is hardly going to interest him. He uses me to scratch his thigh.

Tell your sister, he says, she's a beautiful woman. I love her. I don't even see what she's missing. In all honesty, it's not something that ever bothered me. A lot of other men wouldn't want that.

Armin makes no reply.

Tell Madina from me, I'm the only man who loves her for who she is.

Armin refuses to be drawn.

It was me who set her up, the man says. Without me she would never have become a singer. I got her off the ground. Don't let her forget that. Without me she is nothing.

He stands up and reaches over to borrow a razor from the counter.

Excuse me, he says to the barber. Just for one second.

He begins neatly cutting out one of the pages from the middle of the story. The pain is something else. Now I know what it was like for *Effi Briest*. It happens to be the page where the barrel organ player gets in trouble on the tram. Where the businessman refuses to make room for him and he's forced to fight his way on board, only to be called a faker. Where he's called a Jew and immediately seen as the aggressor. A peace-loving man cast out of the community. For allowing his anger to show on the streetcar, for raising his crutch in retaliation, he will be charged with public disorder and forfeit his right to happiness.

This page contains my author's entire worldview on social injustice.

The man folds the page he has just cut out and places it alongside the money in his pocket. A part of myself has been amputated now, like a severed limb. Any sales description would need to include my true condition. Slight water damage. A spot of thief's blood. A trace of rat's urine containing Weil's disease. A hand-drawn map, as well as a wide selection of thumbprints, dead and alive. Not to mention that faint smoke inhalation from the night of burning books.

And now, this vital page missing.

Before he hands me back to Armin, a flyer falls out from in between my pages and he picks it up from the floor. He takes his time to examine it before he puts it back inside again.

Gallery Fernreich is pleased to invite you to the opening of an exhibition of new work by Christiane Wartenberg. The collection is being launched by *Tagesspiegel* critic Ronald Kolterman. Auguststrasse 89. Mitte. Drinks—5:30 p.m.

He stands up and raps his knuckles on the wall behind Armin's head. Armin sits in a dream, watching him stepping out into the street and going out of sight. One of the barber seats becomes vacant. The barber slaps the chair to let Armin know it's his turn now to be a man.

WE GO IN OFF THE STREET THROUGH THE COURTYARD. The sound of drumming can be heard coming from one of the apartments, followed by the explosive rip of an electric guitar and the howl of a mouth organ. A shuffle of notes blowing through the staircase in the house at the rear. On his way up, Armin is spoken to by an old man who says—this has got to stop, this noise. I have an underlying lung condition. Look, I work on a capacity of forty percent, you probably have eighty percent. I wear this oxygen generator all day. See this fucking tube, the old man says. If I didn't have this under my nostrils, I would collapse.

They're going on tour very soon, Armin says. They're only in Berlin until Monday of next week.

I can't eat while this is going on.

Why not?

It's too unsettling.

The old man with his pulmonary condition is right. Music gets into the lungs. He's got his own harmonica solo keeping him company day and night with a run of howling notes. I have the incessant wheezing of a barrel organ coming from inside my chest.

Armin opens a door and the full volume bursts out like a phys-
ical assault. The musicians carry on playing while he goes over to
kiss his sister, Madina. She is playing the guitar and doesn't even
stop for a second, talking to him without losing a beat. Keeping
the rhythm going like two separate rooms in her head, one for
music, one for language.

The harmonica player has the lungs of a whale. He submerges
himself into a recurring riff with his eyes closed. He seems to have
no need to refill his lungs. He has the power of a dozen oxygen
generators. He is like a diver who is able to reach inhuman depths
underwater. Nowhere can you detect where he breathes in, as if
his respiratory system replenishes the oxygen from an unknown
source. In a further insult to the pulmonarily challenged man
downstairs, he's a smoker. And it's clear why the old man with the
tube in his nostrils is so upset. It's lung envy. He wishes he could
squander a breath, even one puff.

The music stops. The musicians lay down their instruments
like a cease-fire and go out for something to eat, leaving Madina
alone with Armin. The man downstairs must be breathing like a
whale. The silence spreads like clean, unused air down the staircase, out into the courtyard.

I met him, Armin says to his sister.

Uli?

I paid him.

Jesus. You should have ignored him.

He follows me around.

How much?

It's nothing, Armin says. All done now, you don't have to
worry.

Madina sits down behind the drum set. She picks up the
drumsticks and unleashes a sudden rage, lashing out in all directions, right to left and back again.

The money has nothing to do with it, she says. He's getting

his revenge for me bringing this fucked-up relationship with him to an end. Like I've taken something from him that he owned. And you know what, this is the funny part, Armin. He's married. I only found that out recently. He's married with two kids. What does that tell you?

She gives the bass drum a solid kick.

He even got me to go for counseling, she says. I had to attend a group therapist, like it was my problem that his affair was not going well.

Armin sits down on one of the speakers.

It's all right, he says. He's been paid off.

That's what kills me, she says. I've already paid him back. I booked his flight to Warsaw. His hotel cost me a fortune, well over what he ever spent on that guitar.

You owe him nothing, Madi.

I don't know who he met in Poland, she says, or what they put into his head. When he came back, his language was altered. Spouting all this stuff about white Europe, closing borders and not letting any more in. Migrants are only good for wiping the asses of an aging population. I had to remind him that his own father was Russian—Bogdanov.

That's his pressure point.

He started calling me his Chechen girlfriend. Chechnya. Where is that? We hardly know where it is, right. It's irrelevant where I come from. He calls me his little migrant girl. His Muslim chick. Have you ever seen me pray, Armin? Have you ever seen me wearing a veil? We don't know a word of the Koran, right?

The drumsticks are threatening to go again. She does the initial click-click to signal another number coming up, then she holds back.

He made me feel accepted, she says. Like some kind of endorsement. He was validating me, as an artist. As a human being. Made me feel I belonged here like everyone else. He was good at saying there was nothing wrong with me. Good at telling me that he loved me the way I was, you don't notice anything missing when you're in bed. You know what that is, Armin—controlling. Passive aggression. Humiliation by praise. Every time he overlooked my disability, every time he watched me getting dressed and said I was beautiful regardless, it was a punch in the stomach.

Used to put on that song—"Perfect." Like a joke.

Then he wants a refund, she says. And now I find out he's married. I got his phone one night when he was drunk. I had to check out who his new friends were.

Madina drops the drumsticks and walks across the room to embrace her brother.

I'll pay you back.

She picks up the guitar and begins to strum a steady rhythm. A single power chord over and over. Along with the beat, like a spoken lyric, she talks about their adoptive father in Frankfurt and how he used to tell her to put her anger into her art.

THERE IS A PHOTO OF MY AUTHOR AS A SMALL BOY, LOOK-
ing like a girl. Joseph Roth with dropping blond curls and a round
hat on top of his head, a four-year-old cavalryman sitting on a
wooden horse holding a stick.

He came from a place in the East where the Austro-Hungarian
cavalry frequently rode through his town. A place called Brody,
close to the Russian border. He kept the sound of hoofs in his
head. His childhood landscape was like a Chagall painting, with
fiddle players and weddings in the sky. Old Jewish men with
beards and black coats. Men selling roasted chestnuts on the corner. The moon looked in the window at night and laid snow out
on the roofs. A cold hand on his mouth as he went to school. The
window frames shrank and swelled with the seasons, letting in
the heat in summer and the ice in winter. The lives of people living indoors was not unlike the lives of people on the move. They
boiled potatoes in the fields every autumn and ate strawberries
with mud on them in spring.

Juice and mud, exploding in his memory.

In his own words, he grew up with the Gypsies of the Hungarian Puszta, the sub-Carpathian Hutsuls, the Jewish cabdrivers of Galicia, the Slovenian chestnut roasters from Šipolje, the Swabian tobacco growers from Bačka, the horse breeders of the steppe, the Ottoman Siberians, the traders from Bosnia and Herzegovina, the Hanakian horse dealers from Moravia, the weavers of the Ore Mountains, the millers and the coral sellers of Podolia.

An unusual child?

The only son of a single mother. Not much of an athlete, more bookish. He kept pet spiders in his room and fed them flies. Going to sleep, he imitated the sound of hoofs. His fingers were covered in ink. His handwriting was tiny, like needlepoint. At school he got the better of his classmates by copying out an entire poem by Schiller on the back of a postage stamp. He told them his father was good with horses. Fabrication became necessity. He needed a story to go out the door with and so he became the boy novelist who told them his father was a horseman, a cabdriver, a Polish officer, a drunkard, a thief, a vagrant, a madman.

Seventeen different versions, they counted.

The truth was that he never met his father. Maybe that's what happens to all men, he must have thought growing up: they fall in love and go insane. After love there is nothing but fatal illness and death. The loss of his father would become a hidden story, stitched into his characters, writing as his own form of love-madness.

His mother sang sad Ukrainian songs. Dependent on the help of relatives, she pinned her hopes on this gifted child and loved him like an overheated room. A son to compensate for lost dreams. She kept him to herself inside the parameters of a legend, never allowing anyone to come and visit. He loved walking along the wall by the graveyard, looking at the tombstones, but she wanted him to stay at home.

My author has her in his books—a mother who conceals her scheming in tiny complaints about jam. Crystals of sugar starting to form over winter storage. She begins a curse that she cannot allow herself to finish. Her sorrow spreads in hardened glucose across the bread in the morning. Rooms with withered violets and sputtering candles. The manure of horses in the street. Peddlers coming to the door with rain in their coats. A landscape of brown leaves that turns to snow and mush and spring again. Time to go searching for strawberries, even though the foresters will chase the women away and overturn their baskets and stamp the gathered fruit of the empire with their boots. But the forests are so full of strawberries that nobody can stop fresh jam from appearing on the table.

A mother who wears a monocle hanging from her waist and puts it up to her eye in silent accusation, giving her access to his boyhood desires. His thoughts of escaping on the back of one of those cavalry horses off to some distant fringe of the empire. She drops the monocle as though she has seen something unspeakable in his thoughts that cannot be put into words.

A mother who inhales and sighs.

A mother who sits down at the piano to play Chopin. Her face lights up like a young girl's in the candlelight, but when her kind white hands hit the keys, there is no music. The piano remains silent. He raises the lid to look inside and finds the strings have been removed.

A mother who wants to possess her son like a cashbox and thinks all other women are thieves trying to steal him from her. She will never give her consent for him to love another. He will say that his mother was the only source of happiness he ever knew, but still he runs away to Vienna. He volunteers and goes to war.

He witnesses the body parts of men distributed around the fields. He comes back to report on the half-men, the men who only partially return, still wearing their military overcoats for warmth, a brigade of beggars and street musicians that look like bits of fog moving through the city.

Everywhere, that asthmatic whine of the barrel organ.

And Friederike.

He meets her in a café in Vienna. She's eighteen. She's with a friend. After an exchange of jokes, he runs out into the street after her to get her name—Friederike Reichel. Her laughter is infectious. Her dark hair is cut short, dropping in a straight fringe across her forehead. Her eyes are full of provocation. She has already promised herself to another man, but that will not stop her from changing her mind.

She's afraid to tell him that she is Jewish, in case he might not like her. He tells her nothing about being Jewish either, until he finally meets her parents, then he calls them his mother and father.

He goes to see his own mother, dying of cancer in a Viennese hospital. Surgeons have removed her uterus and she is in extreme pain, but she notices that his shirt is torn and gets up to mend it. She wants him to look right. When she's finished, she climbs back into bed and dies. Once her body is taken away for burial, he learns that the medical staff have kept her uterus for examination, so he wants to see it with his own eyes. He stands there saying goodbye to his mother's womb in a kidney-shaped dish.

His Jewish place of origin, with lovers flying over the rooftops and strawberries bursting with mud and potato fires burning in the sky and the roasted chestnut vendor arriving in town with his dog-drawn cart.

They will call him a perpetual traveler. His letters reveal how frequently he can cross the city like a bird. He avoids public transport and prefers to walk so he can talk to people in the street as if the world is full of relatives. He is more at home in hotel rooms now, with a small suitcase by the door containing the most essential things—some clothes, cravats, a notepad and a dozen sharpened pencils.

He loves Friederike like no other.

Frieda.

Friedl.

There is little time left. They must live urgently. A quiet Jewish wedding—Joseph and Frieda—in happiness beyond imagining. He takes her to Berlin. They stay in hotels and eat out in restaurants, like a honeymoon for eternity. She accompanies him on assignments. Sometimes he leaves her alone in her room and comes back late. There is something fragile about her health that is like a forecast of the time they live in. Like some unknown illness spreading through the streets.

In a letter to his cousin, she writes to say that she's been having some trouble with her arm. My arm got very bad, she writes, and hurt a lot. The swelling has begun to go down at last. She still has a cough and takes a hot bath, aspirin, gets into bed to sweat it off. She's worried about him. He's gone out to the theater. It's already twelve midnight, she writes, and he's not back yet—what do you think of that, shocking!

13

HE LIKES WATCHES. HE CANNOT WALK PAST A JEWELER'S shop without stopping to stare in the window. He spends the money earned from writing newspaper columns on a new watch, then he goes for a drink to celebrate, proudly taking it out to make sure it's still working. Then he brings it back to the hotel and takes it apart, just to see how it's made.

Friederike observes him laying the microscopic parts out on the bed one by one. Each component placed in order on the white sheet like parts of his mind. The world reduced to these tiny metal fragments in a hotel bedroom next to the train station. The sound of a late train arriving from the East bearing the scars of giant hailstones on its roof. People with suitcases checking in downstairs. The rattle of a key in a door.

How is he going to put all those fragments back together?

He can read what's coming.

There is a weakness in the people after the war. They are open to slogans. The boundaries between fact and fiction have become so dissolved it's hard to tell the difference. As if people have now developed an appetite for dishonesty. The lies they like to hear. Rogue words to match their resentment. They want the blame for their losses to be placed on the vulnerable, the unwelcome, those from elsewhere.

He has been out collecting what he sees. The streets are filled with people like the organ grinder playing the national anthem on demand. Refugees in police stations needing help to fill in the forms. Paramilitary gangs fighting in the courtyards. The trial of the assassins who murdered the Jewish foreign minister Walther Rathenau. And the trial of the Munich Beer Hall Putsch, which has turned Germany into a carnival. The tomb of history, he calls it, out of which the dead have arisen and made their way into court to speak up for Hitler. A grotesque dream which the people have begun to accept with indifference.

On a train through the Ruhr Valley he meets a young black man with blond hair and blue eyes. Describing this tall, confident, half-French, half-African man is like describing a version of his own contradictions, a Jew born with blond hair and blue eyes. The passengers are perplexed by this paradox. The black man speaks fluent German, his mother tongue. To rub it in, the black man is a reader. A lover of German poetry. He reads passages of Goethe aloud to his friends. He doesn't need blue eyes or blond hair to be German.

Never have people of difference been under so much suspicion. The language has become twisted. Everyone is either a friend or an enemy. People are waiting to see what will happen before they can decide what needs to be done. He will accuse the literary community of being submissive. What right do writers have to be any more reluctant to scream than ordinary people on the street? How can they be so passive now, so fearful of losing sales? He will say that never before have writers been as loud as they are now silent.

The public has been taken in by a new kind of impartial reporting in the media that gives falsehood equal billing. The balanced view. This is the era of distortion, when everything can be instantly refuted. A numbness has entered the vocabulary. All information has become unstable, as though everything contains an equal opposite. If something is said to be safe, then it must also be implied unsafe. The lie appeals to your fears. The truth is too much trouble.

Why am I so concerned about separating truth from lies? As a novel, I belong to the invented world in which you wish things to be true. It's a little secret we keep, between me and the reader, we agree to suspend too much questioning. It's like watching the scene in a movie where they never inhale the cigarette. Where a woman is seen pouring tea without steam. Where she holds the scalding teapot with both hands in such a way that would normally make her drop it and scream.

He spends hours putting the tiny parts together. Little by little, the cogwheels line up in a pattern that seems so arbitrary. He sees how beautiful and complex this is. Like trying to fit bits of memory together in a story that will spin again. The fragments make no sense now. The parts laid out belong to watches not even in the room. Mismatching components rolling off the bed, out the window, scattered throughout the city, on the streets, in bars, in silent rooms where people are afraid to sleep because they worry about waking up again.

Friedl watches him with love in her eyes. Her female conviction shines in a room full of chaos. He looks up in disbelief, as if the watch is made up of more parts than required. He is left over with a wheel that doesn't belong. He sees missing fragments that no watchmaker has imagined.

She stands at the window and sees her reflection in the madness that has taken over the streets.

And then he suddenly has it. The watch is functioning again. Yelping like a boy, he holds it up and makes her listen to the ticking. It's well past midnight. She kisses him. Her happiness is measured in hurried minutes. He lays her out on the bed like a disassembled watch.

14

IT'S FIVE THIRTY IN THE EVENING. ARMIN IS ON THE U-Bahn. The passengers are making their way home or heading out for the evening. An accordion player gets on with a small drum machine on a porter's cart. Once the train is in motion, he plays an upbeat country wedding tune. He might be from Ukraine, or maybe Romania, Macedonia—his music evokes remote places with traditional haystacks on stilts, potatoes baking in the fields, and chestnut roasters.

We hear his music over the clacking noise of the train rushing through the tunnels. We hear his drum machine like a heartbeat. A coin drops into a plastic cup which has been cleverly attached to the top of the accordion. The accordion has also been decorated with a series of small cymbals which ring like coins to create the further illusion that people are being exceedingly generous.

The musician times his departure perfectly at each station so he can rush around to the carriage behind and begin the same routine again. Each carriage brings its own luck. The passengers can look through the glass in the connecting doors and see him playing the same country wedding tune without any sound.

At the next stop, a young woman comes into the carriage holding up a street newspaper. In a hoarse voice, she politely apologizes to the passengers for the disturbance, but if they had some spare change she would greatly appreciate it; if not, she wishes them a pleasant evening all the same. Her voice seems detached. The words are like foam in her mouth.

Armin gives her a coin and she thanks him, staring for a moment into the cup in her hand as if the single coin cannot even begin to address her needs in life.

At the next station, with the usual turnover of passengers getting on and off, the homeless woman becomes suddenly desperate. She spots a woman coming in with an attractive brand-name handbag that gleams with prosperity. She is so taken by the sight of the handbag that she cannot help seizing the opportunity of reaching out to pull it off the owner's shoulder before the doors of the carriage close again. In shock, the owner of the bag tries to hold on. A silent tug-of-war develops in which the homeless woman and the owner of the bag have time to look each other in the eyes. It seems as though the homeless woman wishes not so much to get the contents of the handbag as to step into the life of the handbag owner. For her part, the handbag owner is determined to hold on to her own life and avoid turning into the homeless woman. It would not take much for these lives to be exchanged.

The doors are prevented from closing and the train is held up.

Passengers both on and off the train are simultaneously reporting what is going on as if they are watching a clip on YouTube. For a moment it is no longer clear which of the women is the true owner of the handbag. Bystanders are unable to intervene. For fear of being punched, or sued, or contracting some disease. Everyone stands back. Finally, a man shouts the word— *Polizei*. This seems to re-establish true ownership. The homeless woman is forced to let go and they are both sent stumbling back in a jolt by this sudden release of forces for and against.

The train doors close and the lives of both parties in the standoff race apart in such different directions. The owner of the handbag is reassured by kind words from other passengers, while the homeless woman stands on the platform as though in a dream, just waiting to be apprehended.

If Joseph Roth were alive today, he would be writing about what happens next to the homeless woman. How she is taken into custody by the police. They ask for her identity papers and her address, though one of the officers already knows her from a previous incident. They find witnesses on the platform who tell them what happened. Not unlike the barrel organ player, she faces the same rigors of the law, everything is written down in the records. She has now become a danger to passengers on the U-Bahn and needs to be taken away.

In the case of Andreas Pum, our fictional antihero of a century back, his altercation on public transport leads to him being sentenced by default to six weeks in prison. He leaves his home and his marriage. The barrel organ is no good to him now that he has lost his license. He goes back to stay with his friend the sausage thief. The sausage thief tells him to remain in hiding, the law will never catch up with him. But then there is a knock on the door one morning and the police come to take him away. It turns out that his wife has revealed his hideout.

The homeless woman vehemently struggles to retain her freedom. Appealing to bystanders for help, she screams at the police officers—you're hurting me. Help. Brutality. They're breaking my arm.

One of the officers picks up the tattered issue of the *Motz* off the platform.

As gently as possible, they lead her up the escalator, past

the kiosk selling kebabs, into the waiting police vehicle. She is brought to a place of safety and offered medical assistance so she can wear off the effects of the drugs. Instead of being formally charged with attempted robbery, she is cautioned and eventually released, but her life is not unlike the story of the barrel organ player, leading to an accelerated death.

Armin gets off the train. After a short walk, he enters an interior space where a small gathering of people is standing around holding glasses of wine, listening to a woman making a speech. It's the voice of Lena's friend Julia Fernreich, the gallery owner.

In my view, Julia is heard saying to the crowd, the work here represents a significant shift in how the artist takes on the world in which we live. Those of you familiar with her previous work will no doubt be aware of how she uses random words taken from literature, such as Kleist and Fontane, transposing them into her art in a way that one reviewer described as pieces of silver dug up from the earth. In this current show, Julia says, the artist is questioning where we have come to in our time. The most compelling take on our present world is to be found in the piece at the end of the room.

At this point, all the people in the room turn around.

This series of prints, Julia says, contain words taken straight from the web. From Google Maps, she has transposed specific directions to a place called Paradise in California, where many people died as wildfires engulfed the town. The words map out the linear route from Berlin via JFK airport, all the way by road to the site of the fires.

After the applause dies down, Armin reaches into his bag and takes me out like a lost glove. He stretches his hand up in the air and holds me high above the heads of the crowd for everyone to see, with the title facing out—*Rebellion*. It doesn't take long before Lena comes rushing toward him through the crowd and speaks with some excitement.

The book, she says.

Armin brings his arm down and passes me over into her hands.

How did you find us?

The flyer, Armin says with a smile. I found the gallery flyer inside. So I took a chance.

15

A BOOK KNOWS. I'VE SEEN THAT LOOK CROSSING THE room between Effi Briest and Major Crampas. It's there in the glances of Madame Bovary. In Molly Bloom's thoughts. It's there in thousands of novels, the libraries are full of chance encounters, new beginnings, those breathless possibilities of attraction, people running toward each other with a huge volume of little things unsaid. It's there in many of the books written by Joseph Roth. In the story about a man falling in love with a woman who is brought to his house in shock after surviving a nearby train crash.

They spoke in English. Lena pulled Julia over by the arm and made Armin tell the whole thing again from the start, how he had found the book in the rain, how he had discovered the flyer for the exhibition inside. Julia shook hands with Armin and Lena offered him a drink. She held me under her arm as she carried over glasses of red wine. I could feel the excitement in her lungs.

Two people brought together by a book.

In the follow-up conversation, after Julia had gone to introduce more people to one another, Lena told Armin how I had been rescued from the book burning by her grandfather, and now, obviously smiling at the coincidence, she said I had been rescued all over again. Making that direct link between Armin and her grandfather seemed to say that she was welcoming him into her family.

My father gave me this book, Lena said, before he died. He told me to look after it like a little brother and I went and lost it. I'm so grateful to you, Armin. She began leafing through to find the hand-drawn map at the end and said—look, this little map, I want to find out where that is.

The manner in which she moved closer to Armin and held the page out for him to see appeared like a gesture of intimacy. She might as well have been holding his hand.

I'm sorry, Armin said, somebody cut a page out in the middle.

How did that happen?

It's a long story, he said.

She waited.

My sister's boyfriend. He's not much of a reader.

Don't worry, she said.

As they continued talking, I found myself taking on the role of intermediary, turning loss into luck, matching the finder with the seeker.

Lena revealed that she had read me in translation before she left New York, though sometimes, she said, you can find yourself reading a book without knowing what to look for. There was warmth in her voice. She said it was a sad story, but somehow uplifting in the end. She wondered if you could still find a barrel organ in some antiques shop.

You want to buy one?

See how much I can make.

Why not?

A woman playing a barrel organ, she said.

You'd clean up, he said.

The story of the organ grinder had finally become relevant to the living world. She said she loved the part where he's in prison, when he finds a section from a newspaper in the exercise yard and brings it back to his cell to read the announcements in the personal columns. Like he's smuggled in a piece of the outside world. The people are brought to life as he calls out the names.

The engagement between Fräulein Elsbeth Waldeck, daughter of Prof. Leopold Waldeck, and Dr. med. Edwin Aronowsky. Between Fräulein Hildegard Goldschmidt and Dr. jur. Siegfried Türkel. The bank manager Willibald Rolowsky and his wife, Martha Maria, née Zadik, announce the birth of a son.

Then he sits in his cell and gets depressed. He feels excluded from their joy and cannot be part of their celebrations. He might have been better off not finding that page of the newspaper.

Armin said he loved the passage where the barrel organ player asks for a ladder to be brought to his cell so he might feed the sparrows at the window. The request has to be made in writing. The organ player is given pen and paper. That gives him hope as he crafts the letter. But after careful consideration his request is denied on the grounds that it would be inappropriate for a prisoner to have a ladder in his cell and that feeding birds would violate the principles of punishment.

Lena suggested going for a drink. A couple of us are going to a place down the street from here, she said. The gallery crowd and the artist. A small celebration. Would you like to come with us?

Sure, thanks.

It's a nice evening. We can sit outside.

Sounds good, he said.

They spoke only very briefly about where they were from. He told her he was from Chechnya. She tried to discover more but he said it was a long time ago, he came to Germany as a child. She told him that she was living in New York and had come to Berlin to track down some relatives.

There was a warm glow in the sky. Waiters coming to take

orders. People eating schnitzel. Beer being brought to tables and empty glasses ringing. A woman slapped her ankle and said she was being bitten. A man was overheard saying—okay, I'm going to say nothing more. There was music coming from inside and a string of festive lights hung between two trees. The tables were set out as though they were on the deck of a ship. While they were waiting to be seated, Julia said she had something to show them. She linked arms with Armin on one side and Lena on the other.

Come on, she said. A small touristy thing.

She brought them both inside the building to show them the ballroom upstairs. A tango lesson had just come to an end and the dancers were standing around talking. It was a spacious room with high ceilings and giant mirrors. She pointed at the bullet holes in the mirrors, dating from the Russian conquest of the city at the end of the Second World War. The cracks in the mirrors were like huge cobwebs radiating out from each bullet hole. Imagine them coming up the stairs in their heavy boots, she said, drinking and dancing and firing off their weapons.

16

EVERYBODY SAYS FRIEDERIKE IS BEAUTIFUL INSIDE AND
out. The most attractive woman ever seen in Berlin literary cir-
cles. Her heart is open to the world. Her unaffected smile makes
everyone feel welcome. It's the dimples that spring up on her
cheeks, the schoolgirl mischief in her eyes. The freedom in her
long white arms.

She's in every one of my author's books.

Here she is in a novel called *The Blind Mirror*.

Fini, a young woman who works in a warehouse, falls in love
with a violin player whom nobody warned her about and who
soon betrays her. She is heartbroken. She then falls in love with a
talker, but he's no better because he leaves her and goes traveling
on endless writing assignments. He sends her money, but she's
only interested in love and puts the money aside. She stops eating.
She walks out of the city and comes to a river, where she drowns.

What does Frieda make of this story?

Friedl.

Like the character in his novel, she used to work in a fruit-
and-vegetable warehouse in Vienna and supported her parents.

She married a talker who sends her money whenever he's away working as a journalist. She buys new clothes. She likes to look good. But she gets lonely and stops eating. Living in hotels makes her feel estranged. She doesn't like to go into restaurants alone, pacing up and down outside the entrance without going in. Fearful of his friends talking about literature, to which she has nothing to say, only that she is married to a writer whose manuscripts she reads in his absence. His stories are all she has to hold on to until he comes back. Sometimes she's afraid to go out and sometimes she's afraid to stay in, because the radiators start making noises like people whispering.

She is not cut out for all this traveling. His disfigured idea of home is making her ill. He is a man with no borders, in fear of standing still.

He decides to get an apartment in Berlin where she might feel more at home. But he can't stand it. He's afraid of family life. Afraid of being confined to the real world. Afraid to be found dead in a conventional apartment, so he buys a dozen penknives to defend himself against imaginary intruders. His publisher finds him pacing up and down the living room in his overcoat as though he's waiting for a train.

They continue traveling, on to France. He loves that mix of Saracen, French, Celtic, German, Roman, Spanish, Jewish, and Greek. It reminds him of his own diversity. In the French naval town of Marseilles he feels the welcome. Every onion seller is my uncle, he writes. My mother's forefathers live here. We're all related.

He walks around the Old Port at night. Something in the design of the harbor reflects his restless heart. The lights on the water. Seven hundred ships at berth. The names carry his imagination away to distant places, to the sand dunes of Africa, to where those vendors on the quays come from, selling dates and spices. He wishes to jump on board one of those ships and step into their traveled lives. He is full of leaving and returning, with a cargo of ideas for new novels that he can never hope to unload in his short life. The smell of fish and fuel and wet ropes, the clanging sounds of chains, full of sadness and longing for places not yet visited.

He sits in late-night cafés and drinks Calvados. He talks to sailors, he hears their songs, their stories. Their yearning is placed right next to his own. Wishing he could join them and disappear onto the open sea.

He goes on assignment to Russia. He comes back and writes a novel called *Flight Without End*. The main character, Franz Tunda, is a prisoner of war in Russia after the First World War and begins his journey home to the woman he loves. Along the way he is taken in by other lovers who delay his return. The story of a vagrant husband. There is no such thing as returning, only going further away.

Frieda has the manuscript laid out on the bed.

Who are all these women in his book? she wants to know. Now I know what you were up to in Russia, she says. It's here on paper, in your own minute handwriting. You slept with them all, didn't you?

These women are invented, he replies. They are based on people I have encountered, they do not correspond in a literal way with my life.

Tunda. That's a stupid name to give yourself.

I am not Tunda, he says. The story of Tunda is told to the writer. The writer is me, Joseph Roth, the observer, the reporter. Tunda sends me a letter. He gives me his diary. I put it all down faithfully in the novel.

That's a trick, she says. Your clever modernist way of presenting the story within a story. You are this man who leaves his bride waiting while he falls in love with all these other women. It takes him months to get back home. How do you think that makes me feel?

Every woman I write about is a version of you, he says. Each description is an attempt to get closer to you.

Ha, she scoffs. That's so convenient. Hiding behind author omniscience. Trying one minute to pretend you were there in the bedroom to make the reader think it's real, then telling me you imagined it.

The book is deliberately written that way, he says, to throw the reader off the idea that it might be invented. It's mimicking the truth. You can't take it for real. You can't be jealous of characters in fiction, Friedl. That's like shouting at the screen in a movie. That's what Stalin does. He even calls for actors in a film to be arrested.

She walks around in a circle and comes back to stand over the manuscript laid out on the bed. She goes through the loose pages and begins to read a couple of lines at random—Natascha. She's twenty-three years of age. Her arched forehead, the soft skin of her nose, the narrow nostrils, the lips always round and open. She didn't want to know about her own beauty, rebelled against herself, regarded her femininity as reverting to the bourgeois.

Who is she in real life?

If you want to know, he says, she is based on a writer I met on my trip, a woman with the character of twenty men. I thought she would make a good fictional model for the madness of the Russian Revolution. Every man she sleeps with is a conscript in this great struggle. She even apportions a specific time of night to lovemaking, after all her work is done, looking at her watch and giving it no more than an hour to make sure it doesn't interfere with her sleep. She's pure fantasy. The dream of socialism taken to the point of insanity.

Frieda reads more.

His bride disappeared from his thoughts, like a country left behind. Her photograph was like a postcard of a street on which they had once lived, his old name on some police document, kept for the sake of order.

Is that me? she wants to know. The woman left behind in the past. Tunda shows that photo of his bride to the revolutionary woman and what does she call me—a proper little bourgeois type. Does she have any idea where I come from, the conditions I grew up in?

She continues pacing the room, looking out the window, going back to leaf through the pages again. He stands by the door like a man trapped in the witness box, ready to flee back into a world of drink and fabrication. She waves the pages around like a prosecution attorney.

You're a hand-kisser. You walk the streets with your little cane and think you know the inside of a woman's mind. You're afraid of beauty, isn't that so? You tell me I look in the mirror too much. You think of love as an act of pity. Listen to your own words. His letter took a long time coming, it got fatter, put on weight. You think I'm going to keep waiting for your letters all my life. I hardly recognize you when you come back. It takes me days to get to know you again. Then you'll be gone and I will be left once more with the heating pipes and the people whispering in the corridor and your friends in the restaurants talking about me like a woman who is going insane because I love you too much.

She throws the manuscript back on the bed and puts her hands over her mouth, holding back the tears. She is preparing for a long silence, staring out the window at a country with no meaning.

Without a word, he gets down on his knees. He turns himself into a quadruped on the floor. A dog going up and down the room barking. From the chair in the corner, he picks up her loose stockings in his mouth and flings his snarling head from side to side, then he drops them at her feet. His tongue is hanging out. He sniffs her shoes. He licks her legs. She pulls back and tells him to get up, this is not helping, he will not get around her like that. He is no more than a thinking animal. An animal full of memory. An animal that knows the future. He continues running up and down the room on all fours, looking out the window with his paws up on the ledge, back to the door, barking at the suitcase, then back to sniff her feet again and look up with sad eyes waiting for love.

| **17** |

IT'S EARLY EVENING HERE IN BERLIN, SO IT MUST BE lunchtime where Mike is now. Lena has got herself ready for a video call. She's put on a small bit of makeup. She's wearing a blue shirt with yellow dragons, or trumpets, or maybe it's birds migrating across her chest.

Mike—is that new?

Lena—just got it yesterday.

Cool.

I like your beard.

I want to give you one of my bear hugs.

Come over, she says. You'll love Berlin.

Mike is a hard worker. He loves nothing more than getting things done. His work in the area of cyber-fraud has made him a contemporary detective. A sleuth who never leaves his desk. He has uncovered some major scams in recent years and been hailed among his colleagues as the new Sherlock Holmes. His knowledge of coding makes him almost clairvoyant.

At times, Lena wonders how he can know things about her that she has not told him yet. She even wonders if he has hacked into her phone, though she would never accuse him of that. It would break down that level of trust between them to suggest he might be keeping an eye on her.

My bag got stolen, she says. I lost the book. My precious book. Then, luckily, a very kind young man came to the gallery and handed it in.

Armin, this guy from Chechnya.

She changes the subject and tells him about all the historical landmarks in Berlin she wants to show him when he comes over. Mike tells her that when he was growing up in Iowa City, he had the feeling it was one of those cities that had been bombed during the war. Which, of course, it hadn't. He had read too many stories about the Second World War and began to imagine ruined cities everywhere. He believed Iowa City had been destroyed and rebuilt from nothing.

I'm here with my mother right now, he says.

How is she? Lena asks.

Guess what, Mike says. I get here last night and find all this mail that she's been sent from a firm of lawyers. She refuses to talk about it. You won't believe this, Lena. It's the neighbors, right next door. They're suing my mother for trespassing. They claim she has no right of access to the parking lot at the back. I don't know if you remember, we park around there all the time, we come in the back door, we've been doing that ever since I was a kid.

Sure, I remember, Lena says.

Yeah, so it's these new neighbors. They want to squeeze my mother out of her legal right to park there. They've been living there now for how long, five years, Mike says, not a word. Then suddenly all this legal stuff, like a hand grenade thrown in the door, saying she's been trespassing on their property all this time.

That must be so stressful for her, Lena says.

It's killing her.

What's she going to do?

She wants to do nothing, Mike says. She wants everybody to be friends and just get along.

This is the last thing she needs at her age.

It's the legal stuff that gets to her, Lena. The language they use. Makes her feel like a criminal. Trespass. Words like desist. Encroaching. Invalid. With immediate effect. Terms she's never used in her life before.

Where does she stand?

Solid. Rock solid. It's in the deeds. Goes back decades. When the property next door was a bar. I remember growing up, watching people out back from my window, coming into the parking lot, staggering, laughing. I would see couples kissing. Some of them going a whole lot further. Couples arguing and screaming at each other. The fights. The cops coming. It was better than TV.

Then the premises next door turned residential, people did their drinking downtown, or out of town, who knows, the owners sold up and the parking lot was empty. Only the adjoining residents still had the use of the bays, one each. Three others apart from my mother have all been put on notice.

Why are they doing this?

We even have a photograph of my father painting in the white lines.

They won't get away with it.

My guess is they want to build on that lot. She's a real estate agent, the woman next door. Lydia. She sees a big opportunity here. She wants to build, or maybe she wants to sell up with increased value, vacant possession, no encumbrance, whatever you call it.

They're just trying it on, Lena says.

Exactly, Lena. They're hassling the neighbors in the hope they'll run scared.

She's got to fight this.

Well, here's the deal, Mike says. She doesn't want to. She's afraid of going to court. To her, it's like going into a casino. You never know when your luck might run out, you can't bank on winning, no matter how good the odds are.

The other neighbors are fighting this all the way, Mike says. I spoke to one of them at the back, a retired cop. Dan Mulvaney. He says to me—what are these people doing, pushing us out. He's in his seventies, around the same age as Mom. But he's much more aggressive. He's used to the rough side of the world. He's seen it all. I swear, Lena, he had all this white spittle around his mouth. He was sweating heavily. He's going to fight this tooth and nail. And if he doesn't win, he said to me, there are other ways.

Other ways?

My mother is freaked out hearing this.

What other ways?

He didn't say, but you can imagine. He says he's not going to get pushed around by some Russians. He's got all these guns in the house. We ended up talking about hunting—he goes up to Montana a lot. Said he would love to take me out there. The only thing he hasn't shot is moose.

Now he wants to shoot the neighbors.

We'll see, Mike says. I'm going to speak to the lawyers now, this afternoon.

I thought they were so friendly next door.

They were, Mike says. That's what I can't get my head around, Lena. Christmas, they came around with a gift for my mother. They celebrated the New Year with her. The most perfect neighbors you can imagine. Always greeting her in the morning, asking if she needs anything. Lydia, her father is a good handyman, he fixed the washing machine for my mother, he mows the lawn for her.

Like they've been trying for five years to get close to her. Not a word. Everything is fine, he carries out her garbage one evening, and next morning, wham. The legal letter arrives. Like a punch in the stomach.

Tell your mom I'll camp out in that parking lot day and night with a big protest sign.

Let's see what the lawyers say.

You're going to win this, Mike.

How's your art going?

Not bad, she says.

Listen to this, Mike. You know what I saw yesterday. I was in this café, right, and there's a wedding going by on the street. A big stream of cars with ribbons attached, all of them honking. And then, guess what, they stopped. For no obvious reason, like there was a sudden traffic jam.

I saw the bride getting out, Lena says. She looked amazing. People with their shopping bags were staring at her standing in the middle of the street. And I'm thinking—why are they getting out here, this is a big shopping street. I couldn't believe it. The wedding guests all started dancing, Mike. Right there on this busy avenue, with a couple buses held up behind them. The car doors were left open so they could hear the music, a solid beat, these woofers going, it's like a nightclub. What a sight! The entire wedding party dancing in a wide circle. Big men in black suits linking up with their pinkie fingers in a chain. Some of the women were shrieking, she says. It was like a wedding taking place in a small village somewhere in Turkey, everybody standing by to watch. And the traffic was backed up all the way down the street.

Try that on Fifth Avenue, Mike says.

Nobody was complaining, she says. No cops. No sirens. Like they had permission for this street performance, in front of all those shoppers with their bags standing by. It lasted for about two or three minutes, then they got back into their cars and drove off again. Racing away with the tires squealing. All honking at once. One of the women was riding shotgun with her butt out the window.

No, Mike says. Can't see it taking off here.

It's a regular thing here, Lena says. They even do it on the autobahn. Everything comes to a standstill. There's not a whole lot the cops can do. Or maybe even want to do. A joyful act of civil disobedience, that's what Julia calls it. All the inhabitants of Berlin forced to join in that moment of happiness before it's gone again.

18

THE BALCONY DOOR OF JULIA'S APARTMENT IS OPEN. A car door is heard ripping along the cobbled street. Some hammering too, and the voices of men coming from scaffolding being erected against the façade of a neighboring building. The morning sun reaches across the floor, throwing an oblong shape onto the blue rug at the center of the living room. A light breeze comes in, lifting the leaves of a standard plant in the corner.

On a table, there is a column of large-format art books, one of which has been opened on a stand. It's part of Julia's routine, displaying a different page each morning, like an inspiration for the day. Today it's the image of the young woman turning to look behind her. Or is she turning her face away, not wishing to be seen?

What else? Some unopened mail, including a letter from Amnesty International asking for support to free a human rights lawyer in Iran.

In the kitchen, Lena and Julia are talking. One of those late-morning conversations with Lena still in her dressing gown, her bare knees up and a cup cradled in both hands. Julia is wearing a loose shirt and a pair of tracksuit bottoms. She pours some more coffee and says—we should be out on the balcony. But they decide to stay where they are in the kitchen because of the hammering outside.

Julia says to Lena—I have a studio for you.

Wow. Thanks.

It's a nice place, Julia says. A loft, at the top of a building, no lift though. An artist friend of mine, he's gone to live in Melbourne for a year, so the place is free.

That's amazing.

There's a small kitchen. Enough to boil up soup, that kind of thing, Julia says. Lots of space. Worktables. You'll love it. There's a small daybed as well. That's where he brings all his lovers, so I believe.

Sounds a bit like Lucian Freud.

Exactly, Julia says. He was asked how come he had two children in the same year by two different women and he answered—I had a bicycle.

What do I owe him?

No way, Julia says. He doesn't want money. He's happy to have another artist use the place while he's away.

The woman in the painting on the stand is not turning around to look at anything specific. The space behind her is empty, indistinct, nothing more than a pale gray distance. She is caught in that backward glance, looking around at the past, unable to return to the present. That's what you are given to think. She may come from somewhere else. She's looking around at something that has gone blank, something she has left behind.

Julia begins to tell Lena about a man she met at the gallery recently. It's been keeping me awake at night, she says. Something really stupid. He was in my class in school. The boy in front of me. I used to poke him in the back with my pen and he never complained. I would never have remembered his face. I knew him only from behind. His broad back. Why was I so obsessed with hurting him? Some jealousy, maybe, printed in red marks across his back.

He's a highly successful lawyer now, Julia says. He was very friendly. He gave me his card and asked me to contact him if I ever needed any help. I should have said sorry for making his life a nightmare in class. I wondered if it was those jabs that helped to make him such a success? Or was it the opposite? He became a successful lawyer out of some determination to get even with all those times I poked him. Every case he wins takes back one red mark at a time.

No way, Lena says.

Now I'm asking myself—why did he come to the gallery after all these years? Was it to show me that he had succeeded in defying my bullying?

I'm sure he's forgotten, Lena says. He would not have come if he was holding a grudge.

Julia's laugh holds a hint of capitulation.

It's in his power to forget, not mine.

It's so long ago, Julia.

I should have spoken to him about it, Julia says. Cleared the air. Now I wonder, should I call him, explain to him that I had nothing against him? I liked him. He was my friend. Maybe I fancied him. I just thought boys didn't feel anything. The way he turned around sometimes and smiled at me without saying a word, as if he wanted more. Maybe it was some weird kind of love we had for each other, with no other way of showing it but through this painful messaging. He's happily married now with three children, so he told me. His name came up in the paper just the other day, she says. Some trial in which he is defending a man on charges of attempting to set fire to a hostel. That's what lawyers do. This sounds crazy, I know, but I keep thinking he may have been so desensitized by that experience at school that it brought him to this point where he can defend the indefensible.

Julia, you're thinking too much, Lena says.

I know, Julia says. It's the way I was brought up, feeling responsible for things by association.

Let it go.

If I hadn't subjected him to that daily torture, Julia says, he might have done something kinder with his life, like medicine. Maybe he would have become an artist, a writer, done something creative. Maybe that's why he came to the gallery, because he loves art and he hates being a lawyer defending people who burn other people.

Lena offers to make more coffee.

Julia's son, Matt, walks into the kitchen wearing earphones.

He has the presence of a ghost, not quite in this world. It must be Saturday if he's not at school. Julia speaks about him in the third person—wait till you see, she says to Lena, he will grab some cereal and not even bother with a bowl, hand to mouth. He's a vegan, she says, self-proclaimed. I had to bulk him up with protein last summer because his teeth had gone gray. He was with this theater group in the country and they forgot to eat, just weed and love.

What about saying good morning to Lena? Julia says.

Matt lifts one of the earphones to say hello.

Lena smiles—hi, Matt.

For one moment he's back in real time, then he replaces the earphone and disappears again.

The sound of hammering has come right into the room at this point. The art books have all begun to take it personally. They would happily drag one of those workmen into a studio and silence him in art. Photos taken of artists in their studios often make them look like murderers, their overalls splattered with paint. We are relieved when Julia crosses the floor in her bare feet to close the balcony door.

You can't help looking back, Lena says.

No choice, I suppose.

I'm no better, Lena says. I still find myself getting worried about my father. He's been dead a couple of years now, but I can't help wishing I could undo some of the stuff I did. The trouble I caused him. I was sent to live in Ireland with my mother after they got divorced. I hated it. Couldn't wait to get back to Philadelphia. I thought my father was punishing my mother by foisting me on her. I thought he wanted me out of the way so he could start a life with his new girlfriend. And guess what? I got my revenge on them by taking up drugs. They were everywhere. First thing I came across. Skibbereen is the drug capital of Europe, she says.

I went on this binge of self-destruction.

After he brought me home and got me straightened out, Lena says, I wouldn't let him see his new partner. I refused to let her in the door. The scale of resistance was unreal. I couldn't stand him paying attention to anyone else. Even the sight of a woman's name in his address book made me mad. I tore them all out. I read their letters and cried. He was getting on very well with a woman from Madison named Grace. She was lovely. She would bring chocolates for me and I threw them on the floor, saying—what's this, bribery?

Honestly, they would have had a good life together, but I would not allow it. I got her number and called her one night. I think it was two in the morning. I told her she was ugly and fat and full of poison. She was making my father ill. He was dying because of her. I told her he was throwing up the whole night after she kissed him.

Shit, Julia says.

I was fighting for my life, Lena says.

That's rough.

It's unbelievable, Lena says, the power a child can have over a parent. I could smell the guilt. I could feel him thinking it was such a mistake to send me to Ireland. I could sense him being worried about doing the best for me, making up for lost time. I played his love against him. I held him to ransom. I chased away any possibility of a happy life. I insisted on being his only happiness.

That's the sacrifice, that's what a parent does.

You can't go back and change things, Lena says.

I'm sure you meant everything to him, Lena.

Julia stands up and puts her cup into the sink. She puts her hand on Lena's arm.

Come on, Lena, she says. Let's go and have a look at that studio.

19

THE APARTMENT REMAINS SILENT ALL DAY. OTHER THAN the hammering coming from the building site nearby, there has been no sound, until the key is heard in the door late in the afternoon. It's Julia's son, Matt. He walks into the living room and stands for a moment staring at the North Sea in one of the paintings as though it has spoken to him. He opens the door of the balcony to stand outside and look at the street below. The noise of hammering seems even more furious for having been kept out. When Matt comes back inside, he collapses on the floor by the wall. Before he goes down, he performs an inspired dance routine which includes leaping onto the sofa and sliding in triumph along the bare floorboards like a football player after scoring a goal. His collapse is graceful. Accompanied by a shout that might be heard by workers on the nearby scaffolding.

He appears to be lifeless.

What has he taken? A small spillage of mashed gherkins and bread pulp has emerged from his mouth. His eyelids are not quite closed. His arms have an accidental layout. The positioning of his head against the baseboard gives his body a caved-in appearance. He seems neither deceased nor asleep, making his slow descent from that fantastic peak of lonely pleasure.

He has been stealing from himself. He's like that great junkie in literature—Faust. The pact with the devil. All that stolen knowledge to be repaid.

Hold on, Matt. You have nothing to worry about. Everything will be fine, just hang in there.

My author was addicted to alcohol. Joseph Roth drank himself to death. His life was hard and he had a lot of sorrows to drown, but he still managed to write a stack of books before he left this world. He sat at a table in a restaurant with a flask of wine or a double schnapps, what they called a ninety-percenter. It gave him artistic clarity. He kept listening to the conversations going on around him and managed to keep all that talk of politics out of his novels. He would not be in a position to provide much reassurance on addiction, but it might be worth hearing what he had to say about identity—I am a Frenchman from the East, a humanist, a rationalist with religion, a Catholic with a Jewish mind, a true revolutionary.

Matt is African European. His father is from Nigeria and Julia is German. They met when she was on holiday and he agreed to conceive a baby without any further commitment to each other. She later managed to bring him to Germany and helped to set him up with a career in marketing. Matt grew up without his father, though he sees him from time to time and they occasionally go on holidays together. Last year they all went to Nigeria to meet his family.

Perhaps Matt is not unlike Joseph Roth. He has the elsewhere inside him. A different here. A different back home which is often defined by his skin color. Like Roth, he tries to shake off the construct of identity imposed on him from the outside. He is the true revolutionary at the forefront of a fluid world, free to travel back and forth among various places of origin, some real, some imagined.

Julia has quite a number of books by African writers on her shelves. One of them was written by an African American author who was raised in Nigeria and emigrated to the United States when he was around fifteen, the same age as Matt is now. It's called *Every Day Is for the Thief*. In the book the author describes going back to visit his country of childhood as an adult. He writes with despair at the level of corruption and picks up the Yoruba proverb about the thief for his title. His journey home is written from the viewpoint of a man who has become used to living in New York and feels angry at having to pay a bribe for every small transaction. Everybody smiles and says—have you got something for me. The writer has outgrown his own people. He has taken on the values of his adoptive country and resents their thieving customs. While he managed to escape, they remain burdened by the history of their once colonized country, by the theft of the landscape on which their ancestors walked. The ground beneath their feet did not belong to them until they achieved independence in 1960, fifteen years after the end of the Second World War. The country had been plundered, some of its most precious works of art taken to museums in London and never returned. The people themselves were stolen to be sold as slaves. Theft was an inescapable part of the world order. Their relationship to property became distorted by that brutal history and the writer discovers, by going back after so many years in the United States, that a person can own something for one day, but that every day is for the thief.

And what about those people who go and live in another part of the world. Are they not thieves too, stealing themselves from the place where they grew up? Each person leaving home takes some vital piece of information from the landscape that cannot be replaced by those who stay behind. By the time they go home again, everything has changed.

It's the paradox of the revenant. Going back to where you come from can give you the feeling of being cheated. It all looks so familiar and so different, the grass is lying to you. A person returning feels robbed.

When Julia gets back, it's dark. The light from the street shines across Matt's body and it takes her a moment to notice that there is something wrong. She rushes over to find his eyes open. She feels for his pulse and calls his name a dozen times, trying to wake him up by holding his face in both hands. Telling him where he is and who he is and who his mother is. His breathing is that of a diver coming to the surface. She sits down on the floor with her back to the wall, cradling him in her arms and stroking his face.

Matt, my boy, my baby Matt. Look at you.

He opens his mouth, but he has no words to offer.

She calls the rescue services. When the paramedics arrive, they check his pulse and take his blood pressure. His blood sugar levels have dropped. They ask him what he has taken and he tells them it was skunk, nothing heavier than that. They speak to his mother and tell her that, if she wants, they can take him to the emergency room for observation, but that would mean staying in the hospital overnight. In a gently reassuring voice the paramedic, a young man not much older than Matt, says he will be fine if he gets some sugar. Every junkie will pass out now and then, they tell her. When they're gone again, Julia goes into the kitchen and pours a glass of pomegranate juice. She comes back and makes him drink it all.

Come on, Starman, she says.

She gets him on his feet and leads him straight into the bathroom. Once he is sitting on the floor of the shower with a warm flood of tropical rain coming down on his head, she goes to clean things up. A fictional scent of pine fills the air. She closes the balcony door to keep out the late-night traffic tearing along the cobbles on the street below and allows the room to recover. She gets him out of the shower onto his feet again and dries him off with a large white bath towel. She reaches up with furious love to dry his hair, leaving it in standing stacks, then she rubs his back. She kneels to dry off his long legs and then steps back to examine him.

Matt, look at you. Any woman, she says. Any woman or man on this planet would be crazy about you.

And here, she says, knocking with her knuckle on the top of his skull, what you have in here is infinitely more beautiful than your body.

She wipes her face to make sure he can't tell she has been crying.

Remember all the magic tricks you did for me, she says. And what about your drawings.

His art showed such promise. He has an improvised art cart with trays designed to hold vegetables now filled with paints and brushes. She wants him to find a story for his longing. Now she is forced to check her credit card history and ransack his bedroom to find his secrets.

You know what, Julia says. We'll get you straightened out. We'll go swimming. Let's go to the pool tomorrow morning. Then we'll go up to Hamburg. You need to go and live with your other mother, it will be good for you to be around Irena for a while, going for lots of walks in the forest with her dog. You love that dog, don't you?

20

LENA ARRIVES BACK LATE. JULIA IS STILL UP—SHE CAN'T sleep. Sitting in the kitchen, holding an all-night vigil, checking every now and again to see how Matt is doing. Lena keeps her company and they drink chamomile tea in buckets while Julia talks about her son, how she will have to bring him up to Hamburg, a new school, a new start. His other mother is a doctor and will get him into some kind of drug rehabilitation program.

Lena tells Julia that she went to meet Armin.

I wanted to give him something, Lena says. A small gift, just to thank him for returning my book. A lot of people would not have bothered even picking it up, or maybe would have brought it to some antiquarian bookseller and sold it. I'm sure it's worth a few euros, though it's missing a page.

What did you give him?

It was hard to decide, Lena says. A gift voucher would have been too much like something your aunt would give you. I found a lovely brown scarf with a houndstooth pattern, but that's more like a birthday present, she says. I'm going to keep that for Mike when he comes over. He's planning a walking trip to Romania for us both. He's been growing a beard, by the way, it's quite impressive, makes him look rugged. Like a pioneer. He wants to go hunting, that's his thing.

Lena says she thought of giving Armin two tickets for a Nick Cave concert, but that might have implied going together. If he doesn't have a partner, that is.

In the end I went for the obvious—a book.

That makes sense, Julia agrees.

He brings me a book, so I bring him a book, right?

What book?

Took me ages to decide, Lena says. I can't read them in German. The woman in the shop recommended a novel written by a Bosnian man who came to Germany to escape from the conflict in the former Yugoslavia.

Ah yes, Julia says, good choice.

After I gave it to him, Lena says, I had second thoughts. I felt a bit stupid. Like, hang on, what do you give a migrant, obvious: a book written by another migrant. With a couple thousand titles to choose from, nothing comes to mind, only a book that basically tells his own story. How dumb is that?

No, Julia says, it's an uplifting story.

Like, here, Armin, have a good look at yourself.

Believe me, Julia says, he'll love it. There's a great scene in the book about the writer's grandfather accidentally stepping on his grandmother's foot while they were dancing. It could have changed the course of history and the author might never have been born.

Armin is a good reader, Lena says.

It's thoughtful of you to give it to him, Julia says. He'll appreciate that.

He doesn't have a whole lot in the line of memories, Lena says. There's no home to remember back there in Chechnya. He doesn't have much to say about Grozny, apart from the smell of diesel fumes. The engines of armored vehicles spewing out dirty black smoke. And gunfire. He used to play with empty shells. He can remember queues for food aid. He can remember the curfew where nobody was allowed onto the streets and a group of mothers stayed up all night in the house talking and talking, sometimes all laughing together, until there was an explosion heard in the distance and one of the women said—that's one that missed us.

He lost his parents in that war, Lena says. He still carries injuries from the explosion at the market. He's got some shrapnel fragments in his body. He has a sister who lost her leg in that bombing. There's a piece of newsreel footage of them both in a hospital, he told me, though he's never seen it himself. They were brought to Germany by an aunt when they were young, with the help of traffickers.

He had nothing much to say about that journey either, Lena says, apart from being on the train for hours. It took days; to him and his sister it seemed like months.

He's working with a group of city planners. Goes around measuring, you know, those tripods you sometimes see on the street, don't ask me what they're for.

It was mostly his adoptive German family we talked about. That's a happy story for him to tell. He and his sister grew up in a large family that was full of chaos. A huge apartment in Frankfurt where they could wave at each other through the windows across the courtyard. It was a great place to play hide-and-seek, he told me. Rooms off rooms off rooms—you could get lost. They used to cycle around on bikes.

His adoptive parents were hippies. New Age, neo-hippies. His mother was from the former East, from a place near the Polish border. She was a nurse by profession. She liked to wear those long flowing cheesecloth dresses and went out in the summer with a floppy, wide-rimmed sun hat. She had long red hair. She never shaved her underarms, so they looked like red nests of hair.

The scent of a bakery, that's how Armin described her. A warm-hearted woman with big breasts, like a power station, he told me.

His adoptive father was from Augsburg. A professor of philosophy at the university in Frankfurt. Over breakfast he would ask the children questions like—what will happen when robots take over the world? He was big into John Lennon. The parents met when the Berlin Wall came down, she says. Armin told me there was a large photo in the living room of her stepping through a gap in the Wall.

Her name is Hendrika, mostly Henny. His name is Thomas, mostly Tom. To Armin and his sister, they were Mama and Papa. The apartment was full of books. They had no car. The entire family went everywhere on foot, like a troupe going through the city, with people staring at Madina on her father's shoulders missing her leg, Armin told me. In summer they often went walking in the hills and had picnics out in the fields, all of them naked, the entire family.

They had two biological sons of their own, a couple of years older than Armin. They were permitted to do anything they wanted. It was basically a house without rules. They got away with murder. They were caught smoking weed in school. They were caught stealing in shops and were brought home in a police car. They used to tell Armin he was not allowed to do anything bad because he was adopted. Now they're both highly successful, he told me. One of them a producer working in the film industry, the other in genetics, something to do with stem cells.

He started reading a lot, Lena says. That was the only way he could keep up with the older boys, picking up all the books his adoptive mother and father had around the house. It was his way of getting closer to them.

Then they split up, Lena says.

Ah, that's sad.

I get the impression, Lena says, he's grateful for getting that wonderful start in life. Only that it made him feel like an orphan all over again.

What caused the breakup?

It was an open marriage, Lena says. They both had lovers. It was no big deal, apparently. That's what Armin told me. She had this man who used to come to the apartment in the mornings in his tracksuit, like he would stop off during his daily run, then have a shower and continue running. Another man from Ireland would come in the afternoon with his guitar and start singing ballads; he would never leave.

His father had girlfriends at the university. He would bring them cycling in the hills, or hang gliding.

Then he won a big prize for a book he wrote on philosophy in everyday life. She started writing a novel about a hippie family going on a ship to Australia. They seemed to go their own ways after that, claiming back some privacy after all that open living. She went to live in Turkey with their two biological sons. Armin and Madina were looked after by other families around Germany until they were out of school.

As a boy, he told me, he used to tickle his sister's foot. The amputated one. He would tickle her phantom toes until she pulled it away and begged him to stop.

That's so sweet, Julia says.

He wants me to meet her, Lena says. Madina. She's a singer. I looked her up, she does tours of Germany with her band. People love her, she's begun to build up quite a following. One of the images I've seen shows her onstage with long hair and long legs wearing silver shorts, like Beyoncé. Only that she has a prosthetic leg, a lightweight metal design, attached at the knee. There's a photo of her with a prosthesis made of wire mesh. I'd love to hear her sing. A couple tracks I've heard on YouTube. Armin says he'll get tickets when she's playing in Berlin next; we might go if you're free.

21

THEY SEEM TO HAVE NO INTENTION OF GOING TO SLEEP. Julia smiles when she hears her son snoring. He's alive and well, she says. They sit drinking more and more mugs of chamomile tea. Lena with the fridge at her back, shuddering now and again when it switches off. She tells Julia that she and Armin ended up in a small bar with a disco ball hanging from the ceiling. A late-night place where they sat at a table that had been converted from an old bumper car.

They got talking to an English couple who had moved to Berlin recently. The man was drinking whiskey and soda, Lena says. The woman was doing a mai tai. They were terribly funny. They had us laughing a lot, she says.

They offered to buy us a drink.

His name is Geoff, he's involved in some start-up company. Her name is Gill, she's in food supplements and alternative medical products. They used to run a very successful health food business in a place called Stroud. They drove to Berlin in their car with two husky dogs.

They told us about their wedding, Lena says. Before they left for Berlin with all their stuff and the two dogs packed in the car, they stopped off at Stonehenge to re-enact the wedding vows. She described how he went down on one knee, asking her to remarry him. He's such a laugh, Gill kept saying, talking about her husband in the third person. Look at him, you'd never think it, he's the king of romance.

Gill put her arm around him and winked at us, saying—we had to wait for the full moon.

They assumed that me and Armin were a couple, Lena says. She asked us how long we'd been married.

She must have seen the ring on my finger, but then, for some reason, I laughed and said nothing. Instead of explaining that I was married to Mike back in New York, or going through a long story of why he wasn't here, that he was coming over to Berlin soon, I kept it all to a minimum.

Maybe out of politeness to Armin, she says, I told them I was visiting relatives in Germany. I found myself telling them the story of the book, given to me by my father, and then stolen. It was Armin who found it on the ground in a park and brought it back to me. And then, guess what, they interpreted that as a major sign. Oh my God, Gill said, so that's how you two met, it was the book that brought you together. She turned to Geoff and said— isn't that amazing, they found each other with a stolen book. That book made up its mind to connect you, Gill kept saying.

Which is all true, Lena says, but I didn't know how to stop them from putting such a romantic spin on it. Armin eventually brought it all down to earth.

We're friends, he said.

The English couple thought that was even more hilarious—oh fuck, Gill said.

They're not married, Geoff said.

Mistaken identity, Gill said. I swear, you look so bonded, like the real thing.

Armin was totally cool about it, Lena says. He just started talking about the book, how it was about a man with a missing leg who plays the barrel organ. Armin said he happened to have a sister with a missing leg, he didn't say why exactly, he made it sound like an accident. The English couple thought that was such an extraordinary coincidence, true life meeting up with fiction, like there was something in the book that had the ability to align the universe, Lena says.

Gill said—oh my God, what a beautiful story. That's mind-blowing, Geoff, don't you think?

Geoff got out his phone, saying—you know, I don't think I've ever actually heard a barrel organ, live.

He spent a moment searching and came up with that familiar melody of "The Teddy Bears' Picnic." Like a carousel, Lena says, with wheezing notes rolling along, stopping and starting. There was a sadness in it, even though it was meant to be happy. We listened to it for a moment over the sound of jazz playing in the bar. Gill said their son Dwyer had a children's book about a man with a barrel organ. The story of a monkey and a parrot who escape from the organ grinder and make their way off to the Caribbean, stowed away on a navy ship. After a big sea battle with pirates, Geoff said, they run aground on a tropical island, back where they came from.

We had to read it every night, Gill said.

And because they had been so funny earlier, Lena tells Julia, we were expecting a joke to come out of all this. But Gill started crying. Geoff put his arm around her. He then explained to us that Dwyer was dead. He was sixteen, Geoff said. He was beaten up one night in a random attack in the town, a very quiet place where you would never expect that kind of thing to happen. It was such a shock to the whole community, he said, nobody could believe it, not in Stroud.

He was in a coma for weeks, Geoff said. Gill stayed with him all that time. I looked after the shop. Then we had to make the decision whether to keep him on life support or to let him go. He had no life expectancy.

Gill was crying all the time, Lena says. Now and again she would take a drink to gather herself. I think she was on her third mai tai. She was taking out tissues from her bag, blowing her nose, trying to smile again.

The whole thing was caught on camera, Geoff said. The attack. We saw it in court, he told us, when they played it to the jury. We could have stepped outside while it was being shown. It was hard, he said, but we did it for Dwyer, to make it right for him, to be with him through those terrible moments. So that he wouldn't be alone.

Geoff took her hand and kept looking at her, speaking for them both, Lena says.

Two boys around his own age, Geoff said, from well-to-do families in the same neighborhood. Determined to carry out this act of mindless brutality. We say mindless, he said, but it was totally deliberate. You think they have no feeling, no empathy, but it's the opposite, they got their kicks out of his pain, they could feel his suffering, our suffering. The shock of the whole community is what they were after. They wouldn't have done it if they didn't understand pain. The violence was unbelievable, he said, we will never forget it. We can still hear the sound his head made. I know that's an illusion, he said, because there was no audio. We must have imagined it. When we got home, Gill asked me if I heard his head knocking against the pavement and I said yes.

We saw the fear in his eyes, Gill said.

There's no such thing as justice in a situation like that, Geoff said, holding her hand as though they had just come from the court, Lena says. No amount of prison time is going to bring our son back. We had the impression they apologized for their actions only to get a shorter sentence.

I made a victim impact statement, Geoff said, and it was hard to put my anger aside. All I could find myself saying was that it had now become impossible for us to live in England. The smallest thing would remind us of what had happened. Every time we saw each other, every time we had breakfast or met each other on the stairs, we could only think of him missing. It was like we had begun to turn on each other. Like we could do nothing but blame each other for bearing a resemblance to the boy that was now dead. The brutality was in our eyes. The entire landscape was tainted by this one act of madness. In court, with the murderers of our son listening and staring at the floor, I found myself saying that England was not a country we could live in any longer, they had made it uninhabitable for us. We had everything going for us, a thriving business, a son who was a talented actor. After this, we had no option but to sell up and move abroad.

That's why we went to Stonehenge, Gill said. For Dwyer, like a pact we made around his death. We would never split up or drift apart, no matter what happened. That's why we went to Stonehenge, to sort of get married all over again.

She was trying to lighten things up, holding up her mai tai glass. We still have his monkey book, she said. We keep it open on a side table in the hallway, by the door. I change the page every day.

We go back to visit his grave once a year, he said, on the anniversary of his death in December.

He was a sweet boy, Gill said, really, really sweet. And so funny. A real comedian.

I'm sorry for telling you all of this, Geoff said. We've just ruined your evening, haven't we.

Born comedian, Gill said. He would sit at the table over breakfast and have us in a heap. I don't know where he got it from. He saw a funny twist in everything. He would have had a great career in stand-up, Gill said, he was so utterly natural, with this expression of incomprehension on his face, like nothing in the world made sense, she said, I think that's what made us laugh so much. I'm still cracking up at some of the things he used to say, Geoff said.

Gill got up and started dancing, Lena says.

Oh, quick, she said, the Rolling Stones.

She made her way out onto the dance floor but she could hardly stand. She swayed with her elbows out. You know, Lena says, she was very graceful, smiling and crying at the same time. Her face was covered in those moving light spots from the disco ball turning overhead. She could not keep her balance. She collapsed gradually, with her hands up to her face. As if it was her son's funeral and she was standing by his grave after the coffin was lowered. Armin went over to help Geoff get her up on her feet again. The barman called a taxi. They helped her out the door and I ran after them with her bag.

22

LENA AND ARMIN SAT FOR A WHILE LONGER AT THE BUM-
per car table, listening to the music. They were absorbing the
story of the English couple. Or maybe trying to talk about something else. She wanted to dance, but it didn't feel right.

And then, Lena says, a man came in and started watching
us from the bar. I would have paid him no attention, only that
I sensed Armin was anxious. I got the impression that he felt
threatened by this man. Big guy, wearing a leather jacket. At one
point, Armin went over to speak to him. They stood at the bar
looking at the row of spirit bottles in front of them.

I assumed it was some kind of business.

Who's your friend? I asked him when he came back, Lena
says. Would he like to come over and join us?

My sister's boyfriend.

Is he the guy who cut the page out of the book?

Ex-boyfriend.

I looked over and saw him leaving, Lena says.

Armin gave her the man's name. Bogdanov. Ulrich Bogdanov.
It's become a bit obsessive at this point, Lena says, he's stalking

her in places where she performs in public. Armin said there was nothing she could do to stop him from turning up at her gigs. He behaves like a fan. But then he interrupts her performance.

Madina went to meet Bogdanov in a café one afternoon, Lena says. She told him once more that it was over, there was no going back. She berated him for extracting money from her brother. If he ever did anything like that again, she would go directly to his wife and tell her they'd had an affair behind her back.

Don't push it, she said to Bogdanov. I will tell your wife the whole truth, believe me.

And guess what? Lena says. The guy just laughed.

It's over, but Bogdanov doesn't get it. From what Armin told me, Lena says, Bogdanov even tried to get her to go to a psychotherapist to fix the affair. He was never going to leave his wife and kids. She didn't want to break up a family.

This is the thing, Lena says. He thinks he owns her. In the café where she was warning him to stay away from her and her brother, he kept saying he loved her. He's never been with anyone like her before. His life is meaningless without Madina. He will do anything to get her back, walk out on his family, kill himself, all that stuff. Armin says he's good with words. Totally credible. She had gone back to him a couple of times. Then he started saying to her that she was nothing without him. She couldn't function, couldn't be a singer, couldn't make her own coffee. It was thanks to him that she made it in the music business. Her career was going nowhere until he discovered her.

She told him to fuck off, Armin said.

Without his backing, Bogdanov insisted, she would come to nothing.

She shrugged him off, Lena says. Told him it was over, finished, end of story. Then he threatened her. Bogdanov must have realized that her weakness was not inside herself but in somebody close to her. She was exposed by having a younger brother. Leaning across to look straight into her eyes, he said—I'll take it out on your brother.

Something to that effect, Lena says.

Asshole, Julia says. I know the type.

Armin's sister said she would go to the police.

Bogdanov laughed. He said the police were his friends. They keep the law so he can break it.

Madina said to him—Uli, have you no heart?

She turned to the other customers in the café and said to Bogdanov—tell them what you just told me. I'll take it out on your brother. That's what you said, Uli. Isn't that so? Your brother gets it. That's what he said to me.

Everybody in the café was watching. Bogdanov sat with his arms folded, insulting her with a comical face. Instead of being embarrassed at hearing his own words, he turned around to the other customers and said—

She's Muslim.

That did it, Lena says.

Madina reached under the table and unhooked her prosthetic leg. It took no more than a few seconds, like taking off her shoe. She stood up on her good leg and brought the artificial leg down on the table with a furious crack. It smashed Bogdanov's cup to pieces. There were specks of coffee on his face.

The customers in the café must have been astonished at the sheer velocity of the leg coming from nowhere. Not to mention the accuracy with which the heel of her shoe hit Bogdanov's coffee. The noise alone brought an immediate silence. Everyone stopped talking. How does a woman do that kind of thing? they must have thought. Swing her leg one hundred and eighty degrees? The athleticism was inhuman. Standing there on one leg while the other leg performed an impossible arc over her head, more like a baseball bat coming down with a smack.

Bogdanov didn't bother wiping his face. He grinned. He

turned to the customers and held his hands out in a gesture that seemed to say—look what I have to deal with, blaming her for making such a spectacle.

She was crying at that point. Crying in anger. She repeated the whole raging maneuver, just to show Bogdanov that she meant it. Also, perhaps, to show everyone else in the café that it hadn't been a fluke, she could do this kind of circus show with her leg as often as they wished. It had nothing whatsoever to do with being Muslim, which she isn't. She brought the false limb down once more with an even better second swing. There was nothing left of his cup and saucer. Then she sat down and began to fit the leg back on again.

Everyone was waiting.

Bogdanov didn't mind being stared at. He calmly stood up and pushed his chair back into position. He allowed her time to finish putting her prosthetic leg in place and sit up to look at him. He leaned slowly forward and knocked on the table with his knuckles, a minimal applause. Then he pulled his leather jacket around his stomach and left.

Julia says—bet the customers were on her side.

The café staff wouldn't take any money, Lena says. They told Madina it was on the house.

And then he turns up at the bar, Julia says.

He's not going to let it go.

Did she tell his wife?

No way, Lena says. She would never do that.

Armin began to talk about the possibility of going on tour with his sister. Rotterdam. Antwerp. He's thinking he might take up the job as their roadie. He could map out the best routes and plan out the logistics, what places to stop for lunch along the way. Where to stay overnight, what the band needs in terms of riders. He could design their stage show, lay out the equipment, be the rigger. Have her accordion ready on a small stand, get the guitars tuned up. He would be good at keeping the crowds back, Armin joked. Good at slipping her out the stage door unrecognized, wearing sunglasses.

Lena and Julia agree it might be a good idea to get some sleep.

Can I borrow your book? Julia says.

Rebellion.

I wouldn't mind reading it.

Sure, Lena says.

So, I find myself staying awake with Julia as she lies down beside her son in his bed. He is quietly breathing in and out. Now and again he snorts and his legs jump as though he's running in his sleep, then he utters a startled sound like a word half-formed. Julia puts her hand on his arm to calm down his nightmares and turns him on his side for a while. Then she continues reading until dawn, until she finally falls asleep herself and leaves me lying face-down on the bedside table like a sunken roof.

23

FRIEDA HAS BEEN ILL AGAIN. A HIGH TEMPERATURE KEEPS her in bed for days. It's impossible to know what's wrong. It's in her lungs. In her arms. Inside her head. It's in the suitcases, in the screech of wheels, in the train stations, in the view from each new hotel bedroom window. It's in the emptiness when he goes on assignment and she's left behind with nothing but the curtains moving. He asks his friends to write to her while he's away. It would make her feel better.

He comes back to find her lying facedown on the bed. She hasn't eaten a thing in days. She needs protein and minerals, so he goes out to the market to buy liver, which he brings back on a bloodstained sheet of paper and cooks in the hotel room for her. The corridors are heavy with the smell of liver. It's in the carpet like a lingering trace of previous occupants.

He begins to shape her like a novel.

He puts her on trains to faraway places. He takes her walking, early and late, across the bridges of Paris. Arm in arm, from one side of the city to the other, with his coat draped over his shoulders and a cane in his hand, they walk as newcomers, arriving and never arriving, stopping only to move on again. He makes her laugh. The boy inside him does imitations of horses' hoofs. Entire regiments of cavalry horses with high black feathers sticking out of their heads. Like an athlete in black patent leather shoes, lifting her dress for the freedom of her knees, she clacks along the cobbled pavement until she is forced to stop with a breathless laugh and hold on to him because one of the shoes has come off.

He keeps reinventing her late into the night in his books, sitting at a small table at the back of a restaurant with a glass of brandy while she tries to sleep. The strain of being written down is beginning to show. She has become quiet in company. Afraid of gatherings. Sitting in a corner waiting for him to fill the pages, her reflection in his mind.

She has stopped being herself.

In the restaurant with his friends, he becomes easily jealous. Even to see her laughing at another man's joke is enough to make him think he's lost her. He cannot bear her watching the violinist in the string ensemble playing onstage. He rewrites her as a more restrained woman, not the daughter of a poor Viennese family but a woman of means in wealthy clothes, less openhearted, less innocent, more calculated in company with writers who can see into her head and imagine her most secret thoughts. He likes the honest, worldly comments she makes on his work, but he wants her to shroud her opinions in academic language. He turns her into somebody she is not. At times he can no longer tell the difference between the woman he married and the woman he describes in his novels.

A courier arrives at the restaurant with a special transfer of money for him. He continues talking to his friends and asks Frieda to go and sign for it. Three thousand marks. A sizable amount he's earned from his newspaper reports. He has become so popular that readers have begun to say—whenever Joseph Roth writes, something will happen. While he continues talking to the group around him without dropping a word, she goes out to deal with the postman delivering the money.

She steps out of his novel, free of the author. There is dramaturgy in her movements across the floor of the restaurant and out into the foyer. It gives the sound of her shoes a self-fabricated quality. She comes back inside a while later and lays the banknotes in a pile on the table. He sees only two thousand marks. What's happened to the rest of it, a thousand marks missing? She smiles and shrugs her shoulders. Her dimples spring to life with delirious optimism.

The violinist, she says. He has such sad eyes.

He shouts at her in front of the other writers at the table. In a drunken rage he stands up and accuses her of having slept with the violinist.

How can she deny what he invents?

His imagination is closer to the truth than he knows. While he was away on assignment, sleeping on trains going all the way to Albania, he kept imagining her slipping out at night like one of his fictional characters. He thought of her standing in the street at night waiting for the violinist to come out of the restaurant with his case under his elbow. He could see them linking arms. Their feet in unison. Their laughter like coins rolling along the street. He imagined them arriving back at the hotel and the concierge keeping it all quiet with a wink. In the room from which he was so often absent, he could see her lying naked on the bed with her long white arms and her long white legs while the musician played a sad Polish mazurka for her and everyone in the hotel sat up to listen.

With the other writers around the table looking on in shock, he continues shouting his accusations at her. She sits with her head in her hands, crying. He gets her up on her feet and takes her away by the arm, like a criminal being led out of the restaurant.

Onstage, the violinist continues playing.

And then!

That terrible cloud of writer's guilt comes over him when he returns to the hotel bedroom and steps back into the real world, where everything is beyond his authorial power. He wishes he could withdraw the words left behind in the restaurant. But the living world cannot be torn up and rewritten. The words are gone to print in her memory and the affair with the violinist cannot be retracted.

She can't sleep and she can't wake up. She looks in the mirror and fails to recognize herself. She can no longer trust her own face.

You're making me ill again, she says.

He goes out to get more liver. The spongy meal clogs up her mouth. Between her teeth, she can feel the rubbery arteries that once carried the animal's blood. She coughs it up like a knot of medical tubing. The pulp of organs makes her choke. The smell of liver is in her hair, in the sheets and the pillowcases, the taste of it in their kisses.

| 24 |

HE WENT TO SEE HIS PUBLISHER IN BERLIN. WINTER,
early in the new year. That heavy overcoat of sky across the city.
The cold coming up through the shoes. The streets were empty.
The cafés were full. His suitcase was back in the same hotel by the
train station, as close to the channels of departure as possible. His
editor told him—Roth, you must become sadder. The sadder you
are, the better you write.

All his sadness came from Frieda's illness. The hotel bedroom
was full of books and magazines on psychiatry. The frontiers of
the mind. He read Freud, his fellow countryman. The subconscious. Psychoanalysis. Was that not the science of literature? A
novel bursting its banks.

He read Joyce, the literary stream of consciousness. He dis-
missed that revolutionary device, not only because it inspired
him and scared him like all great literature, but because he felt
disbarred from doing anything similar in his own writing. It was
too close. Too much like what was already happening to Frieda's
mind. Her thought progression sometimes came spilling out in
a confession. She spoke like a clearheaded child, blunt and right,

naïve and insightful to the point of fortune-telling. She had the ability to see things back to front. She could take pleasure from life without thinking too much. Be head over heels in love. Be sad and happy in the same moment. Tear the stockings. Wake the neighbors. She could say what it was she wanted most in her life.

Then she would suddenly become silent. She would go from happiness to regret like a person crossing the street. The furniture in the room would begin to move with the sunlight coming in at new angles. The clothes she left on the chair would be misplaced. She would hear voices in the corridor. The rinse of water turning in a drain. She would speak of being homesick for places that were no longer home. Read letters that stopped carrying any news. She would break into a stream of sudden anger at the people who had let her down, at herself for not living up to what she had wanted most. She would speak with her hands. She would descend into a deep solitude that lay across the room like a million words unsaid.

How could he step inside her head and paraphrase those thoughts in fiction? It was not in his gift. He was too worried about that flow of unrestricted disclosure. He felt guilty for leaving her, for causing her condition, for all the unspoken things in her memory that could not be cured, for not having been there to protect her when she was a child.

He failed to see the warning signals. He continued to believe she could be remade like a new chapter, with new smiles drawn around her silent mouth. New gloves. New clothes. He wanted to believe the winter winds blowing through the Rhône Valley made her sick and the Côte d'Azur would make her better. The sun, the beaches, the seafood, the life in the cafés of Saint-Raphaël would keep her well while he was away.

She got dressed in her best clothes. She took her time getting ready. She packed no traveling case and left the hotel as though she was going for a walk, leaving the key at reception on her way out. She made her way through the streets. She found herself standing in the train station as if that was the only place her feet could take her. At the ticket counter she was forced to make up her mind where to go. Would she go back to Vienna to see her parents? Would she go back to Paris? Was there anyone else she could stay with?

For hours she sat on trains, waiting for connections on platforms in the cold. Late in the evening she finally made it to Frankfurt, arriving at an address she had for his newspaper editor. Benno Reifenberg and his wife, Maryla, answered the door to find her in such a distressed state they could hardly recognize her. This young woman who was normally so well dressed, they said, now looked like a human wreck. Her hair was disheveled. Her clothes crumpled. Her posture was full of fear, as though she had been attacked. What had happened on that journey that made her look so distraught?

She spoke with her hands constantly moving.

In a deep panic, she told them how she had come from Saint-Raphaël. The room at the hotel there was right above the central heating system, she could hear the voices of ghosts coming up through the pipes. There were toxic vapors rising into her room. She could no longer stay on her own in a place where nobody spoke but the radiators.

I can see through them all, Frieda said.

All those writers and intellectuals in the cafés, that cozy literary community. I can see into their hearts, she said. They're all so fake. All rotten with jealousy. They hate me and they hate my husband. They hate any sign of talent because they have none of their own. They only praise things to get the better of each other.

She mentioned them all by name.

Friends pretending to be friends.

They booked her a room in a hotel. They called her husband in Berlin to let him know what had happened. They stayed with her through the night, afraid she might harm herself or throw herself out the window. She could not sleep. She continued her deranged ranting until dawn, getting it all off her chest, those awful things she had been storing up for years.

She spoke out against her mother and father. She began disowning her own childhood. She finally calmed down when the sunlight came in and the night of fear came to an end, falling into a state of exhaustion and lethargy.

He came to collect her. It was just another episode of homesickness, he thought, now that she was smiling again. He took her to Paris and bought her some more clothes. He spent most of his time in her company, afraid to let her out of his sight. Whenever he had to go somewhere alone, he would lock her into the room.

A prisoner in her illness.

To a friend he wrote—she has contracted a chronic weakness, utterly defenseless. I know it must be my fault. Her condition is caused by so many unspeakable things I cannot begin to mention. Maybe in ten years I might be able to describe them, if I am still a writer then.

Did he poison her with his dystopian view? Did he make her ill with his dark vision of the world in ruins? His rage at the rise of Nazism? His unabridged forecast turning them both into lifelong fugitives in small hotel rooms with the sound of trains running through their sleep.

Only when she tried to take her own life did he finally come to realize that she could no longer be left alone. He sought professional help and the doctors diagnosed schizophrenia. The terror in that word struck him with a hollow feeling of guilt that would never leave him.

In desperation he turned to witchcraft. While they were staying with friends in Berlin, while she was in the constant care of a live-in nurse, he brought in a rabbi to exorcise her illness. After hours of torment and shouting in the room, she fell into a comatose state. When she awoke from that torpor, she broke out in further episodes of rage at everyone around her. She forgot who she was and where she was. He brought her back to her parents in Vienna, but that didn't work out either because she continued vomiting, losing weight by the day.

To a friend he wrote in great distress—my wife is very ill, psychosis, hysteria, murderous thoughts, she is hardly alive—and me, surrounded by demons, headless, powerless, unable to lift a finger, utterly helpless with no sight of improvement.

There remained no other choice but to bring her to a sanatorium. An institution in the country, just outside Vienna. The day left him gutted. He was filled with unspeakable guilt, leading her by the arm up to the main door, speaking her name, handing her over like a prisoner to be incarcerated. Filling in the documents, writing his signature, taking possession of her jewelry in a small brown envelope with the name and address of the institution printed at the top. A small parcel containing her lovely clothes tied with twine. In the waiting room, he saw her staring at the floor in front of her without a word. He heard the sound of doors and keys. The sight of other patients in their blue gowns being led along the corridor. A kindness in the voice of a nurse that was more frightening than any brutality he could imagine.

Friedl—his great love. He was forced to let her go. Kissing her goodbye. Speaking to her one last time. Trying to let her know he would be back soon. She would get well and everything would be fine, he would come and collect her, they would be together again, he would take her back to Paris. What could he do but stand outside on the street in tears? What could he do but find a bar to stop himself from thinking about her as she turned away?

25

I'M ON THE MOVE AGAIN. TRAVELING INSIDE LENA'S NEW bag with a copy of *The New York Times* she managed to pick up at the train station. It's the same journey from Berlin to Magdeburg that her grandfather made the day after the book burning. It feels to me like we're in that same expanding moment, as if the years keep swapping seats on the train until they eventually get to a carriage at the back called History. Each year brings events never before thought possible.

What can we do about the unimaginable?

Lena spreads the newspaper out on the table in front of her. She likes hard copy. I've heard her say to Julia that reading the news on the printed page makes it feel more truthful. As if the path of knowledge into memory is more secure when it has been converted into solid form. As if digital information is more equivocal and has the option of retracting the facts after they have been read.

As a book, I belong to the fixed-down world. Not yet deleted. The good news for me is that I have now been read by Julia and she loves the ending. She's even decided to nominate me for her next book club.

From what I hear, Julia intends to hold her book club in a bar that has been devoted to Joseph Roth, right next door to where he once lived briefly with Friedl, where he paced up and down like a prisoner unable to check out. It's a ground-floor café on Potsdamer Strasse, same side as the milliner's where Yoko Ono buys her hats. It used to be an undertaker's, where people got measured for coffins, and is now called the Joseph Roth Café. It's a reconstruction from the 1920s, with old photographs of Berlin on the walls and checkered tablecloths and a large mirror from a theater dressing room suspended at an angle. His books are stacked in piles around the café. Quotes from his work around the ceiling—*Hyla Hyla, white geese, Hyla Hyla, on the Danube*. There is a baby grand piano on a small elevated stage at the back and the menu offers good hearty food such as wiener with lentil stew, at prices any organ grinder could afford. They open only on weekdays. Always busy. You can't get in the door at lunchtime.

A buzzing inside the bag brings Lena's hand down to take out her phone. She's talking to Mike in New York. They say some intimate things to each other. She tells him that she's on the train, heading down to see her uncle Henning in Magdeburg. Mike is having his breakfast. She takes out a pastry from her bag and joins him.

She finds herself telling Mike something she remembers from childhood. An incident when she was around twelve years of age, in Philadelphia, just before her father sent her to Ireland to live with her mother for a year. I put a big scratch on a brand-new car on the street, she says, totally deliberate, like I hated that car. It was a protest. I was on my way home from school. I saw this beautiful convertible, blue and shiny. I made a mark right along the paintwork with a coin, she says. The owner saw me doing it. Like, he was at the window watching his car all day and I looked up and smiled at him. Then I kept going, completing this piece of insane vandalism. He complained to my father, but I denied it. And you know what, my father believed me all the way. The owner of the car sued for the repair. It was his word against mine. A police officer came to the house and I pretended to be completely innocent. I was good at looking innocent. The police officer said—so you didn't do it. And my father said—we have got to believe her.

Then I said—it's a beautiful scratch.

That blew it, Lena says.

I bet it did, Mike says.

My father had to pay, but he went on believing me and said it was a terrible miscarriage of justice.

What else could he do? Mike says. You keep faith with your child.

I told him the truth later, Lena says, and I think he was so hurt by that. I should have kept it from him. He didn't need to know, but it was on my conscience all the time. I wanted to be honest.

Bet he forgave you, Mike says.

How's your mom doing?

Aw, I don't know, Lena. It's tough.

I thought the lawyer said it was in the bag.

Meant to be.

It's a pushover, you said.

We asked for mediation. The neighbors refused to enter any kind of negotiation. Their lawyers are intent on going all the way to court.

And then, Mike says, out of the blue, while I'm down there, she came over one day. Lydia, next door. I answered the door and she was standing there all smiles, asking me to drop in to her house so we could maybe discuss this thing with the parking lot in a rational way, like friends. My mother didn't want to go, so I called around myself. I thought this might be a chance of solving the problem amicably.

What a turnaround! She was so polite and friendly, Mike says. Offered me coffee. A slice of apple tart, which is not like me to refuse, but I left it, just to keep things simple. She introduced me to her father. I had met the son before a couple of times, nice boy, Jake, out there in the parking lot throwing his basketball into a hoop all day.

So, I'm sitting there with Lydia, letting her know that my mother is a bit upset about this whole thing with the parking lot, naturally. It was the legal stuff without warning that gave her such a shock. And then Lydia starts apologizing. She had no idea. It was the way lawyers talk, there was nothing meant by it. She said she would speak to them and see if there was a different way of dealing with the whole thing. The last thing she wanted was to upset my mother. We shook hands and she stood at the door saying—tell your mom not to worry.

Big mistake, Mike says.

You will not believe this, Lena. No more than twenty minutes later, the cops called around to say they had reports of a disturbance. Our neighbor—Lydia, that is, the woman I'd just had a pleasant chat with over coffee—had called to say that I had gone around to her house and threatened her. I had been shouting. Using abusive language. She now felt unsafe. She was afraid to leave the house.

Three days later—listen to this, Lena—there was a letter from her lawyer accusing me of forcing my way into her home. She claims I pushed my way right into the living room and started shouting at her, so the lawyer said. They have video footage of me waving my arm. I can tell it's been doctored. Speeded up a fraction to make me look aggressive. She's a single mom and she now feels afraid to go about her business. Her lawyers advised me to desist from these acts of intimidation or else they would have no option but to seek a restraining order.

That's so fucked up, Lena says.

I'm going to see the lawyers right now, he says, just to deny all of this. What exactly am I denying? It never happened. It's like fake news, Lena. Some of it always sticks. How can you deny what is false?

She's borderline, Mike.

Crazy is the word I had.

Keep away from her. She's borderline. One hundred percent. I know people like that, Mike. They can't deal with reality. They constantly make things up. They will lie. It's all a fantasy to suit their purpose.

Her word against mine, he says.

Some creative instinct gone wrong.

Let the lawyer deal with her, Mike says.

I'm serious, Mike. She wants to manipulate. She wants to micromanage the world. She wants to damage you. And your mother. For no reason other than to get some sense of achievement. Some victory. Imposing her invented reality to take control. Who knows what she might do next?

Look—it's all going to be okay. Don't worry, Lena. Got to go. Call you later.

Stay on it, Lena says. You're doing the right thing.

I miss you, he says.

After she puts the phone down on the table, she begins crying without a sound. The landscape becomes blurred. The trees are like orange balloons. The fields have turned into waterways, the wind farms look like ships. A sandy path sways as it runs away into a forest. A level crossing surges up from under the earth with a group of schoolchildren waiting.

Lena reaches into the bag for a Kleenex and continues staring at the world traveling past. She feels the absence, the separation, the lack of certainty. She may be concerned about the direction her life is taking. Some unspecified anxiety. The motion of the train has left her exposed to a galaxy of memory. That's what trains do. They put the passengers into a dreamy state outside time. That great human protector has suddenly lost its ability to shield her.

An older woman sitting opposite Lena asks her in English if everything is all right. Lena puts the inside of her sleeve up to her eyes and smiles back—it's nothing. The woman says—it's the distance. She begins telling Lena that she has a son now living in Thailand with his wife, Pla, he's a guide on adventure holidays, taking tourists down the rapids. They have a small boy who is so sweet you want to sit all day and talk to him. They have a conversation twice a week on FaceTime. He sings pop songs to her. One minute he's there in front of me, the woman says, then he's so far away. She shows Lena a picture of the boy sitting at a table with plates of food laid out.

Is this your first visit to Magdeburg?

Yes, Lena says. I'm visiting an uncle.

Oh, that's nice, the woman says. You're from here.

No, Lena says. From the United States. My father was from here. He emigrated after reunification.

The woman begins telling Lena some of the places worth seeing in the city. Such as the cathedral. It has two organs now, she says, one that was built during the GDR times in place of the one destroyed in the war. Now they've put in a new organ, in the nave, where the original one was, she says, because the one built in GDR times was in the wrong place. They could play both of them at the same time, theoretically, the GDR organ and the post-GDR organ. You wouldn't know which is which.

It's worth having a look at the famous sculpture of the happy maidens and the sad maidens.

And the green citadel, of course, you can't mistake it, a crooked sort of building with trees growing out the windows and a waterway inside.

And there's a small Stasi museum. If you have the time. It used to be an interrogation center. On our way to school we passed by the gate where the flower delivery truck went in with the prisoners concealed inside. Our classrooms were directly overlooking the windows with the bars. But we never saw any faces.

26

IT'S NOT A LONG JOURNEY, AROUND TWO HOURS. WHEN the train begins to cross the Elbe River, the passengers seem to be struck by the need to stand up, as if the presence of water beneath them has set off a biological sense of arrival. They get ready long before the train reaches the other side and the announcement is made that we will shortly be arriving at Magdeburg main station. Lena gathers up the crumbs of pastry and places them in a paper bag. She finds the refuse bin, then she folds up the newspaper and puts it away in her bag and stands up to get her case. Her uncle Henning is standing on the platform waiting.

He embraces her like a daughter coming home. He picks up her case and leads her out through the station hall.

In the car park in front of the station entrance, two police officers burst into a sprint and come running past. One of them is fitter than the other, holding on to the gun at his side as he leads the way. The less fit officer runs a couple of paces behind, taking off his hat as though it's too heavy. They make it to the side entrance of the station and then come back moments later in no hurry, walking calmly side by side as though they've changed their minds. The faster officer is on his phone. The slower officer is putting his cap back on.

A man is seen walking away from the station holding a bunch of flowers upside down. Lena will mention this to Mike at some point later, how she has observed people in Germany holding flowers the wrong way around. It leaves her wondering if they have been taken straight from a bucket of water at the station flower shop and the idea is to stop the drip from running into the sleeve, or is it to make sure the remaining sap flows to the flowers, keeping them fresh longer? Or maybe the bringer of the flowers only turns the display upright at the last minute, for the right person, the true recipient.

Henning's voice is familiar. His words are old, full of authority and patience. They go to an Italian restaurant and Henning talks to her about the floods, when the Elbe rose one year and the restaurant they are sitting in right now was underwater up to the ceiling. Lena tells him about her life and how she has access now to a small studio in Berlin where she has begun to work on an art project. Henning wishes her the best of luck, encouraging her to go at it with great daring and confidence.

Strike another match, he says.

Another match?

Bob Dylan. Go start anew.

At the house, Henning brings her case upstairs and shows Lena to her room. She takes me out of her bag to show him. Then he gives her a tour of the library.

The books all begin cheering in a collective hum. It's the greatest welcome you can imagine. Like the sound of a thousand monks or nuns in a monastery awaiting the return of one of their own. They call out my title—*Rebellion*. My author's name—Joseph Roth. They have a place ready for me to fit back in among them. Their voices emerge from deep inside a prolonged silence, full of gasping and whispering. As if the outside world from which they were once forged has come back to revisit them. Home again. The familiar scent of other books, the static air, the tranquility. This gathering of human insight. This sanctuary filled with an infinite volume of thoughts and segments of imagination. They break out in a moment of unrestrained joy. The arguments among them are put aside. They go back to being themselves again, giddy as children, cut off from the real world for so long they want to dance around the library in celebration.

They can't wait to hear the news.

Things have changed beyond recognition, I tell them. People do most of their reading on phones now, in smaller installments. Life is too short and books are too long, but they continue to be as relevant as always, I assure them, on the cusp of being rediscovered like an ancient archaeological find. The world is full of confusion and people need stories more than ever before.

They give me the latest news in Magdeburg. A man recently performed a re-enactment of the book burning in public. On the main square, on the exact same spot where books were burned in May 1933, a hate-motivated individual took it upon himself to douse the diary of Anne Frank with gasoline and set it on fire in front of a small crowd of like-minded supporters. It was reported in the paper. The police were said to be making inquiries. No arrests have been made.

The books are packed in floor to ceiling, spreading into further interconnecting rooms. There is a copy of Anne Frank's diary on the shelves and it feels safe. No need for her to be hiding anymore in an attic. She has sold many millions of copies around the world by now. The public burning of one single copy is not going to silence her.

Henning goes straight over to find *Effi Briest*. The book that became my protective cloak after the book burning. Since then it has been reused as a disguise for a Russian novel which was in danger during the GDR years. At one point, he tells Lena, that

Joseph Roth book you have in your hand was no longer banned, but this one was. He opens the copy of *Effi Briest* and shows her the hidden book inside. A slim volume called *One Day in the Life of Ivan Denisovich.*

It tells the truth about Stalin's gulags, a story still not acknowledged in Russia, Henning says. He describes the scene in the Siberian camp where the narrator finds a fish eye in his soup and faces that moral dilemma, whether he should declare this great piece of luck and share it with the other inmates, or whether he should quietly eat the fish eye and keep that piece of glorious protein to himself.

Henning tells Lena that, during the GDR times, after the Berlin Wall went up, her grandfather used to receive books from the West through friends. The parcel would always be opened and checked at the border, but sometimes a banned book would get through without being noticed. Possibly, Henning tells her, because the title had not yet been placed on the banned list, or because the customs officials didn't read books and thought any book by a Russian author had to be okay. Or maybe they were more interested in consumer goods.

As you know, Henning says, your grandfather was a schoolteacher, liable to have his personal library examined at a moment's notice every time a banned book or record was found among the incoming parcels. He occasionally forgot himself and mentioned some literary detail in school which a clever student then reported to a parent, drawing suspicion. He once recited a section of George Orwell's *Animal Farm*—that got him into trouble. He was not a member of the party. He was active in other ways, running athletics clubs, chess tournaments, drama groups that gave him a status within the community.

Rebellion, he says, taking me into his hands and leafing with affection through the pages. A century old. We should have a birthday party with a cake, one candle.

What about the original owner? Lena wants to know.

Professor Glückstein.

My father didn't tell me a whole lot, she says.

We don't know what became of him, Henning tells her. Your grandfather made repeated attempts to find out. He was unable to travel once the Berlin Wall went up, so he got his friends in the West to investigate for him. Nothing. The Glücksteins disappeared like so many other Jewish people. There was no mention of their names on the register of camps, he says, and no evidence of them having emigrated.

If only books could speak.

If only I could tell them what I know, what I witnessed. David Glückstein was a good cyclist. On weekends he could travel up to two hundred kilometers, right across Brandenburg, up to the lakes of Mecklenburg. Some weekends he went all the way to the Baltic coast. In his mid-forties the journeys got even longer. He cycled to Breslau. He cycled up to Kiel.

I was with him one day when he cycled out toward the Oder River. He was going to visit his fiancée, a young woman by the name of Angela Kaufmann. She had studied philosophy in Jena. They had met at the theater in Berlin, after *The Threepenny Opera*, and she had told him that she was interested in writing. He was cycling out to visit her on the farm where she lived with her brother and her mother. Glückstein was up early that Saturday morning in April, before the city began to wake up. It was still cold out, but he soon got warm from cycling. He had me in his pocket, so I could feel the rhythm of his legs pumping up and down. I could hear his breathing. I could measure his heart rate gradually slowing down whenever he stopped to have a drink of water.

This was before the map was drawn. My last pages were still blank, as they were when I was first printed.

He cycled along the straight avenues with the trees lined

along each side, planted to shelter horse-drawn carriages from the winds across the open fields. He got to the farm and met his fiancée. He was invited for lunch. They served goulash. For dessert it was coffee with Streuselkuchen, followed by a single praline each and a small glass of liqueur.

After lunch they walked around the farm together. Angela brought him into the walled orchard, where the apple trees were in blossom. They went to one of the farm buildings where a swing had been erected in the doorway for the children when they were small. He watched her swinging like a child. They walked as far as the bench under the oak tree and sat down.

He noticed that she had ink on her fingers. She told him that she had been trying to write a novel but that there was more ink on her thumb than on any paper. He asked her what she was writing about.

She said she was working on a novel about the woman who smuggled Chopin's heart from Paris back to Warsaw underneath her dress.

She laughed and said she sat down to breakfast one morning with a blue ear.

My author would have described her laugh as something that flew up into the trees. Perhaps a pair of colorful things with a swift flight that didn't stay too long in one place.

Glückstein then took me out of his pocket and placed me into her hands as encouragement.

You'll love this book, he said to her.

Rebellion.

It has a new tone of urgency, he said. What other writer would have thought of making a barrel organ player his central character?

I can't wait to read it, she said.

When it was time for him to go, they returned to the house. He stood in the hallway while she went to her room to get a letter that she asked him to post for her on his way. She wrote the address of her aunt in Prague on the envelope with a blue fountain pen, but the nib was broken. He took out his own pen and gave it to her. He told her to keep it while he got the nib on her pen replaced.

Oh—thanks, she said.

He examined her pen and said there was something aeronautic about the blue design, as if it could take off and fly like a rocket.

That's a cheap pen, she said. Be careful it doesn't ruin your jacket.

She walked him to the farm gate, where his bike was leaning against one of the red-brick pillars. After they embraced and he set off on his journey back to Berlin, she sat down right away in the living room to begin reading. Her mother could be heard speaking to the dog on the doorstep and the chickens came running across the yard for food. Her brother walked in after dark and put some wildfowl on the kitchen table. The light was left on in her room until late.

27

HENNING FINALLY COMES TO THE MAP AT THE BACK AND speaks about how they found the place. It's out there near the Polish border, he says. Near the Oder River. Your grandfather eventually worked it out by studying the annotations in the margins. He was too old to undertake the journey himself at that stage, so he asked us to find the place for him.

We went there, your father and me, one day in the summer after your grandfather died. It was a matter of honoring his wish more than anything else. We found the religious shrine. We found the small river with the bridge, just as it is pictured in the diagram. Henning shows Lena the map and says—we followed that path and came to the farmhouse. We were quite certain we had the right place, but then a lot of those farms out there look the same. The single-story house, the barns erected in an oblong around the inner yard, the walled orchard.

The people living there had taken over the farm during the Nazi period. The family of Angela Kaufmann had been dispossessed, so the records showed. At first we were of two minds whether to go up to the farmhouse itself, but your father was braver than I was and insisted we talk to the new owners. There was a dog on a chain in the yard. He started barking at us and pulling on the chain, which was attached to an old water pump with a long handle.

A woman came out of the house and stood on the steps by the door. She wanted to know what we were doing there, so we told her we were out walking and that we had lost our way. We were looking for a path that might lead us to the next village, and she pointed us in the right direction. She told us to keep going along the path, we would come across an oak tree with a bench underneath. All we had to do is carry on, then we would eventually come to the village, a walk of maybe half an hour, she said.

This confirmed that the place corresponded with the map in the book.

We thanked her and apologized for disturbing her.

She said it was not a problem, then she continued watching as we made our way back out toward the path.

At the last minute, Henning goes on, your father turned around to ask another question. He just wanted to make absolutely sure that we had found the right place. Ideally, we would have loved to take out the book and show her the map, perhaps ask if we could walk around to have a look. But she was not all that friendly and the dog was continuing to lunge at us, making a lot of choking noises as the chain cut into his neck. And then your father decided quite spontaneously, since we had come all that way, to ask the woman something that would put everything beyond doubt.

Is there a barn here with a swing in the doorway?

The woman stared with instant suspicion. Her eyes narrowed. She took a long breath and said—how do you know that?

Her answer told us everything. It confirmed to us right away, however unwillingly, that there was a swing in one of the barn doorways.

The woman said—who are you?

In a raised voice, she wanted to know what we were doing there and why we had come all the way to her farm to ask such a specific question. Perhaps she thought we had come to accuse her of taking over the farm from the original owners. She became quite agitated. The dog almost strangled himself. She turned back into the house to call her husband—Karl, Karl.

We left as quickly as we could. We found the path and made our way past the oak tree. There was no time to sit down on the bench, Henning says. We had to keep moving. We heard shouting from behind us in the farmyard, and when we looked back there was a man running after us carrying a farm implement. Perhaps it was a scythe, we couldn't see with the sun in our eyes. He was joined by two young boys also carrying farm implements as weapons.

We had no option but to run, Henning continues. It was a while before the dog was released from his chain, so we had a good head start by the time he came bounding out of the farmyard and overtook the man and his sons. We continued running along the path toward the village and then we decided to split up. Because your father was carrying the book, we thought it best that I run across the open fields to distract the dog, so that he could make his way back through the forest. I was worried when I got home to Magdeburg and he was still out. He got lost in the forest and only returned late that night.

We were glad to have found the place. We told ourselves the map had been drawn to remember a good day. We never thought of going back there again. When the Wall came down, there was too much else to think about. Your father went away with the book and I stayed behind with the library. Maybe it was the only thing your father had to connect him to his place of birth, like an unsolved memory.

| 28 |

THE MORNING BRINGS A PINK GLOW INTO THE LIBRARY.
It overlooks the herb garden with its low red-brick walls and a
single pear tree in the center. The fruits have now been removed.
Henning has them lined up to ripen by the kitchen window like
ornaments.

Lena is still asleep upstairs.

The library is awake. The books are quietly talking among
themselves while the house is still silent. A low hum of voices, like
a swirling cloud of pollen, hoping to take part in newly invented
ecologies. Einstein compared the attempt to understand the universe to a child walking into a library. How can you figure out all
those books at once? It's like getting your head around the idea of
God, or the concept of infinity—impossible to grasp that entire
constellation.

Books stacked on tables, some left on the windowsill, some
yet unread, some in columns beside piles of newspapers and magazines waiting to be assigned places on newly built shelves in an
adjoining room.

All of them taking turns to tell their stories.

An English poet says people fall apart after love, like two halves of a lopped melon.

An Irish poet describes the act of love as two people getting the measure of each other.

Then there is an older Irish drama in which a woman falls in love with an outlaw on the run from the police for murdering his father. When the father appears and the outlaw status evaporates, her love dies and she loses the only playboy in the Western world.

And Tolstoy, the great Russian novelist who wrote about love as a dance between war and peace. He and his wife both secretly read each other's diaries. They became mind readers in the same house, stealing from one another to get ahead in that lovers' guessing game.

And the German writer who felt love could not be love without an ending. After leaving behind their farewell letters, Kleist and his lover, who was dying of cancer and had agreed to take part in a glorious suicide pact, walked a short distance from their hotel to a lake where he first shot her and then shot himself.

Effi Briest tells how her husband invented a ghost in the house to keep her from stepping out of line. It was only a matter of time before the ghost became real in the form of her lover. Effi ended up falling in love with a ghost in order to escape from a dead marriage.

Is there a ghost in every marriage?

Maybe it's only in dissolution that marriage is interesting in literature.

An American writer tells the story of a boy watching his father and mother as associates planning a serious crime. He finds a gun on the back seat of the car. His parents carry out a bank robbery and get caught. They are put on trial and go to prison, leaving him an orphan.

Another American novel describes the pregnant April Wheeler engaging in a moment of meaningless sex with her neighbor in the back of his Pontiac. Afterward, when he tells her that he loves her, she says—don't say that. It's the last thing she needs to hear. She is still out of breath when he says it again—it's true, I've always loved you—but she tells him to be quiet—take me home. In the darkness outside the dance hall she can't see his face and says she doesn't know who he is, because she doesn't know who she is herself.

A memoir written by an Englishwoman talks about marriage as a fraud. Both parties are forced into extraordinary levels of self-deception just to keep the family enterprise afloat. A man is either a predator or a provider. She describes herself traveling further and further away from her disbanded marriage into places where love is never spoken about.

An Italian novelist describes a woman whose husband walks out on her, leaving her with two children and a dog. The dog plays a central role in the story as a witness to her grief and abandonment. He is eventually poisoned and found dead in the park.

A writer from California tells how she gave her husband's clothes away after he died and then ran in grief to the charity shop to ask for his shoes back.

Does the pain of loss not describe love better than all signs of happiness?

The old man with his tape recorder comes across a love scene in his memory where he was once rocking in a boat with a woman. The brightness of that memory is too much. He can't take it. He quickly spools forward to a more bearable part of his life.

The great Norwegian dramatist tells the story of a woman who murders a book. It contains all the pain of a lost love. She kills what she loves. When the murdered book is brought back to life by her husband with the help of another woman, she goes into a room next door and shoots herself.

And the contemporary Norwegian writer who murders his girlfriend with a poem. He describes how she ran off with his older brother. When she comes back to him, everything is set for a wonderful reunion. But instead of forgiving her, he takes out a poem written by the Romanian-born writer Paul Celan. The poem is called "Todesfuge"—"Death Fugue." It begins with the words—Black milk of the morning, we drink it in the evening. A powerful description of the Nazi terror, when people were forced to drink their own death. As he reads out the words, it becomes clear that he is using the poem to let her know that she is nothing in comparison to this enormous event in history.

And the murdered story written by the American poet whose husband wrote the poem about lovers falling apart like a lopped melon. She loved him so much that she wanted to be one of his ribs, right next to his heart. Her collected letters talk about the day the two of them found an injured starling and took it in, feeding it milk and diced-up raw meat. But the starling got sick and weakened. Out of mercy, they placed the dying bird into a small box and gassed it in the oven. It was a shattering experience for her and she saw in it some fatalistic portent of what was happening to their love. The story was called "Bird in the House." It was never published. It disappeared. Like a missing person. Presumed dead.

And the book in which a mother murders her own child out of love, to protect it from slavery.

And the story of the artist who lost all the people he loved in the Nazi years. He painted their portraits and then erased them again. When a painting was finished, he began to scrape at the paint until the features became unrecognizable and he was left with nothing but a studio covered in human dust. The artist, described in a book called *The Emigrants,* went to live in Manchester, where he almost vanished himself, covered in a fine layer of dust that made him look like one of his own paintings, translucent, resembling a photographic negative.

Now it's time to be quiet.

The library has become silent because the bell has begun to ring at the cathedral. The sound comes in waves through the streets, slipping under the doors. It enters the morning thoughts of people waking up in their beds. It enters the library and steps into the bookshelves, a familiar sound that has been ringing ever since the Middle Ages. Carrying the stories of the people who lived in this city, their sorrow and their happiness, the children, the adults they became, those who left and those who stayed, the living and the dead, the love they had and the memory they left behind.

There were twelve bells to begin with, but most of them disappeared over the centuries. The main bell, weighing as much as six elephants, crashed to the floor during the Second World War.

The science of bells could fill the library many times over. Sound patterns that can be worked out mathematically and written down in a score, like music. But there is also, inside each bell, a unique set of frequencies that remain imaginary. Layers of subtones that cannot be measured. Like hearing things that are not actually there. Here we are, a couple of thousand books debating all night about the intensity of love, and this is our answer. The famous Apostolica bell of Magdeburg. A scale of harmonies and musical shapes coming and going on the morning breeze, like a choir performing the "Ode to Joy."

HERE IS WHAT HAPPENED TO JOSEPH ROTH'S MARRIAGE.
In his novel about a Jewish family emigrating to America, he writes about his wife's mental collapse. He calls her Miriam. She lay in a wide white bed. Her hair was loose, black and shining across the white pillows. Her face was red, her dark eyes had bright red rims.

She began to laugh. Her laughter lasted a couple of minutes. It sounded like the clear ringing of relentless sirens in train stations, like the beating of a thousand brass rods on thin crystal glasses. Suddenly the laughing stopped. Then Miriam began to sob. She pushed back the covers and her bare legs were kicking, her feet hitting the soft bed, becoming more and more urgent and regular, while her fists swung through the air in the same steady rhythm.

He describes the doctor arriving. His voice issuing the ominous words—she is insane. They hold her down while the doctor administers an injection—soon she will be quiet.

She is tied to a stretcher and taken away.

At the asylum, through the glass door separating the waiting room from the corridor, he describes seeing patients in blue striped robes being led past two by two. First the women, he writes, then the men. Occasionally one of them will throw a wild, contorted, worried, menacing face through the glass into the waiting room. He finds himself looking away in rotation at the floor, at the door handle, at the magazines on the table. In that moment of separation, handing her over into the care of the nurses to join those patients in their blue gowns, he is left staring in grief at a vase full of golden flowers.

To her parents in Vienna he writes—don't let Friedl read this book. It would not be good for her.

To his friend and fellow author Stefan Zweig he writes—I am terribly sad. So cut off from humanity.

To her parents—if Friedl happens to talk about me, whatever she says, good or bad, true or made up, the details should be related to me at all costs. Don't say she's wrong, that's nonsense. Listen to everything. Please. Promise.

Friedl, thank God, he writes, appears not to be suffering from dementia. She probably has hysterical psychosis. If it weren't for the fact that she is so intelligent and acutely sensitive, the whole thing might have been over within a few weeks. But she is obsessing over a small detail, can find no way out, and, in despair at this, it seems, is losing her mind.

Her heart is sound, she can drink good strong coffee.

Her weight must go back up to fifty-five kilos again. If she can tolerate liver and will take it, give her liver, as much as possible, and slightly underdone.

At the sanatorium outside Vienna, she has come under the care of Dr. Maria Diridl.

She sits in the consultation room, staring into the distance. Her eyes bear a catatonic expression, the eyelids drooping, half closed over. Her hair has had to be cut short because she tends to pull it out in big clumps. She remains listless, refusing to answer questions. At times she complains about "degradations"—having to take a bath, being told to eat, being told to sleep. She has been refusing her food, leaving most of it on the plate. Her weight is down to thirty-two kilos, she has to be "spoon-fed" on some days. At lunchtime she threw her food on the floor and picked it up with her hands to bring it to her mouth.

Doctor Maria is patient with her.

Frieda, why don't you tell me what happened.

She stays mute, hurting herself again, bending her legs back underneath her body to make them disappear. This has already resulted in a malformation or fusion of the knee joints which prevents her from walking properly. Doctors tried to correct it surgically under general anesthetic, but she goes back to this slow self-harming as though she wants to have no legs at all.

Frieda, you were married for ten years.

It's none of your business.

Your husband is a writer.

Frieda looks up and smiles.

The visitors are waiting for me outside, she says. They have nice legs and nice hands, but they have no heads.

Was it a happy marriage?

Russia is the biggest swine of all, she says.

She begins making faces. Grimacing and laughing out loud. She suddenly shrieks and starts reciting lines of poetry, linking a variety of remembered verse together in a long stream that makes no sense. She throws in bits of Goethe with Schubert's *Winter Journey*. Lines of Rilke followed by lines of Heine. Shouting literary junk around her at the walls, defending herself with these powerful words and saying there are people watching her—Christian eyes and Jewish eyes staring at her.

Doctor Maria waits for her to calm down.

Frieda, tell me about your wedding day.

In a coherent moment, she begins to speak about herself unguarded.

I was on my own, she says. In Paris, in Marseilles, one of those cities. He was away on assignment for the newspaper and I was left with his manuscripts and the voices of people in the next room and the smell of liver in the curtains and the different languages in the streets and nothing to do but talk to the violinist and ask him to hold me.

You met somebody?

It was a comfort.

Did you have an affair?

I told my husband when he came back. I confessed everything.

She is crying now.

It's all right, Frieda. You were lonely. It was a mistake. You told him what happened.

The baby, she says. I had to abort.

You were pregnant?

We had no children. He's infertile. He's told the whole world that he can't have children. It was not possible for me to have the baby. Are you in your right mind? Keep a baby in a hotel bedroom and go on traveling, what kind of mother would I be?

Doctor Maria holds her hand.

It's all right, Frieda. Everything will be fine.

Doctor Maria has many more questions. Was it one of those backstreet abortions? Was it done in the hotel bedroom? Did he come back from one of his assignments and find her lying on the floor in a pool of blood?

By now, she has dropped back into her silence again, staring out the window, waving her hands around. She cannot sit still and begins pacing up and down the room.

Doctor Maria puts it all down succinctly in the case notes—she has been ill for one and a half years. Married for ten years. Seems to have stepped outside her marriage. Marriage apparently happy, though she had a brief affair one and a half years ago, resulting in a tragic decline in her self-esteem, all of which she revealed to her husband in a big confession. Abortus. The marriage remained childless.

When the nurses come to take her back to her room, she bares her breasts and shouts—guess what I have between my legs. As they guide her out of the consultation room, she turns to point at one of the nurses and says to Doctor Maria—you should take a photograph of that woman's arse. It would be interesting. And insert a pencil.

She shrieks and laughs as they lead her along the corridor. She refuses her medication and has to be held down. She lies on the bed, covering her face with the blanket. She sleeps for a long time and refuses to eat. At night she sits up for hours in a comatose state with her knees pulled back in pain underneath her.

She likes it in the sewing room. Always sits in the same place. Calm and polite. She has made a shirt with no buttons. Says her visitors waiting outside should be sent to Germany, maybe they can smuggle back some stockings.

On May 11, 1933, she is officially declared a ward of court—*voll entmündigt*. She has lost the ability to speak for herself.

30

HE GOES TO VISIT HER. INSPIRED BY GUILT FOR NOT HAV-
ing gone sooner. He worries about how she is being treated and
cannot stop thinking about her wearing the blue striped robe.

As a journalist, he has written about standards of care at
psychiatric facilities and published a news story about a semi-
paralyzed patient who was placed in a bath with the hot water
running, scalded to death. Difficult patients are pacified with sco-
polamine, he writes, morphine, cold compresses. They are terror-
ized with injections and abused with harmful poisons. The school
of psychiatry seems slow to understand that mental patients are
like normal people, they suffer emotional pain, they can be made
angry, and irritated, and sad.

He speaks to the chief psychiatrist about her condition.
They have tried everything but her symptoms continue to dete-
riorate. He is provided with an outline of her present medical
status—psychomotor inhibitions, given to agitation, absent-
mindedness, sexual arousal, manic fantasies, acute paranoia and
wild imagination, hallucinations. She speaks in a High German
accent one minute, then falls back into a rough Viennese dia-

lect. She is often lewd. She talks to people that don't exist. Flies into sudden rages. Smears her food onto the walls. She has been exhibiting suicidal tendencies and frequently has to be tied down in a cot with bars at night—the patient is suffering from serious schizophrenia.

The chief psychiatrist sits behind his desk going over the reports, hoping to unlock the secret to her suffering. Frieda, he says, reading from the report, does not allow herself to be examined. Refuses to answer questions. She is frequently silent and distant, unable to recognize people. She is troubled by the brief affair she had with a violinist and the abortion that brought an end to her pregnancy. She says there is a cesspit inside her and describes herself as perverse.

He tells the psychiatrist that Friedl experienced traumatic sexual episodes in her early life. He confirms the pregnancy that was terminated during their marriage. Is there a possibility that her affair and the resulting abortion triggered her illness? Did this event kill off some vital avenue to happiness?

The ghost in the marriage?

The psychiatrist explains to him that there is no known cause for schizophrenia. There is no known cure either, but there may be some therapeutic way in which a husband can influence her condition.

Everybody is following Freud and Jung. People in white coats exploring the unknown frontiers of desire and sexual intelligence. Every experience, every orientation, every deviation to be explained and corrected. Literature is full of women thinking about sex.

There is a concerned look in the psychiatrist's eyes as he discusses these clinical matters with her husband. Her behavior has become increasingly lewd, he says, both in action and in words. Her sexual fantasies are often accompanied by an urge to be freed from all human restraints, running naked through the sewing room. He suggests a practical way of helping to alleviate those patterns of distress and arousal.

You should try to pacify her, he says.

Pacify?

She may be seriously ill, but she has normal desires. There are moments when she is completely lucid. Have sex with her. Please her. Satisfy her. Only you have the power to assuage those passions.

But is she in her right mind?

That's up to you to find out.

How?

Only you can get inside her head, the psychiatrist continues. You can enter those wild areas in her consciousness that we have failed to reach.

She's a ward of court.

She is your wife.

My wife? It's impossible for me to imagine that the person I love most in the world can have anything wrong with her mind. It's such a cruel contradiction. I cannot understand how a woman so beautiful can be mentally ill.

The psychiatrist closes the case notes and offers a piece of personal encouragement.

Look, he says, there is a degree of guessing involved in every sexual encounter. None of it is entirely rational. It's two people agreeing to suspend disbelief. Lots of emotional trading. Lots of assertion and surrender in both directions. We're all crazy when it comes to love.

How do I know it's love?

Love, lust, need, sexual healing, call it what you like. Make her happy.

Here, in this place?

You're a writer. Use your imagination.

He is brought to her room. He describes the corridor with a

series of numbered doors, like vertical coffins. He hears the keys rattling and the door to one of the vertical coffins being opened. She sits with her back to the wall and her eyes fixed on the far corner. Her legs are folded back to the breaking point underneath her. The door is locked behind him and he is left alone with her inside a padded cell. There is no furniture, no bed, nothing but a wooden stool bolted to the floor.

31

OVER BREAKFAST, HENNING TALKS TO LENA ABOUT HER grandparents.

Their marriage was lived in a wonderful flow of silence, he says. Her grandfather spent most of his time in the library. Now and again he would come home jubilant, having found a great treasure, some classic which he got for a bargain and instantly became immersed in. Her grandmother was a qualified fashion designer. She could have made a lot more money than her husband did as a teacher, but she didn't like running a business. Their marriage was devoted to knowledge.

On the wall by the door of the breakfast room there is a framed photo of them, taken shortly after they got married in the 1930s. It was done by a professional photographer. They are shot in profile. In the pose of courage. Her face overlapping his a little. His face a fraction beyond hers. Both looking out with great belief in themselves, as if they are listening to an opera, gazing into the lives that lie ahead of them with passion and resilience.

I love that photo, Lena says.

You know, Henning tells her, they lived the life of that picture. All through the war. All through the GDR years. Not for one minute did they stray from that sense of self-belief. It carried them through everything, good and bad.

Lena takes one of the ripened pears from the windowsill in the kitchen. She places it on a plate with a blue design around the rim. Henning stands up and searches through a drawer. He comes back with a dedicated fruit knife and she cuts the pear into four equal shapes, like long canoes lined up before a race. She looks at the pleasing design of these boats for a moment before picking up the winner.

Henning tells Lena that her grandfather once helped a young student when his parents got into trouble. During the GDR years, he says, the parents of one of his pupils planned to escape to the West. All their hopes were placed into that one great dream of getting out. The father managed to make it across on his own, hidden inside a truck carrying rolls of paper. He could easily have started a new life there, but he kept devising ways of getting his family out. A year later he returned under a new name with false passports for his wife and son, but the plan was naïve. The trap had been set. The Stasi agents understood the force of love better than anyone. They were good at guessing human weakness. The three of them were caught when they reached the border checkpoint in Berlin. The parents were sent to prison and the authorities decided to send their son to an orphanage to be re-educated.

Lena's grandfather offered to keep the boy in school and find him a place to stay with a relative.

The request was refused. Your grandfather, Henning says, kept trying even though it seemed futile. The officials he dealt with were coldhearted. The more representations he made on behalf of the boy, the more he became associated with the couple who had made the escape attempt. They accused him of being a collaborator. They brought up a list of contraband literature which had been confiscated in his mail, as if that proved his complicity. They came to search the house, and I remember them in the library for hours, an entire morning and afternoon. It was a terrifying day, mostly for my mother. My father kept calm. He had gone through this kind of thing before. They were wasting their time. They failed to find anything. It was all too well concealed.

Your grandfather continued pleading on behalf of the boy until they finally released him from the orphanage. It was his standing in the community that made him so persuasive. The boy, his name was Max, went to stay with our aunt in a suburb on the other side of the city. He went to a different school there. Occasionally he was invited to our house and we got to know him as a quiet type, not saying very much, waiting for his parents to be released so he could go back home again.

Some years ago, Henning recalls, I ran into him, by accident, here in Magdeburg. He was working as a caretaker in a house where a friend of mine lives. On my way in, he recognized me and asked if my name was Knecht. He spoke about my father, the schoolteacher, giving the name of the school. He had heard that I had stepped into my father's shoes and become the principal at the same school. It had been relocated when Russian troops took over the original building, Henning says, but then it moved back after the Wall came down and the Russians went home. We spoke for a while in the courtyard. His parents had gone to live in the West, but they were not happy there and returned to spend the rest of their days back here in Magdeburg. The escape they planned so many years ago as a young married couple may well have seemed irrelevant by then.

Henning wonders—was it worth trying?

Max told me he was glad they made the attempt at least. What else could they do? If they hadn't tried, they would have spent the rest of their lives regretting it. Even though it caused so much trouble and loneliness for each one of them while they were separated from each other, he said he would tell them to do it all over again.

These events were never spoken of very much in our house, Henning says. It was one of the many things my father got involved in over the years. I hardly remembered it until this man stopped me at the entrance to the house and introduced himself as Max. I didn't recognize him, Henning says. As though I had expected him to remain the age he was when he came to visit us as a boy, before his parents were released from prison. Max spoke to me with some excitement in his voice—it was clear that he was delighted to find the opportunity to remember what my father had done. There were tears in his eyes. My father meant so much to him. It felt to me that I had taken my father for granted. To me, Henning says, he was my father. To him, he was the man who rescued him from the orphanage. To me, he was a man sitting in the library reading. To him, he was the man who treated him like a son while his parents were in prison. We both remembered him on a trip down the river one day in the summer, reading out a passage from Dostoevsky on deck to all the passengers.

THERE WAS A REASON WHY LENA WAS SENT TO LIVE IN IRE-
land when she was thirteen. She tells Henning how her father said
it was for her safety. There was no further explanation. I thought
it had to do with me being a teenager out of control, she says. I
had got involved in small acts of vandalism around the city after
they separated. I tried to stop him from getting to know anyone
new. I had become a burden. An intruder in his life, watching him
eat, watching him picking his teeth, waiting for him to clap his
hands at the end of a meal to signal that it was time to move on.
I knew too much about him, his words, his clichés, his linguistic
mistakes. His German accent was an embarrassment, I thought.

You're going to Ireland, he said one day, it's in your best interest to live with your mother for a while. She has a nice school
picked out for you over there, you'll love it, he said. It was just
for a year, so I could get to know my mother's side. He packed
my case, each item laid out on the table and ticked off the list.
That was it, she says, we were on a flight the next day, handed over
into my mother's care in a house full of drugs, looking back home
across the Atlantic.

I loved my father, Lena says. We used to have great fun together. He could be very funny. He would tease me about the way I came in from school and left my shoes and my coat lying on the floor, like a snake shedding its skin. And I would get him back about his hair, telling him he looked like a parking lot full of weeds.

He was having some trouble at work at the time, he told me, but he never went into that very much. He worked in a large bakery where everything was mechanized, it was a waste of his baking skills. They mass-produced doughnuts and Danish pastries, and those rolls for Philly cheese steak sandwiches. Some of the workers began to victimize an African American employee, calling him names, throwing flour over him, telling him he looked better white, that kind of stuff. It was years later that my father told me all this. I think he was initially glad because they stopped calling him a Nazi. They turned on this Black man from Houston, his name was Julian, I remember—Julian Ives. One day they covered him in dough, like human pastry, then threatened to bake him. My father intervened. He called the supervisor and the men told him to get lost, what was a Nazi doing in a place with ovens. When the supervisor arrived, the men said it was all a joke. Everybody shook hands and that was the end of it—no hard feelings. Julian was told to get himself cleaned up and he was given the rest of the shift off. They chipped in and gave him some money so he wouldn't make an official complaint. Nothing was ever put down in any report. And then one day, Julian was found on the floor with head injuries. My father called an ambulance. The production line kept going, nothing was held up. The Black man was in the hospital for some time after that.

Lena describes how she and her father used to go on the train to a suburb called Bryn Mawr on Sundays, visiting friends who spoke German. I loved that journey, she says, the time it took going through different town centers. On the way back, the train stopped every couple minutes at each station. As we got closer to the city, the train went through a series of derelict stations where it didn't stop and I asked my father why? Don't the people here take the train? Don't they need to go into the city? We passed through all these boarded-up stations, no lights, lots of graffiti, like nobody lived in that part of the city anymore. My father said they were the African American neighborhoods and I thought they were like dead stations.

One night, she says, coming back from our Sunday trip, we came out of 30th Street Station in Philadelphia onto the street and a car pulled up beside us. One of the men inside leaned out to ask me what age I was. We took a different route home but the car caught up with us and the man called out—hey, Lena, look at you, I bet you're sixteen now. My father told me to pay them no mind. He took me into a diner and we sat there for an hour while the car kept passing by every now and again. I asked him what they wanted, and he told me they were workmates, probably drunk, it was nothing to worry about.

Then I suddenly found myself in West Cork, thinking—what did I do to deserve this? Like I was being sent to the rainiest part of the world as punishment for letting men talk to me out the window of a car.

Ireland was a foreign country to me, she says. He might as well have sent me to live on Pluto. Even though the language people spoke was English, it was totally different, everybody calling each other boy. I hated the landscape, the hills, the narrow lanes. I hated the school, the weather; the sight of the sea made me sick. I wrote letters to my father begging him to take me back. He replied each time, saying he was missing me and asking me to hold out. At one point, because I refused to speak to the teachers, my mother opted for homeschooling, but that was an even bigger disaster.

After I got back to Philadelphia, Lena says, my father finally told me what happened at the bakery. He opened up one day and said the Black man had been pushed off a steel platform by two of their work colleagues. The police were brought in to investigate and my father told them he had seen them forcing Julian Ives over the railing.

My father made little mistakes in his sentence structure. That's what made him so convincing, like everything was being translated simultaneously from German in his head while he was speaking. He used some ancient words that he must have got from books and nobody used anymore. Like the word merriment. After the men had pushed Julian Ives over the railing, they were full of merriment. He heard them laughing over the sound of the kneading machines.

And that's when the trouble started, she says. They began to threaten my father and follow us in the street. The Black man, Julian Ives, recovered from his injuries and went back to work. Nothing more was said about the incident. My father quit his job and found work in a small bakery further away. He carried this alone. He didn't talk much. Maybe he was trying to shield me from the truth by sending me to Ireland.

What would it take to bring those stations back to life? Lena wonders.

I go visit people I know in Philadelphia from time to time, she says, and they're still there, the dead stations we used to pass through when I was a girl. Nothing has changed. The hoarding is still there preventing people from getting in and out. The train still goes through without stopping. It's like passing through a different country, like train stations that don't belong to America. Like some faraway place has been lifted up and put down at random in the middle of Philadelphia.

I've taken a series of photographs from the train, Lena says. I've gone there in a taxi and taken pictures of the entrance to some of the stations, all the graffiti and the dust of traffic layered on the walls, some with the scorch marks of fires in the doorways. I try to imagine them back in service, with people standing on the platforms and the trains stopping as they once did before I was born. I can see them painted up in bright new colors and people so proud of their station they will add hanging baskets in summer, maybe an old wheelbarrow with a display of flowers, like they do in some of the other stations further on the line out to Bryn Mawr. What would it take for that to happen? she wonders. What would make those stations viable once more? A whole country would need to change. All I can think of doing is to take more photographs. Next time I get back, she says, I will go and talk to the people who live there. Maybe I can put it together as an exhibition. Call it something like—*Bringing Up the Dead Stations*.

| 33 |

ON THE TRAIN BACK TO BERLIN, LENA HAS ANOTHER conversation with Mike. The motion of the train is coming up through the wheels as she takes me out of the bag and places me on the table. She opens out the page with the map. Pointing the phone down, she takes a photograph and sends it to Mike.

Mike, she says, you've got to come over.

It's a bit difficult right now, he says.

I have it. Henning gave me directions.

Where?

The map I sent you, she says. In the book—*Rebellion*. On the last page. Remember? Henning told me how to get there.

There's a lot going on here, Lena.

Mike, she says, there's something in this. I can feel it. I don't know what it is. But we need to go, you and me. The two of us, let's go out there together. Find out where it leads to. It's like we can step back in time.

Can't do it, Lena. Not right now.

It wouldn't take long, Mike.

It's Mom, he says.

This map, Lena says. This book. It's beginning to open up a whole new world for me, Mike. There's a story here that I want to excavate. Bring it to life in my work. I need you to come and find it with me. Us both. You'll love it.

I can't leave my mother right now.

What's going on?

Do you know what the neighbors have now done? You're not going to believe this, Lena. They've put up this gigantic fence around the parking lot. I know it's their property, they have a right to do that. But it now means my mother can't get into the house around the back anymore. If she parks in the lot, she has to walk back out into the street again to go in the front door.

No way, Lena says.

Yeah, he says. And wait for it. They have now put up security lights. And cameras. It's lit up like a stadium at night. It's not just, like, one or two lights. It's fifteen bright arc lights, I counted them, just to let our lawyers know everything that's going on. I mean, how is this going to look in court? The judge is going to say they're being totally unreasonable. They're creating an atmosphere of hostility.

They must hate themselves.

The place looks like a detention center. I swear, it's like a prison yard. All you need is prisoners walking around in a circle twice a day, and armed wardens standing by. My mother can't even bear looking out there at night. She's embarrassed when her friends come to play bridge and they ask—what's that going on out back? She's got to explain it to them—it's a parking lot, the neighbors have decided to light it up at night for security reasons. Which is entirely their choice, of course, but it now sounds like it's a rough neighborhood, like people are no longer safe if they need all those lights and high security fences. And what's more, they leave the lights on all night. I had to get my mother some blackout curtains.

They must hate their own lives, Lena says. That's the only explanation I can think of. The neighbors. Can they not see how ugly it is, even if it is their own lights?

You don't hear your own noise either, Mike says.

This will backfire on them in court, Lena says. It's pure intimidation. Is it even legal?

This is it, Mike says. My mother is not going as far as the courts. She's had enough.

She's not going to sell up, is she?

What else?

It's your home, Mike.

She's made up her mind.

Does that mean they've won?

What can we do? She was going to have to sell up sometime. A day comes when you leave it all behind. We've all got to keep moving on.

She has been driven out.

The other neighbors have got together in a group to fight this whole thing legally, Mike says. But she's out. She has no time for that confrontation. She's been having trouble with her stomach in the last while. Doesn't eat properly. She used to have a great appetite. She's a mean cook, you know that, Lena. But this has got to her.

And the old cop at the back, he's gone nuts. Dan Mulvaney. He's threatened to shoot the neighbors. If they come anywhere near his property, he'll shoot without warning. Intruders, he calls them. Interlopers. He's standing at the back door with his rifle, day and night, just waiting for them to put their heads over the fence.

It's like war, Lena says.

The neighbor's kid, playing basketball, Mike says. He used to go in there to get his ball back now and again from the old cop. Dan would have a chat with him. I've even seen him in the parking lot throwing the ball into the hoop himself. Now that's all over. If that ball goes into Dan's place, it's gone.

I can see his point, Mike says. The old cop. It's his whole life, that house. He raised four sons there. He lost his wife only a couple of years ago. I see him up there on the roof doing those repair jobs himself. That's all he has now. That and a bit of hunting on the weekends.

It's just sad, Lena says.

Hey, it's not the end of the world, Lena. My mother can have a long life. She's talking about moving into a condo. She's quite upbeat, looking up all these properties around the state. This might be the start of something new. Who knows? It might be the best thing that ever happened.

BACK IN BERLIN, LENA WENT STRAIGHT FROM THE TRAIN station to the music venue. She managed a quick bite to eat, but there was no time to go back to the apartment and drop off her case. Julia was in Hamburg, getting Matt settled in with his other mother.

Lena sent her a message—here with Madina.

She attached a photo of herself standing beside Madina, the Chechen-born folk-rock artist. It showed them onstage with a set of drums in the background and a man behind them on the right with his back turned. The singer has her arm around Lena, both smiling, standing in such a way that it appears as though Lena has the prosthetic leg. The illusion works perfectly. Lena seems to be lifting her knee up to show her prosthesis with an illuminated design along the shin, wearing light blue footwear. It's a trademark image of the singer. She has been photographed like this with her fans, also with some prominent artists like Nils Frahm.

Madina's head is shaved on one side. She has a wave of red hair coming down along the other side of her face which gets tossed around during the performance. Her arms are bare and there is a tattoo that looks like a shadow along her neck. Lena wears a black jacket and a russet dress, from which the thigh with the prosthesis seems to be emerging. Her hair is shorter than before, with a green streak running across the top that could be mistaken for foliage.

A message back from Julia—sounds like a great night. What happened to your leg?

Lena's reply—if only I had her voice.

Followed by a quick chain of messages. Hope all going well in Hamburg. Doing a lot of swimming. Lots of walking in forest with the dog.

Lena sent the same photo to Mike in New York with these words—amazing Chechen singer. Plays the accordion, totally mind-blowing.

Mike's reply—you cut your hair.

Lena—you like it?

Mike—love the leg.

She sent him a link to a track on YouTube. A recording of the band in which the trumpet and accordion appear to chase each other in a circle, while the singer's striking voice comes striding across the top with the chorus in English—"No Time for Bones."

Just imagine how the ex–barrel organ player feels right now, in his prison cell, hearing that somewhere in the future, at a well-known Berlin music venue, a young Chechen-German singer with a titanium leg plays the accordion like an absolute demon. Her dancing is inhuman. He would give a raucous cheer and start dancing around his cell himself, stamping his good foot. He would dance to his memory of marching tunes, and children's rhymes, ancient love songs that my author grew up with in the East. A beat of horses' hoofs. The smack of splitting wood. The rhythm of carpet beating. He would jump on his bunk and celebrate this living female artist a hundred years younger than himself with a brilliant roar through his prison window at the night sky. The guard would come running to see what was going on and bang on the door. If only Andreas could start over again. He would take the courtyards by storm. Bring the mothers and children of the city out dancing. Men whistling his melodies coming home late from the bars.

Madina Schneider—just like my author. Endless flight. Endless hotels. Carrying her identity around in a suitcase. Her memory in her songs. Her selection of prosthetic legs in an extra suitcase along with the band's equipment. Always beginning again. Always unpacking. Getting up onstage every time with the performance of her life.

She had the audience banging on the tables.

And then a moment of drama that nobody was expecting. At the end of a song, when she was removing the accordion, like taking a jacket off her shoulders, there was an interruption from the crowd. The band was taking a breather before the next song and the audience had broken out in a wave of conversation, when Bogdanov, her ex-partner, showed up right in front of the stage with a bottle in his hand.

Madina—I love you, he shouted.

At first he looked like an over-devoted fan.

I can't get enough of you. I want you. I need you, Madina. You're killing me.

It was the type of situation where nobody knew what to do. How can you complain about a man who loves her music so much that he is willing to make a show of himself?

Madina leaned down toward him and said—stop this, Uli. There's no point.

Kill me, go on, he said.

Go away, Uli.

Please, he said, going down on one knee. You're the only one, Maddy.

Uli. You're wasting your time.

The band got ready to start up again. The drummer gave the

initial tap of the drumsticks. He set up the beat for the next song, but it lost energy and dropped off. The unfolding disruption was getting in the way.

Bogdanov managed to haul himself up onstage. He stood in front of the microphone and tapped to see if it was working, then he said—one, two. His voice was so loud he jumped back. He began pointing at Madina with the bottle as he declared to the audience—

I started her off. I got her singing. Me—Uli Bogdanov. She loves me. She offers me protection.

Nobody wanted to tackle him. Perhaps they assumed he was her manager, making an official announcement. Maybe they thought this was some big Johnny Cash declaration onstage. The audience finally became irritated because he was not making a lot of sense.

Get him off.

He became aggressive. He threatened the audience with his bottle. You're all wankers, he said, you have no idea how much we love each other.

Asshole.

He turned back to her and pleaded—Maddy, please, please, I'm yours.

He dropped the bottle and made a lunge for her. She pushed his face away with her hand.

Uli, fuck off.

His sense of balance failed. He began to rock on his feet. He slowly tilted backward, knocking over the microphone with his elbow. His weight gathered momentum as he reversed across the stage, tripping over the accordion, getting his foot caught in the straps. He continued staggering into an electric guitar and finally collapsed against the drums. His hand reached out like a drowning man for something to hold on to, pulling down a stand with cymbals on top of himself with a clanging finish.

Silence.

It was like the end of a song. Somebody in the audience applauded.

They laughed. They whistled.

Bury him deep.

Two men rushed onto the stage and pulled Bogdanov away, still protesting, turning around to see Madina, blowing her kisses with both hands as he was dragged outside.

The band started up again with renewed energy. The night was a great success, the Bogdanov display of admiration seemed like part of a singer's gathering fame, the audience loved her even more.

Everyone sat around with the band at the bar after the performance. It felt good being part of the inner circle, hearing them joking about the earlier disruption. One of them remarked that Madina would need a security detail in the future. She was getting mobbed. What she needed was a couple of heavies with big necks to stand in front of the stage with their legs apart and their arms folded, looking out for signs of restlessness in the audience. This could be Altamont. Madina laughed and said she could do her own self-defense, thank you.

They were talking about their touring schedule. Armin put his arm around his sister and said to Lena—she's impossible to catch up with now. Madina and her band were starting a ten-day tour of Scandinavia. She had then been meant to do a tour of Britain but that had been canceled because one of the band members might have had difficulty getting a visa. Instead they were filling in with a tour of France and Italy. Then it would be back to Holland to record an album.

Madina stood behind Armin and put her hands on his shoulders—our new roadie.

She kissed each one of the band members, then she gave Lena a warm embrace, thanking her for coming to the gig. Armin said he would see his sister out the door to the taxi and come back in a moment.

The rest of the band was packing up. Lena was getting ready to leave. She went to the bathroom and then she looked around for Armin, asking the band members if they had seen him come back in. She went outside, thinking he was still with Madina, that they might have been talking before she got into the taxi. Eventually Lena found him a little distance down the street. There was a man holding him by the throat against the wall. It was Bogdanov. Lena recognized him. She shouted at him. He pointed his finger at her like a warning not to come any closer. She had the presence of mind to take a video of him walking away, but it was too dark to make out his face. She was more concerned about Armin. He was spitting blood.

It's nothing, Armin said.

It's not nothing, Armin.

I'm okay, seriously.

You're covered in blood.

She pointed to the cluster of drops on the ground, then took some Kleenex out of her bag and wiped his face. He held an entire packet of tissues up to his nose.

She brought him to a restaurant nearby so he could get himself cleaned up and they could have a drink to recover. The waiter seemed a little uneasy at first. The sight of blood made him back off initially—it's the color of violence. Armin returned from the bathroom like a new man, concealing the bloodstains on his shirt with his arm held across his chest. They sat for a while at a table by the window and had a bottle of Beck's Gold each.

It came from nowhere. As soon as they were back out on the street again, it seemed inevitable. That moment she used to describe, as a child, as "cut between." Whenever she watched a movie on TV with her father as a ten-year-old girl and a couple began to kiss on-screen, she would shout the words and bury her face in a pillow. Here she was, leaning into that movie scene without a thought.

As they moved on again, Armin insisted on pulling her case, that rolling sound of somebody returning late from a holiday in some warm place. They could not find a taxi, so they took the U-Bahn. The smell of the U-Bahn in Berlin, Lena said, was unlike any other underground network in the world. Some unique identity of its own, as distinct as woodsmoke or candle wax. Or was it the inside of a rubber ball? A combination of coffee and chewing gum and hair products and everything else worn by the people who travel on those yellow trains each day.

Back in Julia's apartment, Lena dropped her bag at the door. She began removing Armin's bloodstained shirt. As they stood in her bedroom, she asked about the shrapnel fragments inside his body and began tracing her finger over the scars where the metal pieces had entered when he was a child. They had stretched a little as he became older. She wanted to know if they bothered him, did it ever hurt? He said he couldn't feel a thing, no more than he could feel his own liver.

I wonder what they look like, she said.

They're like any normal body piercings, he said. I've made them safe. They can't hurt anyone else now.

You were lucky with this one, she said. That's close. A few millimeters further over and it might have gone straight through your heart.

Wait, he said.

Armin walked out to the kitchen. His bare feet could be heard slapping across the wooden floor. There was a brightness coming in from the street and no need to turn on the lights. He went to the fridge and took down a couple of magnets, leaving the notes they were holding up—theater tickets, gallery flyers, laundry receipts—on the table. He came walking back through the wide living room and stood in front of Lena.

Here, he said. Why don't you put them on?

Attach them, you mean?

See if they work.

She took the fridge magnets from his hand and began placing them one by one onto those scars that corresponded with the shrapnel inside his body. On his hip, she placed one in the shape of a hamburger. Another on his thigh with the name of a restaurant called Max and Moritz. The one close to his heart was a bottle of Russian vodka. They remained attached. He was magnetized. She threw her arms around him and they fell back on the bed laughing.

| 35 |

WHY DO PEOPLE SHUT THEIR EYES WHEN THEY KISS? IS it because they are too close and everything becomes blurred? Do they need to eliminate the faculty of sight to open up that vast landscape of lips and tongues in the mind? The unlimited distances of the human mouth. Like traveling in space. Infinity. Like walking into Einstein's library.

And how do you describe love?

Fontane kept it short. His description of Effi Briest's frozen fingers being gently prised apart with kisses does it all. Another German writer once cut it down to a single line—then for a while it was nice. A British writer reduced it to a brief tangle of pubic hair. A female author living in the United States describes a woman waking up after a year spent in a drug-induced sleep with the vague memory of her boyfriend's testicles sweeping across her face.

What more is there to say?

It's only afterward, looking back in words, that anything becomes memorable. How it came to a decision to sleep with

Armin is not something Lena discussed with anyone. It may have been a spontaneous thing. It may have been coming down the tracks ever since Lena's bag was stolen and Armin found her discarded book lying on the ground in Görlitzer Park.

She did say one thing. While they lay still afterward with the light from the street spilling across their bodies and some late-night voices coming in from outside, she told Armin that she had felt something sharp digging into her back. It gave her the feeling that one of the shrapnel pieces inside his body had come loose. She laughed and said it made no sense. It was one of the fridge magnets, of course, but she continued to believe it was one of his shrapnel fragments that had been dislodged by all the movement and she didn't want to remove it. She was not sure it could be described as pain. A sensation that kept coming back again and again as a reminder that what was happening was true, it was not imagined.

Look, she said.

She pointed to a bruise low down on her back and said that was certified proof.

Armin patted his hands up and down along his body as though he was checking for his wallet.

They laughed.

She placed her head on his shoulder and they lay silent for a while, dreaming with open eyes.

Inside her bag on the floor of the living room, her phone buzzed a couple of times. The messages were coming from far away, from another time zone.

It was Mike.

Are you still up?

It was early evening over there in the United States and he was calling to see if she was awake and up for a chat. He eventually assumed she was asleep and left a message saying he would catch up with her in the morning. A short while later he followed on with an audio message which she only played back to herself the next day when she was alone again.

It was Mike saying—I'm here in a gas station outside Des Moines. And I'm looking at this man sitting in front of me and he's got three double burgers on a tray and three boxes of fries and three large Diet Cokes on another. Like he's gone for the Mega Meal three times. He's making his way through them all and I'm wondering why he doesn't just get one at a time, it's not like he's getting a reduction. And while he's eating, he's looking straight ahead without seeing me. Like he's completely focused on the food. Going through the whole lot as if it's his job, lifting the hamburger to his mouth, then picking up a couple fries with his fingers, then taking a sip of his Coke through the straw. Every now and then he swirls the Coke around to hear the ice inside, or maybe to guess how much is left.

And it looks like he's not really thinking about anything. It's hard to know. Anyway, Mike said in a low voice that had the restaurant house music playing in the background, you know the way you look at somebody for long enough and you gradually become them. You kind of imagine you are that person. You take on their mannerisms.

Here I am, he said, and I think I've turned into this man in front of me. Like I've just made my way through three of those double burgers and all the fries and I'm just washing it down with the last of the Coke, waiting for that slurping sound to come up through the straw at the end. And you know what, I bet he's desperately lonely.

Jesus, Lena, you won't believe how much I miss you, here in this place on the highway, and I'm not able to say exactly why, but I feel like that guy eating just to stay in the world.

| 36 |

AND WHAT ABOUT THAT DAY AT THE SANATORIUM IN Vienna? The day Roth goes to visit and finds himself alone with his wife inside one of those vertical coffins. Nothing in that padded cell that might give her cause to self-harm. Nothing but the stool bolted to the floor and the cold Viennese light dripping in through the high window, not enough to spread into the corners.

He speaks to her. He says her name and tells her the news from the world outside. He has brought his stories from the streets of Paris, the cafés, the world is still free, people have been asking for her. There will be such a great welcome for her when she gets better.

She remains unresponsive. What is there for her to report but the same routine interrogation by the psychiatric team about her thoughts, her feelings, her dreams, her sexual fantasies. The same greasy smells of dinner lingering in the walls, voices coming and going, faces unrecognizable, echoes following her back to her room and the screaming at night from deep inside a vertical coffin next to hers. The same walks around the grounds of the hospital.

The same avenue of trees and the brief slice of sky, the same windows replicating themselves each day in this house of doubt. In the corridor, the sound of keys always coming to the wrong door.

He has come with his smile to restore her. He has brought the smell of smoke in his suit and laughs as he tells her it was bought for him by his friend Stefan Zweig when he spilled wine on his trousers. He has brought the sound of trains and platform whistles, the click of tracks, the screech of wheels. His eyes are alive with affection. His mustache. His cravat. His calm voice. His jokes will cure what all those psychiatric assessments have failed to understand. His hands are the only viable intervention left, like his own delicate handwriting, touching her face to remove a dried smudge of tear dust from her cheek.

Come on, she says.

Her eyes speak to his. She has it back, that provocative smile in her mouth. She takes his hand and invites him to dance with her around this anonymous room. His other hand is holding on to one of her cold kidneys at the back while she is humming along to the music inside her head, laughing and using his nickname—Mu. The one she made up from his second name, Moses.

Come on, Mu, you haven't danced with me in ages.

His shoes squeak on the rubber floor. Her bare feet are silent. Around and around the stool fixed to the center of the dance floor they swing to a tempo that begins to gather speed, a Viennese waltz that converts this small institutional space into a grand ballroom with ornate ceilings and golden columns. Her madness has purpose now. She flings his name at the rubber walls with accelerated joy and rage. An absurd force in her laughter, like the needle of a compass inside her head pointing to something that needs to be repossessed right away before it's gone again.

You always take your time, Mu.

Her need for human warmth is urgent. Her tormented desires are now free to express themselves. All those possibilities, all the

novels not yet written by her body, come to life with such conviction in his company. She can feel the energy in his lungs. She can
feel the cool buttons of his suit. She can feel the soft weight of
his writing hand. She can feel the padded floor against her back
as they lie down together with the light on the ceiling buzzing
like a trapped wasp. She can hear the sound of keys and doors and
people whispering in the corridor.

She smiles and turns her head calmly toward the stool bolted
to the floor as if there is somebody sitting there watching them.

It's my husband, she says to the invisible spectator. His name
is Joseph Roth. He's a good storyteller. He can make things up
that I could never imagine.

On the squeaky floor of this cell intended to prevent suicide,
they spend the night together. Locked inside a room from which
he has come to rescue her. Their confinement becomes their
escape. Their marriage, their identity, their memory, the forces
of hatred turned against them, the restless places they have traveled to and found freedom, the entire story of their love has been
shaped into this one short, terminal moment of luck and misfortune. Surrounded by harm in a space that allows no harm, they
keep each other close. He kisses her forehead and she lays her
head on his shoulder. With the walls smelling like the interior of
a car tire, they lie awake in a time void.

She can't sleep. She sits up and speaks to the door as though
there is a team of doctors and nurses standing in the room with
their charts observing her. She tells them to write down in the
file—the man who brought her here came to take her away. She
tells them to bring her clothes first thing in the morning, she will
walk out hand in hand with him into the street, they will get on a
tram together, straight to the main train station.

We're going back to Paris, isn't that so?

In a letter written to his publisher, Hermann Kesten, in 1971,
Joseph Roth is reported to have said that he made love to his wife

inside a padded cell on the advice of psychiatric experts. It was a private matter between husband and wife, not entered into the medical records. What is recorded in the case notes on repeated occasions is this statement in her own words—the person who brought me in here should come and take me out again.

WHEN JULIA RETURNED FROM HAMBURG, SHE OPENED the gallery one morning to find a hand-delivered envelope in the mail. It had no addressee. Inside, she found the printed page of a book and a newspaper cutting. An interview with Madina Schneider alongside a photo of her taken on a bridge in Berlin. The loose book page had been defaced with a swastika. The familiar Nazi symbol was scrawled with a red marker that came through like a blurred mirror image on the reverse side.

The missing page. Cut from my rib cage when Armin made his payment in the barbershop.

Weird, Julia said on the phone to Lena. You better come down.

I'll be there right away, Lena said. She was not far away, working in her new studio.

You should let Armin know, Julia said.

What?

It's got to do with his sister, I think.

The interview with Madina describes her as a new talent with limited previous media exposure in Germany. So far, she's better known in Holland, where she is in discussion with a company about recording her first album. The journalist reveals that the singer travels with a collection of artificial legs, each of them different—like you wear different clothes for certain occasions, Madina is quoted as saying. Some of them have flashing lights, others are decorated with various absurd things like medical tubes and bandages, depending on her mood. She is proud of her prosthetic leg, the journalist writes, and she jokes about getting a parrot, if that isn't a bit cruel to take a live bird on tour, maybe a false one would be more appropriate. She talks about the parrot once found by Humboldt, the great German explorer, speaking the language of a lost Amazonian tribe.

The journalist goes into her Chechen background, though the biographical details are thin. The singer lost her family during the Second Chechen War, it says, after which she and her surviving brother were brought to Germany by an aunt. They grew up in Frankfurt with a family that she cannot possibly say enough good things about.

Madina has no intention of going to Chechnya while the leader of that country posts photographs of himself lying around with a tiger.

The interview goes on to say that her music allows her to express the longing for what is missing. The absence of a backstory is what got me singing, she says, something she picked up from her adoptive mother, who is from the former East Germany. She used to sing at the top of her voice around the house to make up for the gaps in her biography. Your life is a bit of a fabrication anyway, Madina says of herself. Like a song. With an accordion solo in the middle. It's never going to be any more than—based on a true story. What was it her father used to say—biography, the story you call your life?

My story is prosthetic.

Her quote is pulled out of the interview for the headline. The caption underneath the photo says the Chechen-born singer is in training to run the Berlin Marathon.

It's raining heavily by the time Lena arrives. I can feel the dampness in my pages. The character in my story feels it in the stump of his amputated leg. Lena gives a shudder as she comes in the door. The water is heard dripping on a steel window ledge outside and I have that sensation of being confined indoors, like a deferred sneeze. She leaves her umbrella open by the entrance, forming a series of pools on the floor.

Shouldn't you bring this to the police, Lena?

Wait. Let me talk to Armin.

Looks like a death threat, Julia says. We shouldn't have touched it, there might be fingerprints.

Let me figure this out with Armin.

While they wait for Armin to arrive, I become reunited with the missing page. It's a great moment for me. That feeling of being intact. Lena goes about fitting the severed page back into place with tiny strips of adhesive paper on each side. It might be somewhat predictable to say this, but it feels like having your leg reattached by an expert surgeon, hinging perfectly back and forth at the knee joint. Julia begins to unpack some of the artworks that have arrived for her next exhibition. A collection of nudes painted by a female artist celebrating the flesh of women with all their pudginess and blue veins showing.

My story is complete again. All my fingers and toes, page numbering correct.

The reattached page begins to tell me where it's been all this time. It sat folded up in the inner pocket of a leather jacket belonging to the man who defaced it with the red marker. Ulrich Bogdanov. He never takes that leather jacket off. I was forced to witness everything firsthand, the rediscovered page says. The way he eats, the way he slouches in his chair with the phone, the way he talks to his wife. I even had to accompany him into the bathroom.

The lost and found page goes on to describe that time in captivity as an eye-opener. Bogdanov, it says, seems at first not to be such a bad person at all. He works in a retirement home for the elderly. You would have to be decent enough to even want to take up a job like that.

I've seen him with some of the patients, the mutilated page says. He can be extremely kind. Their infirmity doesn't bother him. Their smells. Their morbidity doesn't put him off life. In fact, it seems to enhance his lust, knowing that he is young and they are old. I have seen him, for example, the page recalls from its days in captivity, wiping the bum of an old man and then going home to have sex with his wife no more than an hour later. She wanted him to have a shower first. She said he smelled of old people. But he looked on it as part of the same sequence of life, the arc of time going backward, cleaning the shit from an incontinent old man's legs in an operation that lasted twenty-five minutes, followed by urgent sexual activity with his wife, lasting no more than three to four minutes.

Without taking his leather jacket off.

He is terribly generous to his children. He loves them. No doubt about that. He buys them massive Disney dolls, the house is covered with stuffed toys and plastic products—that's where the earth's resources are all heading, the previously missing page says. And his wife. Anna. She has more jewelry than she has days to wear the stuff. He's just got her a TV the size of a farm gate and he keeps saying it's too small—I'll bring it back and get you a proper one.

He is moved by a deep range of feelings. His favorite songs are those describing male humility, such as the big hit about angels. Angels spreading their wings to shield him from harm. He cannot help singing along to the words—protection—love and affection. When he's drunk he sings that song at family gatherings, raising his voice to an emotional pitch on the word waterfall. It brings him to tears and his wife, Anna, consoles him like a baby, stroking his head.

Once or twice, the newly freed page says, you can see the other side of him coming from nowhere. An irrational piece of cruelty breaks out with no warning. Some crime carried out long before his time, something his Russian grandfather did during the war, coming back in some delayed form of trauma. The violence committed in war is brought home by the perpetrators and continues loitering in the kitchens, in the bedrooms, in the uneasy dreams of children, only to resurface a generation or two later like a dormant virus.

Without explanation, he just flips, punishing somebody at random for an atrocity that was never atoned.

He is in a position of power over the people in his care. He can be generous and he can also withdraw favors, like divine justice. I've seen him taking it out on an old woman who is unable to retaliate, the eyewitness page says. She wants her wheelchair to be placed next to her husband in the sunshine when they are brought out into the garden every afternoon. They're all lined up, wrapped in blankets. And just because she asked to be placed beside her husband, he says—no. Bitch. He places her in the shadow of the buildings, as far away as possible from her husband. They have only a few days or weeks or months at most left in this world, but he refuses to grant her that request. He has them sitting apart and she's getting cold, unable to say a word, looking over at her husband at the far end of the universe. She waves but he can't see her with his back turned.

My defiled page describes him as a talented hater. He understands exactly what will hurt this old woman most. He leaves her out there until the rest of them have all been brought back inside again for supper, she's the last, and one of the nurses then says her hands are frozen, they've gone blue, her skin is like thin wax paper. The nurse blows on her hands and rubs them back to life, saying it might be better that she doesn't go outside in the afternoons anymore until next summer. Where, in fact, the old woman doesn't care about the cold, there is nothing she wants more than being out there beside her husband, they don't have to speak, just sitting side by side is all she wants.

The following day, Bogdanov makes an about-face. He is so kind to her she can hardly believe it. He treats her like the most favored person and she cannot trust him. He tucks the checkered blanket in around her back and even asks which side of her husband she would like to sit on.

Then he goes home to spend hours at night on his laptop looking up right-wing sites. While his wife and children are asleep, he's in touch with his friends, discussing ways to create chaos and destabilize democracy. They want to fight the system from inside, infiltrating peace movements and climate activist sites, spreading their message of unrest in the most unlikely places. He followed every word in the epic trial of Beate Zschäpe, the woman whose two lovers went around Germany murdering kebab vendors and greengrocers mostly of Turkish origin. He has online friends in Poland, in the United States, and in New Zealand. He unfurls a swastika and hangs it up behind him on the wall, then takes it down again before going to sleep, folding it up neatly and putting it away on top of the wardrobe, inside plastic packaging that came with a set of pillows.

Armin arrives at the gallery with his jacket soaked and his hair down on his forehead. One eye is still discolored by the blow he received from Bogdanov.

The windows have steamed up.

They sit together over coffee and wonder how to react to this piece of hate mail. Is it a sign of something worse to come, or is it simply the action of a jilted lover?

It's not fair that you two have been dragged into this, Armin says.

Armin, you can't do this alone, Lena says.

We can't let this happen, Julia says.

It has been decided, after Armin helped Lena and Julia to map out each possible scenario like a series of alternative plots, that it might be best to contact the police.

This is serious, Julia says. Let's keep it all aboveboard. I don't want those fuckers coming in here and I certainly don't want them getting either of you on the street some night. I know this city. They shot a Chechen separatist in the head, right here in the Small Tiergarten. His assassin fled on a bike. Then they put out a whole lot of misinformation about the victim being a brutal terrorist. All you do nowadays is reverse the accusation, say the man they killed was a killer, then his killing becomes a good deed.

It has been decided, by Armin himself, that he will give up his job measuring parking spaces and go on tour with his sister instead. He has been offered the job of roadie—that will get him out of Berlin for a while.

And finally, it has been decided, by Lena, that Armin should leave his current place of residence and come to stay in her studio instead. It has a bed and a small kitchen, she says, and lots of light. It's at the top of the building, overlooking the river. He'll never find you there.

| 38 |

TO BE HONEST, I QUITE LIKED THE ATTENTION. IT WAS my first time inside a police station, apart from the fictional arrest of Andreas Pum, that is. Though I have to say it fell short of what I would have imagined. It was a normal police station. A room with desks and computer screens. A police officer's hat left on one of the desks. A coffee machine and a water dispenser. Some posters on the wall to do with drug crime and missing persons. If anything, the familiarity of these interiors made it all seem staged. It's hard to believe things that make no effort to be true. A writer might have made it look more interesting.

There was a squeak in one of the swivel chairs.

A female officer held me in her hands, wearing protective gloves, examining the defaced page from both sides.

Understandably she didn't have time to sit down and read, but I was hoping she might have glanced over the contents of the eyewitness page at least. But the text was irrelevant to their investigation. What mattered was the Nazi insignia. She uttered a tiny hiss each time she turned the page, making sure that she was looking at it the right way around.

Not nice, she said.

She spoke good English. She switched back into German with her colleagues, two male officers, one of whom was busy scrolling through a series of screen images with the faces of known extremists for Armin to identify. The other man was documenting the evidence, downloading a thread of abusive images Armin had received on his phone.

It was impossible to say which one of the swivel chairs was making the squeak.

The officer continued leafing through the pages. She seemed drawn to the unseen. The subtext. A book is like any human mind—it has a story to tell that is not always revealed at first reading. Underneath the printed text there is a complex pattern of subconscious associations. Secrets, suspicions, hints, reflections. It communicates on all those highly intuitive levels that are so crucial to the hunch science of police work.

The past is no longer safe, I wanted to say to her. My time is coming back. Listen to what my author wrote to his friend Stefan Zweig a hundred years ago—the barbarians have taken over.

Don't deceive yourself. All hell is coming.

It was not what anybody wanted to hear.

The police officer calmly went over the details with Armin. The backstory with Madina. The loan repayment on the purchase of a guitar. The scene at the music venue followed by the assault outside. Lena showed them a video of Bogdanov pointing his finger. Unfortunately there was no clear view of his face.

The police officer flicked through the pages and came across the map at the back.

Is this part of it? she asked. This map here?

Lena said—no. That was drawn by the original owner, years ago, before any of this. She then explained how the book had been saved from the book burning. How it came into her possession, how it was lost, or stolen, then recovered by Armin. How the page had been cut out by Bogdanov and then returned with the red swastika intended as some kind of death threat, that's what had to be assumed.

The officer carried me over to her colleague to have the swastika page scanned in.

Technically, she said, there is not a lot we can do with this kind of hate crime without more evidence. I know the threat can be frightening. But look—I'll tell you what we will do. We will track down this man Bogdanov and ask him a few questions. How does that sound? Let him know this is now in the hands of the police, just in case he has any ideas.

Thanks, Armin said.

We need to remain calm, she said. We don't want to switch on the blue light yet.

At that point the defaced page began to make itself heard. Maybe not to the police or to anyone else in the room, but to me at least. After spending all that time undercover inside Bogdanov's squeaky leather jacket, the newly liberated page felt emboldened to outline exactly who they were dealing with. This Bogdanov guy has become a problem, it said. This is no empty threat. A few polite questions on his doorstep is not going to do it, I'm afraid. He's been hurt. He feels aggrieved. He's full of resentment now.

Take it from me, Bogdanov's unauthorized biographer said, he means business. He's managed to purchase a gun. It's all aboveboard. Fully licensed. I've been out there with him on the firing range. It was deafening. He doesn't go hunting. He's only interested in fixed targets, he's a very good shot, he's entered a competition.

The liberated page went on to reveal that Bogdanov keeps the gun in a small box on top of the wardrobe, along with his hidden flag. He has taken it out once or twice to show his online friends late at night. Other than that, he seems to have no particular use for the weapon. I've only seen him threaten his own family with that gun, the mutilated page said. One evening when his wife disagreed with him over something one of the children did. They spilled yogurt on the map of Germany, which he had spread out on the table to give them a history lesson. When he got upset and slammed his fist down on the table, she said—for God's sake, Uli, don't get so uptight, they're kids, a bit of yogurt will do the country no harm. Afterward, while she was giving them a bath, pretending not to hear him talk about respect for nationhood, he walked in and pointed the weapon at the children's heads.

What are you doing, Uli?

The children thought he was joking.

I can't believe it, his wife shouted. You bring a gun into this family to, what—threaten your own children. I hope to God it's not loaded.

We need to be ready, he said.

I want that thing out of the house, Uli. Right now. Never let me see it again.

All these migrants, Anna. Europe is getting flooded. We need to draw the line. Our daughters are no longer safe. They need protection. Don't tell me you haven't seen all those attacks, those murders.

You've lost it, Uli.

She tried to take the gun off him, the defaced page said. There was a moment where it might have gone off right there in the bathroom.

Give me that bloody thing, she said.

Let go, he shouted.

His voice echoed around the tiles. The children started crying as if they had soap in their eyes. Their mother and father fighting over a toy. She had to let go when he held her face in his hand, pointing the gun directly at her head. She looked at him with fear in her eyes and said nothing more. He then pulled the gun away slowly and blew across the muzzle.

I'm their father, he said.

Once he was back in the living room switching on the TV, she could be heard vomiting in the toilet bowl.

Nobody in the police station heard any of this. We were just talking among ourselves.

The officer closed the pages with a slap.

Good, she said. We're going to pass the file on to our bureau with special focus in this area. They may very well get back to you with more questions.

As they were wrapping up, she introduced Armin to one of her colleagues and said—this is Lothar. You know what he does in his spare time? He's in a rock band. Your sister might be interested in meeting him. You should hear him doing "Johnny B. Goode." He plays all around Germany, and you know what he does during the day when he's off duty? He talks to kids in schools about racial hatred and integration.

She winked at Armin, to make him feel better.

She spoke to them as a couple. She advised them against giving in to any further demands. It was essential to take all necessary precautions without curtailing day-to-day activities. She thanked them for supplying the information—if anything else comes up, please get in touch right away.

Life is full of things that never happen, the officer said. Let's hope it stays that way.

The meeting ended on that encouraging note. They even strayed into a light-hearted moment, spinning off into a spontaneous conversation about facial recognition technology. One of the male officers remarked that it might be a handy police tool if it wasn't met with such public opposition from human rights organizations. Lothar, the "Johnny B. Goode" officer, made the point that facial recognition was a natural faculty possessed by crows. If only you could train crows to work for the police, they could keep an eye on everyone around the city. It was probably something the Stasi would have thought of, the female officer added.

Everyone felt reassured. The greatest fear at that point for me was the possibility of being sent away for fingerprinting. Ten days in a queue at the forensics lab while the more urgent cases were being cleared ahead of me. It would have meant missing out on Julia's book club. I was glad when the female officer gave me back to Lena and shook hands, telling them not to worry, just lead a normal life.

39

THEY WALK THROUGH THE CITY. THEY STOP TO BUY A pineapple. They stop again outside a café bar that has not opened yet. The shutters are down. There is a father and a small girl outside. The child is sitting on the wooden bench holding on to a scooter, swinging her legs. Behind her there is a large image spray-painted onto the gray shutters, of a female astronaut in a space suit. The child is wearing a helmet and the astronaut is wearing a helmet. The astronaut has cartoon features and bandages on her face, a crisscross of plasters on her left cheekbone, another single beige strip on the visor of her helmet, and a further one on her right cheek. She looks slightly bashed up, as though she's been through a rough journey and has returned to earth with a cigarette hanging from her mouth and her upper lip curled in an expression of ironic resilience. Beautiful and absurd, a character from a graphic novel, with large eyes and drooping lids. She is indestructible, as though she's been out all night in the clubs, ready and up for more. She could take a lot worse and still come out alive. A white speech bubble emerging in a zigzag from her mouth says—*it's my cosmos, bitch!*

The day is bright and sunny, but also a little cold. Autumn has begun to grip the streets and the air is motionless. Lena tells Armin that she loves nothing more than a good crunchy leaf to step on. It's just the most satisfying thing on earth, she says, don't you think?

As they continue walking, it seems to me that a curfew is about to fall across the city. Time is running out and it will soon be winter in these streets. Soon they will be taking in the outdoor furniture. We will feel it in our pages, that flinching against time. The words will stiffen and retreat into a big sleep from which we might never wake up. As though we're about to be overwhelmed by some great weather event, some world phenomenon, some part of history rising in the streets like something that has never happened before. We come to a place where workers have dug up the street and left a pile of sand at the side of a pit. The pit has been fenced off with planks of wood. The sand makes it look like the workers are at the seaside. Somewhere in the distant past the city must have been underwater. Like a city on loan from the sea. A place where people carry subliminal thoughts of the sea coming back to reclaim the streets.

They pass by a woman sitting in a car putting on her makeup, leaning forward toward the mirror as she applies the lipstick. They pass by a woman standing on the street with her dog on a lead, holding a small yellow sack containing dogshit in her fingers. They pass by a woman sweeping leaves with a wide broom. The broom looks new, with a wooden handle and bright red bristles. The sweeping woman is joined by other street sweepers, one of them with a wide rake, all gathering the leaves into one large mound, and then it's Armin who is the first to speak into that silent walking.

Sometimes the broom shoots, he says.

What?

Lena laughs.

It's a German expression, he says. My mother said it from time to time. I suppose it comes from children using the household broom to pretend it's a gun. You know, building a barricade of chairs in the kitchen and hunching down to defend their territory. It's usually said as a warning, I think. Like, harmless things don't stay harmless. If you pretend something is a weapon, sooner or later it might turn out to be one. Or maybe, if you imagine something bad, who knows, it might become what you imagined.

Shoot the broom, Lena says.

I'm not joking, Armin says. I've heard my boss say it recently. One of our colleagues was talking about his wife meeting her former husband for a drink, just to chat about the children from that earlier marriage. The boss told him to watch out, sometimes the broom shoots, but the man whose wife was meeting her former husband said—don't worry, it's me who's holding the broom.

They come to a bridge and Armin leans over the wall to look at the water below. There are people sitting on benches along the bank, some still wearing light clothing in the sun, holding on to the summer. A child throwing stones into the water. Lena wonders if they should get on one of the boats and go up to the lake. She speaks as though this might be the last opportunity available.

You could walk there faster, Armin says.

When they get to Lena's studio, she takes me out of her bag and lies down on the bed. Behind her, over the bed, there is a skylight through which the light of the afternoon comes flooding down around her. She examines the map and wonders, as Armin walks around the room—is there something buried there, what do you think? Armin comes to lie on the bed beside her to have a look.

I am happy for them.

The room returns to stillness. As if they're waiting for the red glow of the sun to fade and darkness to fall, before they can resume their lives. He tells her that he's got to get a few things done before he goes on tour with his sister.

I need to get a new X-ray, Armin says.

What for?

They won't let me travel without a certificate. The shrapnel, he says. Sets off alarms at the airport.

Armin tells her about a man he met some time ago who was turned back in midair with metal pins in his leg. He's from Nigeria, he says. He had a gunshot wound in his knee and managed to make his way to Ireland, where he was operated on at one of the main hospitals. Then he found himself being deported back to Nigeria because he was unable to produce any evidence of persecution other than his injuries. A human rights lawyer took up his defense and argued in court that they had no right to deport him because the bolts and screws in his knee were the property of the hospital. Quite apart from their indifference to the man's uncertain future, the lawyer said, the immigration officials were, in fact, committing an act of larceny by exporting hospital property without consent. On top of that, there appeared to be no medical experts in Nigeria qualified to remove the complex metal structures from his leg, so the man would have suffered for the rest of his life in terrible agony.

The judge rejected the plea and the deportation officers came to collect the man while he was still on crutches. An officer boarded the flight with him, that's the way it works, Armin says, the deported individual has to be delivered into the hands of the police in the country to which he is being returned. In any case, Armin says, the Frontex flight was turned back over Algerian airspace. The immigration officials in Ireland were there to welcome him back just a couple of hours after he left. They had to wait for an appointment at the hospital before the bolts could be removed and he could be deported successfully.

In the end, Armin says, his lawyer in Dublin pursued a case against the state on his behalf and managed to have him brought back from Nigeria. He's living in Ireland now. Eventually they gave him citizenship.

Through the skylight it is possible to see the clock tower, lit up as the evening light fades. The clock has a black face and gold-painted hands, no numerals. Armin stands up to look out and see what the time is.

Let's go and eat something, he says.

The X-ray, Lena says. Could I have a copy of it?

What for?

Do you think they might give us a copy?

We can ask, he says.

It's your body. You're the patient, you have a right to demand it.

It belongs to the hospital, Armin says. Like the bolts and screws in my friend's legs. My body is my copyright, but the radiology image is their property.

We'll have to steal it, Lena says.

Why?

My art, she says.

You want to use it?

If that's okay with you, Armin. I want it for my work. A life-size image is what I have in mind. Your X-ray will be the focal point, with all that shrapnel, jagged and black inside. The story of a man reconstructed from several locations.

Cool, Armin says.

Are you sure it's okay with you?

Absolutely, he says. I'm with you all the way. You distract them and I'll download a copy.

He laughs—don't worry, they'll give me the file.

Lena kisses him. They go out for something to eat and I hear the door closing after them. The room is silent. The city has come to life with the sounds of night and there is a yellow glow coming in through the skylight across the floor. The clock tower chimes. I have been left behind on a broad desk along with the pineapple and a small stack of books.

At the bottom of the pile, there is a book by a Russian journalist who was murdered for telling the truth. Her life had been in danger for some time and she had been subjected to many acts of intimidation and violence, even poisoned, even once put through a simulated execution when they brought her out on a pitch-black night and fired a rocket launcher directly over her head. All because of her reporting on the war in Chechnya. Despite those threats, she continued searching for the truth, bringing the facts to light in her articles for a free Moscow newspaper. And because the truth could not be silenced in any other way, she was shot in the elevator of her apartment block one day. It happened to be Vladimir Putin's birthday. She was shot four times by a man who got into the elevator with her. Twice in the chest, once in the shoulder, and once more in the head at point-blank range. It is assumed that her killing was carried out on orders from the top, for her outspoken work on the Chechen War, for speaking the truth about Russia, for not giving up.

Her name is Anna Politkovskaya. The book is called *A Small Corner of Hell.*

Her firsthand account of the conditions during the Second Chechen War describes the country as a commercial concentration camp. Villages are locked down. Children become mute after bombings. The Feds, as the Russian troops are known, will not even let people out into the woods to collect wild garlic, their only source of vitamins. The inhabitants of these poor villages pay ransom fees to have their loved ones released from the pits in which they are kept by the military. People go around collecting money to save a neighbor from being killed. A woman is asked for fifty thousand dollars before a surgeon will agree to operate on her injured husband. His skull is an open wound. She has no money. She is forced to look for a friendly taxi driver who might bring him into Grozny. The capital is blockaded, nobody can move. Every morning women stand outside a detention center to plead for their loved ones. Each one of them is given a price to pay for the release of her husband. If she doesn't pay, the figure goes up, because the price of a corpse is higher in Chechnya than the price of a living person. She describes a group of women gathered around a table, sitting out the curfew through the night, listening to the sound of distant shelling.

The women at the table do not cry, although they would like to. You rarely hear crying in Grozny. They've all cried their eyes out long ago.

And the children's hospital.

In the words of the head doctor, Ruslan Ganayev—

As soon as the blockade started, the parents grabbed their children and tried to make their way to the villages to hide from the shooting and the purges. They even took some kids from the resuscitation wards. They simply took out the tubes and carried them away. We had a girl with infantile cerebral paralysis in traction—they took her off it. The only patient we have left in the whole hospital now is a three-month-old, Salavat Khamikov from Alkhan-Kala.

40

THE CATERING WAS DONE BY A SPANISH RESTAURANT. The wine was delivered by the usual Italian dealer, though nobody drinks very much at these meetings anymore. Julia had decided against holding her book club at the Joseph Roth Café—it would have been too noisy. She had opted instead to hold it at the gallery, with a few comfortable chairs set in a circle, and soft lighting arranged around the room. In the center she had placed a bouquet of flowers on a wide coffee table, along with a stack of books from previous meetings. The book club journal containing earlier entries was lying open on a new page.

The title had already been entered—*Rebellion*.

This was it—the psychoanalysis. The trial by book club. On the wall there was an enlarged projection of the first-edition cover with the image of a cripple waving his crutch at his own shadow. A photo also of Joseph Roth in his early days, wearing a cravat and an expression of amusement and curiosity, before he started drinking himself to death.

The guests stood around helping themselves to the food.

The servings were made appealing in tapas portions. There

was a vegan platter with schnitzel made of eggplant as well as some dishes from a local Israeli-Palestinian restaurant with hummus and baba ghanoush. A further table laid with coffee and desserts, small slices of brownie and apple strudel.

Julia asked if anyone had seen the production at the Schaubühne theater where the actor took off his clothes at the end of the play and turned himself into a human schnitzel, rolling around the stage in egg and flour and breadcrumbs—he left his underpants on, thank God.

Guten Appetit, she then added.

Lena is a New York artist on loan to Berlin, Julia announced to the book club members by way of introduction. Two of the other members couldn't make it, so there was Sabina Wilfried, a schoolteacher from Stuttgart originally. Valerie Crosthwaite from the UK, now living in Berlin, running an online medical practice. Renate Frohn, an old friend of Julia's from school, also working in culture management. Yanis Stephanopoulos, he moved to Berlin from Greece, Julia said, but don't mention Greece, please, he hates anything to do with his own country. She put her arm around him and said—look at him frowning already. And finally, Jürgen Kohl, a psychoanalyst, Julia said, specializing in marriage counseling. His wife, Zeta, is Croatian; they have two of the most beautiful children you have ever seen in your life.

Julia took out her phone and showed Lena a photo.

Guess who that is?

It's a grab from Spiegel TV, Julia said. October 9, 1989. Bösebrücke. The famous Berlin Wall crossing at the Bornholmer Strasse. That's the bridge in the song by David Bowie—"Where Are We Now?"

Lena examined the photo. It showed a crowd of people on the move, making their way across the bridge for the first time, just after the Wall fell and the barriers were opened. The people are smiling, mostly young, eager, hopeful, everybody talking. There is a tall man among them, in his twenties, wearing a black bomber jacket and carrying a shoulder bag. He has a bottle of beer in his hand, turning back to say something to a border guard in passing.

Julia pointed to Jürgen. That's him, right here, she said. He was the hundredth person to cross the bridge that night, am I right, Jürgen?

Jürgen nodded.

Lena smiled—yes, now I see the resemblance.

He's a piece of walking history, Julia said. Look at the clothes, Lena. And the hair. What was it you were saying to the border guard?

I was telling him to get stuffed, Jürgen said.

Number one hundred, Julia said. Of twenty thousand. And how many millions more since then.

I'm sorry I wasn't the first.

I love that photo, Julia said.

Once everyone was sitting down, Julia opened the meeting with a formal touch, naming the author and the book, still in print in multiple editions. While I was being passed around, hand to hand, she mentioned the fact that I had been rescued from the book burning by Lena's grandfather. Sabina asked if the swastika was from that time and Lena explained it was a recent addition, the page had been cut out.

The conversation stayed with the book burning and Sabina mentioned a special collection of books housed at the university in Augsburg. After the war, a businessman had gone around spending his money buying books banned by the Nazis until his house was filled with them, and after he died the collection had been taken up by the university.

Okay, Julia said. Let's have a look at the contents of the novel first. Renate, would you mind.

Renate began to summarize the story of Andreas Pum. He has lost his leg in action during the First World War and finds himself in a military hospital in Vienna. I wasn't sure it was Vienna, she added. Pestalozzistrasse is in Berlin.

Renate said the author seemed to have no intention of producing a realistic narrative—the story is more like a legend in which a law-abiding barrel organ player is the unwitting victim of intolerance on a tram. He loses his busking license, causing his marriage to disintegrate. After spending time in jail, his only friend in the world, Willi, the former sausage thief, offers him a job as a toilet attendant in a fancy restaurant. He lives out his days in the men's toilets with a parrot that says hello to all the customers coming in.

He dies in the act of rebellion. He declares himself a heathen. With nobody listening but the parrot, he makes a final speech to the empty cubicles, rebelling against the whole world around him—his country, the state, the nation, God, religion, politics, the war, the society for which he lost his leg, everyone who has contributed to his undoing.

A character rebelling against his own author?

He turns down an offer of a plush job in heaven and says—give me hell.

The suggestion was made by Yanis that Samuel Beckett might have written something like this. A toilet attendant growing old overnight in the company of his parrot.

Some of them had seen the movie version made by the Austrian director Michael Haneke, in which the organ grinder is played by an actor who has a cast in his eye. This makes him look tragic, more like a helpless boy. A prison scene shows him walking around the exercise yard with chickens pecking at the ground as though they were fellow inmates.

Jürgen went to the table to refill his plate.

Valerie said she felt the story was trapped in a male viewpoint.

It was written a hundred years ago, Yanis said.

Lusting after women with big breasts and wide hips.

What's wrong with that? Julia said.

Jürgen turned back from the table and said—men rely a lot on visual stimulation.

It's all so dead white male, Valerie said.

Jewish, on-the-run-from-the-Nazis, dead white male, Yanis reminded her.

Look, Valerie said, it's a nice book. I hate running it down. But I have issues with the male character being cast out by the woman. She's to blame for his downfall. That's a misogynist view, I'm afraid.

I've been kicked out by a couple of women over the years, Julia said, laughing.

It's all men alone, Valerie continued. Men on trial. Men in graveyards. Men looking at the human condition as though it's the woman's fault.

Look at his masterpiece on the fall of the Austro-Hungarian Empire, Valerie continued. *The Radetzky March*. A young cadet, Trotta, seduced by the sergeant's wife when he's fifteen. She unbuttons his tunic and pulls him into the bedroom, kicking the door shut with her foot, as I remember it. It's a good scene, but it all goes back to that basic witchcraft view of a woman's power to corrupt.

There was a silence.

Could I make this point, Jürgen stepped in. He returned to his seat in the circle and held a piece of sweet potato up on his fork like a microphone. In my view, he said, it may have less to do with gender difference than with a more fundamental mismatch of human expectations.

I have it all the time in my practice, he said. I deal with a lot of male dysfunction. Lots of control freaks. Men full of narcissism. Men full of regret. Men who get blamed for not initiating. Men whose performance can be undermined by a sigh. The wrong word at the wrong time. I'm not breaking any confidentiality here.

I had a man the other day who left his wife and child stranded on the autobahn for something she said about his dick. I have another man who claims his partner checked her phone during sex. I have a client who came home last week to find his ex-wife having sex with a man on the living room floor—that's ten years after they got divorced, she still had the key.

I'm getting sidetracked here, Jürgen said. What I'm saying is that sometimes male inadequacy leads to aggression. Other men just bottle it up.

Renate said—please, Julia, take away those cashew nuts. Once I start eating them, I can't stop.

They took a moment to praise the food. Yanis said he never imagined hummus would go so well with calamari. I am going to hand it to you, Julia, the food is amazing. They got swept away into a further discussion about favorite restaurants. Sabina asked if anyone had been to the Russian restaurant near the Gendarmenmarkt, it's quite spectacular.

What is this, a foodie club? I wanted to ask.

Sabina followed on from the Russian restaurant and said—let me tell you something about my husband. Klaus. I drove him mad this morning. I made the coffee and forgot to put the pot underneath the spout. It leaked across the kitchen counter. I thought it was funny. It was so stupid I started laughing. I even took a video of the coffee dripping down onto the floor and sent it off to my friends.

Klaus lost his cool. What are you doing? he said.

His seriousness made me laugh even more, Sabina went on. I couldn't help it. It was his birthday yesterday, Sabina said, so we had a lovely time, out for dinner in that Russian restaurant. And then I did such a stupid thing this morning. Like the intimacy between us, that bubble we were in last night, she said, was suddenly destroyed.

Oh my God, Sabina said, I can't believe I'm telling you all

this. What I wanted to say was just—how easy it is to be misunderstood.

You know—it happens every time. I cry afterward and then I go into a swirl of giddiness the following day. They shouldn't let me drive the car. Do not operate heavy machinery. My head is in a complete daze, it's unreal. For him it's different. He goes into a deep sadness. He's like a blackbird gone silent. He puts on all this somber music. Something hopelessly dark and tragic. Usually it's Mahler. Or Górecki. Guess what he put on this morning, she said, full volume. It was that song about a woman getting shot by the river. Down by the river—I shot my baby, she said, quoting the lyrics of the song. I know it doesn't mean he literally shoots her. I completely get it. It's just the way a man thinks about love, like it becomes weaponized. Maybe I'm reading too much into this. But still and all, she said—*shot her dead.*

Nobody knew what to say.

They sat for a moment without anyone speaking. Each one of them reflecting. Some of them stood up to get coffee and dessert. Julia asked if they would like the strudel heated up—I have some fresh mint leaves if anyone wants tea.

41

HERE IS THE NOVEL THAT MOST CLOSELY RESEMBLES Roth's own marriage. His true masterpiece, that small book he wrote later in his short life, knowing how little time was left to him as a writer on the run from the Nazis. *Das falsche Gewicht. Weights and Measures.* The story of a government official sent to a small town on the Russian border to take charge of verifying the people's honesty. The town, not unlike my author's own birthplace of Brody, thrives on falsehood and corruption at a time when the empire is coming to an end and the new era of nationalism approaches. Eibenschütz is an isolated man, despised by the rest of the community, fighting a lonely battle to uphold standards of truth in a world where order has begun to fall apart around him.

When he discovers that his own wife is being unfaithful to him, his life descends into chaos. She gives birth to a baby boy and pretends it belongs to him. Devastated by this betrayal, he then falls in love with a young Gypsy woman at one of the most notorious smuggling bars. He begins to drink heavily and finds himself joining in with the community, entering into the life of falsehood he has been sent to clean up. Loose and free as any chestnut roaster traveling across borders with his dog and cart.

An epidemic begins to sweep through the country.

He receives a letter informing him that his son is dead and his wife is dying. He goes to visit her and finds her in bed in the care of a nun. She stretches out her arms to say that she has always loved him—do I need to die? He wants to do something kind for her, play some music, perhaps, in her dying moments. He paces up and down in the room, listening to the sound of her body shuddering in the bed. He looks out at the murky rain falling and horse-drawn trucks passing the house, driven by men wearing black hoods, laden with bodies on their way to a communal grave. The hospitals are overcrowded and people are left to die at home. A single candle stands lit on a round table, like the only sign of goodness left in the room. His wife reaches out to him with a searing cry as she dies. He moves toward her, wishing to hold her hand at least, but the nun tells him to stand back. He breaks down sobbing and takes out the bottle from his pocket.

And what about *Rebellion*?

Yanis brought the book club back on track.

For him, the man with the barrel organ was the perfect example of the person on the periphery. His happiness is brought to an end by a racist.

You think it's an allegory for racism? Renate asked.

It's the story of the outsider, Yanis said. The newcomer on our streets. Downgraded to cleaning up after other men in the toilets of a restaurant.

As a book, Yanis continued, I found myself comparing it to *Ulysses*. James Joyce published his masterpiece around the same time, by the way, just two years earlier. The story of Leopold Bloom wandering through the city of Dublin. The outcast. The cuckold. The Jew. Betrayed by his wife, who sleeps with another man while he spends the day out walking the streets. Bloom has become displaced. His country is imaginary. He returns late at night when she is already asleep. He picks up her underwear, and maybe then, holding these fantasy garments up to his face, he realizes that this is as close as he will ever get to home.

I'm not a literary scientist, Yanis said, but I believe James Joyce and Joseph Roth both struck the same model found in ancient Greek literature to describe the stranger. The solitary traveler.

The unrecognized.

They stood up and began putting the furniture back in place.

Leave it, Julia said.

But they all felt the need to bring things back to the starting point. They continued tidying up, covering the remaining food, bringing used plates out to the small kitchen. They folded the tablecloths and stacked the tables away. Small conversations broke out around the room as they carried the chairs over to where they normally were, in a cluster around the coffee table by the reception area. The book club journal was left on the desk for everyone to put in their own rating.

Jürgen began leafing through my pages and came to the map at the back. Lena explained to him how it had been drawn in by the original owner of the book, a place somewhere in the East, close to the Polish border, she believed.

He told Lena that he and his wife, Zeta, had been out there recently looking for a house to buy. Call it nostalgia, he said, something in that landscape I can't let go. Somewhere to escape to. Zeta says we would have a rule—no phones, no devices, we would just walk and make meals and talk and be alive.

Sounds good to me, Lena said.

We found a nice house in the heart of a nature reserve, Jürgen said. It was funny, the real estate agent insisted on showing us the basement. It was damp. We got the smell of mildew. There was nothing to see apart from a couple of shelves with pickle jars. The real estate agent kept pointing out how much space there was. During the war, there were twenty-three people sheltered down there. They all survived in the end. They even went without being detected when the Russians arrived. It was the safest place in the whole of Germany.

The agent spoke about the basement as a unique selling point. The basement is where you will take shelter from whatever the world will throw at you. You never know what's coming down the line, the agent said. Disease, hunger, migrants, the climate. You will be safe, she said. You will never run out of water. Space to store food. Look at the metal doors, you would have no trouble with marauders. Away from the floods. And the summers, the heat, the real estate agent said, the world will be burning up and you will all be nice and cool down here.

Are you going to buy it? Lena asked.

We have bought it.

42

LOOK AT HER IN GOOD TIMES—FRIEDERIKE ROTH. WALK-
ing along the street in Berlin, smiling to herself, wearing a fur-lined
coat with a brooch on the collar. The coat is softly checkered,
long and straight, double-breasted, with four big buttons. One
of those cloche hats down over her forehead, shielding her eyes.
Dark gloves and pointed shoes, a sheen in her stockings. She is
twenty-seven years of age, married to a writer whose career is on
the way up. She is carrying his manuscript under her arm. He's
walking by her side, a fraction ahead, his overcoat open, hands
in his pockets along with a folded newspaper. He's wearing a suit,
also double-breasted, white shirt and bow tie. His eyes full of
invention, his smile defiant, transferring a word from one side of
his mouth to the other. They are walking in unison, right feet lifting off the ground.

I would never have imagined, he writes, that I could love a
small girl so permanently. I love her shyness and her sensibility,
and her heart which is full of fear and affection, always afraid of
what it loves.

That was in 1927, before the Nazis took over. When the world was in the sun for a moment. Before she became mentally ill and was transferred to an institution in Vienna to be closer to her family.

To her parents, he writes—if I can get enough money, I'm sure Friedl will get well without an asylum.

If it's not too much trouble, why not give her a canary to keep in her room. It might distract her.

To his friend Stefan Zweig—I need 1,200 for my wife and 800 for myself monthly.

My wife's costs are fixed, I can do nothing to reduce them. I will work to my very limits, even if it kills me.

My wife is so important, if I am to stay alive.

To her mother—if Friedl pulls through, I will be much older than her. As soon as I feel thoroughly aged, she will snap out of it, I know she will.

People ask after her everywhere in Marseilles, in all the hotels and restaurants.

His life moves on.

To his cousin—I've fallen for a twenty-year-old girl. It's impossible, a crime, to attach this girl to me, and to the awful tangle of my life.

For the first time since my wife's illness, I feel alive.

To Stefan Zweig—life is more beautiful than literature. Literature is a swindle. *Schwindel.* In German, the word covers anything from dizziness to fraud, fake, cheat, con, vertigo, spinning, swirling.

My wife is silent, he writes. My in-laws talk of a cure and of a resumption of the marriage, reporting of her happiness every time they mention me to her.

About his short-lived affair with the twenty-year-old girlfriend, he writes—I couldn't stand another woman suffering on my account.

To her mother—I have money for Friedl until August.

If Friedl were to get better, then I would get better too. It's brutal, I can't bear it.

To Stefan Zweig—my wife has been in a state that makes it impossible for me to go to Austria.

To her mother—I was very glad to see Friedl's handwriting is unchanged.

To his cousin—she's become more lucid of late, asks for me from time to time, and I don't have the strength to go to Vienna. What would that do? And if my wife becomes completely lucid, do I then go back to her?

To Stefan Zweig—the only thing I've managed to keep up are the monthly payments for my wife's hospital.

I must live like a dog until the twentieth of September.

To her mother—I'm thinking of you and your pain, and hope that Friedl's return to health will comfort us all.

In the meantime, he has been living with a new woman. Andrea Manga Bell. Her father was Cuban, her mother from Hamburg. She has two children from an earlier marriage to a prince from Cameroon. She works in the editorial department of a music publishing house. He takes his role as provider seriously. He is good with the children, making up stories, telling them that he was born a crow and that his mother threw him out of the nest.

He becomes possessive. He forbids Manga Bell to dance. Will not allow her to wear swimsuits. Forbids her to visit the hairdresser, claiming that hair salons are brothels, the hairdresser should come to the house. He's against her continuing to work as an editor and she feels he is trying to make her dependent on him.

Manga Bell writes this about him—

He was an ugly man, but he had a strong pull on women, and there were always women who fell in love with him and were after him. I never met another man with so much sexual appeal. He was slow as a snail, holding back, never a spontaneous movement that I noticed, he lurked, every expression thought out. But he was soft, like no other, and I was completely mad about him.

They drink a lot and fight a lot. He claims Andrea carries a gun in her bag. He gets a friend to accompany him to a reconciliation meeting with her to make sure she doesn't pull the gun on him.

The relationship with Andrea Manga Bell comes to an acrimonious end.

He writes frequently about insanity. A group of insane people getting off a train. A mother going insane when she is told about losing her son in the war. A version of himself gone insane, locked in a padded cell with nothing but a stool bolted to the floor, a twitch at the corner of his mouth, still trying to smile, only the rest of his lips have forgotten how.

He describes a circular insanity taking hold of society. Nationalism is the new religion. He writes about Hitler and the madness let loose on the streets. He drinks more and more heavily and writes novels with increasing urgency to keep himself sane.

To Stefan Zweig—my parents-in-law are emigrating to Palestine. It was for the sake of those old people that I undertook so much for my wife; now the mother is leaving her daughter, and I alone will be the mother.

My wife is currently being put up free of charge at an institution in Baden. But the sanatorium is asking for 7,000 schillings.

Love, for me, goes through the conscience, the way it does for others through the stomach.

To his French translator, Blanche Gidon—I suddenly had to leave Amsterdam for Paris [his code word for Vienna] on account of my wife. I'm having awful days here. I am very, very unhappy.

I have initiated divorce proceedings, which is very difficult.

My wife's sanatorium has set the bailiffs on me.

He drops the idea of divorce.

. . .

In Ostend, in a small group of exiled writers, he enters a new relationship with the German novelist Irmgard Keun. She is not Jewish, but her books still fell victim to the book burning for portraying liberated female characters. She took a case for damages against the Chamber of Culture led by Joseph Goebbels, who was personally in charge of selecting banned books, but the case was never heard. She was imprisoned and had to be bailed out for a substantial figure by her father. She fled to Holland and ended up joining that clustering of exiles in a season of celebrated doom before the Nazis took over Europe.

She says of Roth—my skin said yes at once.

Irmgard is young and attractive. Never has she loved anyone as much in her life. Never has she met anyone with such a strong sexual force. She loves his fight, his calamity, his wreckage, his rage at Hitler and everything that is a lie. She says he is a gifted hater. She says he is a child of all countries. They live together and drink together and write together. He is getting steadily worse, his teeth are falling out, his eyes are red. He doesn't eat, his legs are thin, he has a belly like a cannonball. He is like an old man with the mind of a child, calling for his mother. Once again, he is consumed with jealousy. He becomes so possessive that he cannot even let her out of his sight, shouting her name through the corridors of the hotel.

By the time she leaves him, a year and a half later in a cross fire of drunken arguments, Irmgard Keun says the alcohol has robbed him of his manhood. It was a great friendship more than a great love, she says. In truth, he loved only Friedl.

Not a day went by that he didn't speak of her.

. . .

The last time he lays eyes on Friedl is through the spyhole of her cell.

He's back in Vienna undercover. Back on the tram out to the suburb of Pensing, up to the Steinhof sanatorium on the hill. A quick shot of cognac before he walks into this vast compound of sixty buildings with the white cathedral and its golden dome at the center. Fifteen thousand patients housed in three- and four-story houses they call pavilions, all separated by trees into different zones to avoid them running into each other. It's like a city built for the insane. The new lunatic asylum, they call it, a city within a city. Thousands of windows duplicating themselves into paranoid repetition. Thousands of eyes waiting to be recognized. He needs directions to find her. He has defaulted on his payments and they are threatening to transfer her to a facility where she can be made to work for her keep. He cannot get close to her. The locked door of the cell between them.

He calls her name.

She screams at him to go away.

She has fallen into a violent disposition. According to a memoir by Friderike Zweig, Stefan Zweig's former wife, it became dangerous for Roth to be in the same room as her.

She hates me, he writes.

The slender woman who once walked by his side on the street in Berlin, wearing a coat with a fur collar and a cloche hat, now sits crouched on the floor, staring across the empty space in front of her. Her hair has been cropped. Her face is puffed out. She is continuously harming herself, pulling her legs back and warping the knee joints.

Attached to her file, there is a mug shot photo that makes her look like a criminal in custody—one image face-on, one from the side. She is wearing a striped institutional gown with large black buttons. Her eyes bear a menacing expression. Full of defiance and pain. Maybe the hint of a tormented smile emerging in her mouth. The image taken from the side shows her head resting against a metal frame into which a card with her name has been inserted—Roth, Frieda.

The streetlights long for morning, he writes in one of his novels, hoping to be put out.

Who could blame him for going back to his rocking horse days? Back to his childhood fantasies of the cavalry coming through his hometown. It was his way of grieving, his way of trying to dream Friedl back into his life, still hoping that her illness could be cured in some imaginary way by slowing down the march of history.

He believed in the illusion of restoring the monarchy. For him, it was the European dream. With all its diversity and open borders. Where Jews were once safe. Where the chestnut roasters and the horse traders moved freely from country to country, from season to season, across mountain ranges. Where the cities bulged with difference. Where the music followed trading routes from East to West, from the Mediterranean up to the Baltic. His political views began to take on fictional values, to the point where he was convinced that Hitler could be stopped from annexing Austria by bringing back the monarch. In his wildest drunken visions he planned to smuggle the exiled heir to the throne back to Austria inside a coffin. His delusional conceit. The emperor coming back from the dead, stepping out of the coffin into a doomed democracy that was about to be swept aside. A funeral in reverse. A watch ticking backward.

He had reached the outer limits of tragedy. His catastrophe continued to play out alongside world catastrophe. The fall of Europe, that collective descent into madness, is contained in that final sighting of Friedl on the floor of her cell, staring ahead, obsessively bending back her legs to the breaking point.

She was ultimately transferred from the Steinhof sanatorium in Vienna to a country institution in Mauer-Öhling, a place where patients were put to work on farms and employed as cheap labor in homes around the locality. When it was first opened during the Habsburg era, Emperor Franz Joseph said it was a wonderful place to be mad.

Roth fled Vienna the day before Hitler marched into the city. He made his way back to Paris and continued writing and drinking himself to death. He became reunited with her briefly in his last novel. At the age of forty-four, he died in agony of delirium tremens in a hospital for the poor in Paris—May 27, 1939.

On July 15, 1940, they came to take Friedl away from the institution at Mauer-Öhling. She was brought by train to Linz. There she was placed on a black bus. One of those unmarked black buses that were used at night for transporting young people from the small towns into Linz to go to the cinema. The journey from there didn't take too long. She arrived at Schloss Hartheim, a castle which had for many years been in the hands of the Sisters of Charity of St. Vincent de Paul, who had looked after mentally disabled children. When the nuns were being removed from the facility, one of them had asked if she could take some of the children with her, but that request had been refused. The castle was refitted with communal showers and ovens. The chimney stacks were put into regular use, with smoke drifting across the district even in summer when it was warm. People had to close their windows. The human smoke hung around the rooms like a thought that could not be expressed or eliminated. The black bus drove through the open gates into the central courtyard. There she was told to step out and brought inside. She was taken straight to the showers and told to remove her clothes.

Frieda Roth. 1900–1940.

LENA WENT TO THE AIRPORT TO MEET HIM. SHE STOOD IN the arrivals area with her arms folded, checking the flight monitor. She kept her eyes on the doors, watching people being matched up at times in the most unlikely reunions. When Mike came out, it took a moment before she could be sure it was him. His beard, his height, his clothes. His eyes searched through the waiting crowd without seeing her, as though he was looking for somebody else entirely. She rushed forward to embrace him. She kissed him hard on the lips and stood back. She smiled and wiped her eyes with her wrist.

In the taxi they held hands.

Outside the hotel he paid the driver. He had only one single case—he was traveling light. He wore walking boots. Camouflage trousers. A jacket with buttoned-down military pockets across the chest.

They had a room looking out toward the station at Friedrich-strasse, where the various local and long-distance trains were pulling in and out under the arched roof, far enough away to be silent, like a miniature train set.

They kissed.

They said each other's names three or four times.

Christ, Lena, he said. Now I know exactly how much I missed you.

She felt his beard and said—I love it. Makes you look like you've been out in the forest. Your arms, have you been chopping wood?

The Italian restaurant they went to was situated on Rudi-Dutschke-Strasse. Named after the revolutionary who got shot on his bicycle, Lena explained. It was white tablecloths. There was a row of tables along the wall, a long bar and some further tables at the back next to tall windows. The restaurant was quite full. There was a good volume of voices. They kept forgetting to look at the menu and the waiter had to give them more time. She laughed—let's concentrate. He ordered lamb chops, she ordered tuna. They asked for a platter of antipasti to start with and he selected the wine.

It was a matter of closing the gaps. Their conversation was at times close and also dislocated. It was almost a geographical thing. Looking at each other across the table as if it were the Atlantic.

She told him about getting the U-Bahn out to the airport, how a man in the carriage started singing in English. He was so out of it he kept repeating the same words, about lovers being separated by the salt seas. Don't you think that's crazy, she said, the coincidence.

There was a pause.

What's happening with your mom? she asked.

It's tough, he said. I was down there yesterday helping her to pack up. It will take a while for the sale to go through, but I thought it was better to get her settled right away. She's renting for a while. She was eager to get out. The atmosphere is toxic. The neighbors put these dogs into the parking lot, big black security dogs running free.

You know what happened, Mike said. She could find no on-street parking one day, so she drove in around the back. She saw the gates were open. To hell with it. One last time. Then she got trapped. The dogs kept her pinned inside the car. Jumping up at the windows, slobbering all over the glass. Two enormous Rott-weilers. The owners next door must have let them out when they saw my mother arriving, because the gates were closed behind her. She had to sit there in the car. She couldn't get out. Every time she even so much as moved to pick up her phone, they were up again, snarling at her through the glass. The car door is full of scratches, Lena.

That's frightening for her.

She left messages for me, Mike said, but I was in a meeting. She was there for nearly an hour.

Did she not call the police?

This is it, Mike said. She called the retired cop at the back, Dan Mulvaney. And guess what, he came running out with his rifle. He climbed over the fence and shot both dogs point-blank. One of them was lunging at the cop when he got blasted, my mother said. It was like watching some horror movie. Two big black beasts lying dead on the pavement.

One of them with half his head ripped off and all his teeth showing, Mike said, like he had bitten off his own face.

Jesus.

My mother said Dan escorted her past the dead dogs, back to the house. He carried her groceries and she invited him inside to sit for a while and have a coffee. She asked him to leave the rifle outside.

She should sue.

She's glad to be out of there, Mike said. She was beginning to feel like a stranger in her own country. She didn't even want to go back to get her stuff. Everything was still there in my room. There's no way I can bring it up to New York. A big dumpster full of my things. I kept my baseball mitt. The hardest thing was trying to stop myself from looking over everything, remembering every moment of my childhood. That would have taken years, I would still be there.

She has some peace of mind now, Lena said.

She's thinking of moving to California to be with her sister. That's the long-term plan. The weather in Iowa is getting to her. I think she wants a clean break.

Lena took his hand across the table.

How about you, he said. You got to see your uncle in Magdeburg.

Look, she said.

She reached into her bag and pulled me out. She showed him the map at the back.

Henning gave me directions, she said. It's near the Polish border. We can get there by train.

I have a meeting in Frankfurt, he said.

I waited for you, Mike.

It's an important client, he said. I need to get that out of the way, Lena.

So, it's a business trip.

No way, he said. I've got plans. Wait till you see.

Mike, I need you to go with me, she said. I think there's something out there. I don't know what it is, but I want you to come with me and find it.

I have everything booked, he said. Your birthday. Big surprise. Transylvania.

This is something I've got to do, she said.

There was an excitement in his voice as he began to unfold his plans. First thing, he would go to Frankfurt and sort out his business connections. Then he would meet her in Bucharest. From there they would go to a city in the mountains called Brașov. A beautiful old German town, he said. I have a tour guide set up,

he said. Răzvan is going to take us in his jeep to a place where we
start walking through a beech forest that goes on for miles. Then
we stay in a small town, meant to be the most diverse biosphere in
Europe. The farming techniques are unchanged for centuries, still
the same raised stack of hay in every farm, courtyards enclosed to
protect the animals from wolves and bears. Lots of Gypsies, some
of them living without electricity. We'll celebrate your birthday
at two thousand meters, Lena. There's a sheep farm up there,
Răzvan tells me, the shepherds cook up the cheese on-site, so
fresh—that will be our meal, out in the open, with plum brandy.

We'll stay in one of the monasteries, he went on. Răzvan has
it arranged, a place way up at the top of a mountain. It takes five
hours on foot to get there. Slap in the middle of nowhere. The
monks are completely self-sufficient, living on a plateau where
they grow their own crops and keep cattle and sheep. Their bread
is meant to be amazing, so Răzvan told me—he was there once
and the abbot had flour on his hands while he was pointing to his
cell. It's completely off the grid. No tourist would dream of it. Just
the two of us, Lena. Like going back four or five centuries. All you
hear at night is the clacking of wood as the monks are called to
prayer in the dark. It's the last chance to go back that far in time.
It will blow your mind.

We might have to stay in different cells, he added.

She smiled and said—separate quarters.

You can sneak over to my cell in the middle of the night, he
said. After all the clacking of wood and the monks have gone back
to their cells and it's silent again. I'll leave the door open for you.

Hope I get the right room, she said.

The main dishes arrived. His lamb cutlets were arranged like
a tepee beside a hill of shredded cabbage and some french fries in
the shape of a log fire. Her tuna slice was a plinth erected on a base
of potato discs, beside a pool of plum sauce. He began eating right

away. She picked up her knife and fork and cut into the soft flesh of the tuna, chargrilled with crisscrossed black lines.

Maybe one or two touristy things, Mike said. Like the famous Peleş Castle, where the former communist leader Ceauşescu used to stay. He made it his summer house, where he would go hunting. They say his officials used to catch a bear live and let it loose on the lawns so their leader could wake up in the morning and shoot it from his room. And he was such a lousy shot, Mike said, they had a marksman ready in the wings to shoot the bear for him. Their leader thought it was just the echo of his own rifle ringing around the walls of the castle.

Mike laughed as he ate. He picked up one of the lamb chops in his fingers. He chewed with great hunger. Now and then he took his napkin and wiped his mouth, cleaning his fingers before he picked up his wineglass.

I was hoping to do a bit of hunting myself, he said. At the end of the trip. Răzvan has it all lined up. License, shotgun, everything. I know that wouldn't interest you, Lena, he said, so his wife, Gabi, said she would be very happy to take you to see Dracula's castle. That's a bit fake, maybe, you might prefer to go visit one of the salt mines. Amazing, like a huge cathedral underground, where people play soccer matches under lights, really good for pulmonary conditions.

Lena was slow about eating her food, as though her appetite had been questioned and she would rather have ordered something else.

That bear, she said. I won't be able to stop thinking about him, Mike. Making his way around the mountains, eating berries, leaves, grass, roots, happy in himself. All that slow time, and he's already dead.

He sensed her resistance.

Trust me, Lena, this is going to be great. I'll catch up with

you after the hunt. We'll continue going up north to see some of
the painted churches. I swear to God, Lena, we're going to be the
inventors of happiness.

She looked at him in silence and put her fork down. She laid
her hand on my face and paused for a moment before she spoke.

I've got to do this, she said.

Why are you so hung up about that book?

I was counting on you, Mike.

Lena, I'm not going out there to dig up some Jewish people's
belongings, he said. Is that what you're looking for? Some hoard.
If you find something, you have to declare it. You know that,
Lena. You can't just dig it up and own it.

That's not what I'm after, Mike.

The landowner gets half.

The owners of that land took it from the Jewish people who
lived there up to the Second World War. If I find something out
there, I would have no intention of keeping it, Mike. You know
me better than that.

Who owns it, then?

I would try and return it to the legal owners. And if that didn't
work, I would find some other cause.

The state will get most of it.

Look, I'm not interested in treasure.

You could say it was given to you by your uncle, he said.
That way you would keep the landowners out. But the state will
ultimately claim it and give you a percentage. It's not worth the
trouble.

What I want is the story, she said. What this means to us,
Mike, you and me. I want us to go together and find what's out
there.

Mike wiped his mouth with the napkin again and picked me
up in his hands. He started leafing through the pages and soon
came across the page with the swastika.

What's this?

She began to explain what had happened.

Remember how the book got stolen, she said. And this man found it in the park. The guy from Chechnya. His name is Armin Schneider. His sister is the singer, Madina Schneider. With the prosthetic leg, remember. I sent you some of her links. So, there's this thing that happened, you see, one of the pages got cut out.

And then it was sent as a death threat, with that swastika. We had to go to the police, me and Armin.

Mike stopped eating.

It's become part of my art, she said. This man's life. His injuries from the war in Chechnya. He lost his parents. He's got all these shrapnel wounds.

Mike placed his knife and fork down to listen.

I've asked him for his X-ray, Lena said. It will show three black shapes of metal inside his body. My plan is to base my artwork on this X-ray and whatever else I can find out about him. It's going to be a visual story of his life.

Looking across the table into her eyes, Mike laid his napkin down beside his plate.

You don't have to tell me, he said.

He stood up without another word and walked away.

There was some delay before Lena could react.

Mike, she called after him.

He continued making his way out along the passage between the bar and the tables by the wall, putting his jacket on as he went.

Was this a remake of *Effi Briest*? Should I not have held on to the facts a little longer? Should I not have let the story find its own truth underneath the prose, to be discovered later? Here I was, giving away the plot. The whole conceit was being tragically exposed.

Lena picked me up and threw me into her bag as if she was angry with me for letting her down. She walked after him through the restaurant, almost breaking into a run. She stopped to tell the waiter she would be back in a moment to pay. Once she managed to get some cash. He seemed to understand the urgency. He spoke to her in Italian—*prego*.

Leaving behind her coat, she ran into the street and saw Mike walking away, some distance ahead.

Mike, please.

She followed him into the station at Friedrichstrasse. This used to be the border crossing between East and West. It had been part of her plan to show him all those places. The remainder of the Wall, the tunnels, the Stasi headquarters with the desk where Erich Mielke used to sit and direct his surveillance operations. The spot on the opera house square where the book burning took place, where they now had the monument underground with the empty white shelves. Here she was running onto a platform, calling across the tracks to a man who turned out to be somebody else, not Mike at all.

She tried calling him on her phone.

No reply.

There was nothing left to do but go back to the hotel and wait for him there.

This was all my fault. I had made her come to Berlin. I had brought Armin into her life. I had started this blind narrative experiment, marching into an uncharted story without thinking through the consequences. Had I not seen this happen a million times before in all those books that Henning kept on the shelves of his library? Had I not learned enough about life to know that love never stands still, it keeps moving like water, it runs away and comes back, it spins in a clockwise direction?

She stood watching the trains coming and going through the great arch. That bowed roof. Bombed during the war, leaving a locomotive hanging at an angle on twisted metal tracks. She poured a glass of water from a bottle. I could hear the cap twisting off. I could hear the fizz. I'm not sure she even drank any of it. She went back to staring at the trains, waiting for him to arrive on one of those platforms like a passenger from some unknown place in the East, perhaps. After some time, she lay down on the bed uncovered, with her shoes still on, as though she might have to get up at any moment and go.

| 44 |

SOMETIME DURING THE NIGHT, HE CAME BACK LIKE SOME-
body arriving on a delayed train. It must have been around three
in the morning, because the station was quiet now. A reduced line
of taxis waiting at the side entrance for the final latecomers. She
was asleep. The door made no sound as it closed behind him, not
even a click. He waited for a moment with his back to the door,
then he stepped into the room and stood by the window for a
while. The curtains had been left open.

How did she not wake up?

His presence should have entered her sleep and made her
want to sit up and tell him to lie beside her, place her head on
his shoulder and wait till morning to speak. He turned to look at
her lying on the bed, breathing quietly, her eyes closed, facing the
door. Who was she now, with no smile and nothing to say? Her
mouth trapped in the silence of a photograph. One word from
him would have brought them back together, but he continued
watching her like a stranger in the room.

Without the consent of her eyes.

He picked me up from the bed beside her. Her most precious

possession. He held the open pages up to the yellow light coming in from the train station. It was as though he had taken her hand to read her fortune lines. He took his time examining the map at the back in the same keyhole manner with which he had watched her face without her knowledge. Like a thief going through her things, searching for information he did not have the courage to ask her for directly.

What was he thinking? Did the thought cross his mind, as he studied the map, to go and find whatever was buried out there without telling her? Is that the kind of man he was, ready to steal from her? Like all men, robbing little pieces of treasure to file away in their heads. He had already hacked into her phone. He had read all her messages. He was clever enough not to reveal it, but it was clear, even to her, that he knew too much.

Why had he not asked more questions?

Walking out of the restaurant had been an admission of his knowledge. Instead of speaking about his suspicions, he had held on to them as if they were his companions, his armory, the evidence he would present in some eventual courtroom where he would put her on trial.

Once, on a call from Iowa, he had almost given himself away, reminding her that she had left her keys behind at the studio. She asked him how he knew that and he said he was guessing. He loved her so much that he could read her mind.

He was collecting facts he didn't want to know. The pain of finding things out made him feel stronger, as though each piece of proof gave him more and more power. He was like a man with a hunch for negatives, a man who wanted to hear the bad news in every agonizing detail. The more he found out, the more he sank into that fortress of self-pity. One time he'd stopped along the road outside Iowa City and sat crying for an hour with a Subway sandwich that he had just bought untouched on the passenger seat beside him. He could not eat. He could not drive. He spilled his heart out to one of his friends on the phone, listing off the things he had discovered about her. His technical abilities as a forensic analyst allowed him to be present at each encounter she had with Armin. He was a witness to his own worst fears.

He decided to place me back down on the bed beside her, perhaps knowing I was worthless without her.

He picked up his laptop and placed it into his case. He took his passport from the bedside table and must have felt her breath like a feather crossing his hand. Without switching on the light in the bathroom, he tapped with the fingers of a blind man for his toothbrush. He paused to look around the room, making sure he was not leaving anything behind, taking everything from her that belonged to him. She turned in her sleep to face the window. She spoke a word from inside a dream that was not clear enough to take hold. He retreated backward to the door and let himself out.

In the morning she woke up to find his things were gone and sent him a message—why didn't you wake me?

There was no reply.

She waited for him at breakfast, on the off-chance that he might appear, wondering where he had gone to. What streets had he walked through and had he got lost—is that what had kept him out all night? Every time the door opened, she looked up with a smile that faded again almost instantly. He didn't come. She went to the reception and discovered he had already checked out. The room had been paid for.

It was cold. She went back to get her coat from the restaurant. She picked the wrong street. In the light of day, everything seemed to have turned around. She had to check the street sign to find out that she was right after all, that she only had to go on with more conviction to where the failed dinner had taken place. A cyclist came flying past her with a shout right in her face. She jumped back. She had stepped out like a blind tourist into the cycle lane.

They were getting the restaurant ready for lunch by the time she got there. A delivery of vegetables had just arrived and there was a man with a cart of carrots and cauliflower entering backward. The same waiter from the night before came to speak to her at the door. She wanted to pay, but the waiter said her husband had already done that. Last night, the waiter said, he came back just before we were closing. He paid by card. He left a generous tip. Your husband, the waiter said, had only just gone again when we realized that you had left your coat behind. The waiter told her he'd run back to get the coat, then dashed up the street, around the corner—your husband was gone, out of sight.

There was a sadness in the waiter's eyes. It appeared as though he had done his best to fix their disagreement, running as far as the main street to put things right. She smiled and said thanks. That gave him some hope.

Prego, he said as he helped her on with the coat.

She went to a café and sat staring at the pedestrians passing by. The sound of the staff making coffee, knocking the espresso cylinder, switching on the steam, was a comfort at first, then it became a shock that brought her back to reality. She checked her phone again. She left a final message—

Mike, where are you? Are you at the airport now? I went to the restaurant to get my coat. They said you had been there. You're making me cry, Mike. I'm here in a café on Friedrichstrasse and I can hardly see the coffee in front of me.

Twenty minutes later she received a single message back. The message contained her flight details to Bucharest. He would be waiting for her there—we can do this, Lena. We can be happy. It's your call.

| 45 |

WE TRAVELED AWHILE BY TRAIN. NOT MUCH LONGER THAN
an hour. The announcements were made in both Polish and German. We got off at a station that seemed quite rural, somewhere
on the outskirts of a town, perhaps. Nothing but the sound of
birds. A gust of wind in the leaves. The voices of other passengers who got off at the same station—a group of schoolboys
with their Scout leader, an elderly couple, and three young women
returning from the city. At the end of the platform, a man wearing sunglasses got off and stood at the shelter examining the
timetable.

The station house with its waiting room and café had long
been closed down and boarded up. All that remained of that service was a ticket machine and a line of waiting taxis. The three
women were the first to get there and they sped off in the direction of the town. Lena spoke to the second driver. We passed by
the troop of schoolboys walking in single file and drove along
straight roads lined with trees on both sides. Every now and again
we passed by those road signs where a graphic car is seen crashing
into a graphic tree with exclamation marks.

The taxi dropped us off at the edge of a forest. When it drove away, we were left with the horizontal depth in the trees all around us. The screech of a jay could be heard, the bird children call the forest policeman. There was no other sound apart from their footsteps along the sandy path, two people in unison, not speaking a word. Nothing to add to the interior of the forest but more silence.

It was only when we got a bit further into that expanding silence that Lena began to wonder if they were alone. A car door was heard closing behind them on the road. Perhaps it was another taxi. Somebody else being delivered to this remote place for no apparent reason. Once the car drove away and the silence was restored, the emptiness seemed to hold the presence of an unidentified watcher, like the eyes of a predator keeping them in sight without ever showing up.

Lena turned around several times.

Are we being followed? she asked.

She answered her own question with a laugh. It was nothing but her imagination, she said. Coming from such an overcrowded city as New York, she must have found it difficult to believe a place could be so empty of human beings. They continued walking and came to a clearing in the trees with a set of stables and a paddock. The neighing of horses produced an echo of other horses further away. Lena stood at the fence and her hand reached into her bag.

Let's give them an apple, she said.

She threw the apple, but it bounced off one of the horses and she laughed at her own clumsiness while they took fright, galloping away as though it was a stone that had been hurled at them. They made a circle around the paddock and came back cautiously to watch.

She was waiting for one of them to find the apple. Waiting for the crack of it inside the mouth of a horse, the ungainly brown teeth crunching sideways, trying to hold on to all that sweetness spilling across the lips. But the horses took no notice of the apple at their feet.

Come on, Lena said to the horses. What's wrong with you. It's a nice apple.

They don't know it's an apple, Armin said.

Before he could join his sister in Amsterdam, Armin was having to stay in Berlin while he got a clearance letter to board international flights. In the meantime, he was busy with logistics, in touch with tour promoters, arranging accommodation and flights, shipping the equipment to Holland by road.

They continued walking deeper into the forest. At one point they stopped to eat a pastry. Along the side of the path, the earth had been dug up by wild boars. Lena said it looked as though the ground had been plowed by a tractor. How many wild boars did it take to do all that work? The earth was still fresh, turned during the night, maybe that morning at dawn.

When they moved on again, Lena once more felt they were being followed, and this time she turned suddenly to face the unseen stalker.

Mike, she called. Is that you?

There was no answer. She told Armin that she must be going crazy. You could be on a street full of people and not ever think you were being followed or even looked at. Why, in a place so empty and unpopulated, is there always such an illusion of the invisible?

Call him, Armin said.

On his phone, you mean?

She wanted this landscape of trees to remain honest. She took out her phone and made the call. There was no answer. No reciprocal ringtone in the still interior of the forest drawing him out like a man exposed. The trees held on to what was imagined.

What am I doing? she said. He's in midair, on a flight to Romania by now.

A while later, they left the forest and found themselves in the open. They came to an industrial pig farm. A series of long single-story buildings with no windows. There seemed to be nobody around. Only the noise of a thousand pigs, maybe many thousands more, inside those barracks. They seemed to be there on their own, rearing themselves in this remote place without any human intervention, feeding from containers of food that were filled on demand, drinking from automated water troughs. Their pink faces looking up to see if anyone would visit them, like a hall full of children waiting for their mothers and fathers. They were grunting and squealing among themselves, communicating with each other in large separated pens, unaware that there was a world outside with daylight, sunshine, air, trees, mud, stray food to be discovered. What if the rumor of such a world were to spread through the crowded pens? How would the news of freedom impact on their contentment?

I think we have this wrong, Lena said.

No, hang on, Armin said.

They stood awhile looking over the map, then Armin worked out that the pig production plant had to be a recent addition, built on land that had once belonged to the farm. It replaced a section at the edge of the forest where the religious shrine had once stood. Armin found the path leading away beyond those enormous buildings. They followed it and came eventually to the small river with the footbridge. Once they crossed the bridge, they could see a farmhouse that matched the diagram on the last page.

The farmhouse was boarded up. Weeds had taken over the driveway and there were creepers growing across the steps leading up to the door. Nature beginning to reclaim the farm, rewilding bit by bit the places that had once been kept in such good order. A tractor stood abandoned in the yard, with grass growing around the wheels, a sycamore sapling standing in its path. Other farm machinery parts were scattered around the perimeter. The wooden barns had fallen into disuse. Some of the doors had been left open. Inside were the remains of what had once been pens for cattle and pigs, the troughs and the baskets for hay left empty. A dove scattered from the loft and flew away across the fields.

It was Armin who decided to open the big sliding doors to one of the barns. The swing was still there. The wooden seat was warped and cracked, held in place at a slight angle. The two long ropes were suspended from the frame, over four meters high. They were intact, though frayed. Perhaps they had been replaced at some point over the years.

Lena didn't trust herself on the swing—she was expecting it to collapse. So Armin decided to have a go. He cautiously sat on the seat and it remained in place. Lena gave him a push and the ropes creaked as though they were under great strain, aching with the lack of use and about to break. As he got more courageous, it must have felt like swinging right out across the fields toward the horizon. Into the bright sunshine, where his face lit up and he had to blink. Then back inside to the shade of the barn. Swinging in and out, from darkness into light and back again. The swing released small clouds of fruit flies that had been nesting in the ropes.

Lena stood leaning against the frame of the door with Armin passing her by, going higher and higher. She was looking over the map.

The map had been drawn one afternoon in April 1933. David Glückstein had come here on his bike from Berlin to visit his fiancée, Angela Kaufmann. The place was vibrant with life then. The cattle were out. Geese and chickens wandering around the inner yard, the dog asleep on the steps of the house. From the barn, David and Angela watched her brother lead the bridled horse back out after lunch to plow the earth.

They spoke about their plans for a wedding. It should be held at the farm, he said, a simple wedding with tables out in the open, under the stars. They spoke about having a family and living in the country. She sat swinging in the doorway of the barn and the air around her was so calm it was almost too much to bear. As if something would give and one of the ropes would break.

Angela watched her future husband move the granite pillar with the sundial aside. There was a stone slab underneath to provide a base. He lifted the slab and began digging the ground underneath with a spade. Once he had dug deep enough, he went inside and came back with a metal box. Angela jumped off the swing and left the two long rope shadows moving on their axis along the floor of the barn. She stood beside him as he placed the metal box into the pit he had dug.

Let's disown everything but ourselves, he said.

He took his time covering the soil back over again. Finally, he spread out a small sack of sand followed by a bag of pebbles on the surface, like the top layers of a cake. He replaced the stone slab and she helped him move the pillar with the sundial back into position. He pulled a handkerchief out to clean his hands.

On a warm day in spring of that year when Hitler came to power, they stood by the sundial looking across the field at her brother with the horse. He waved at them and she waved back. The professor then reached into the pocket of his jacket and took out the stub of a pencil. It was no longer than a cigarette. Something a carpenter might have kept tucked over his ear. He opened the blank page at the back. It was the only thing to hand, his copy of *Rebellion* by Joseph Roth. She had read it and given it back to him that afternoon when he arrived, saying she loved that passage where the barrel organ player was cranking up his melodies and the money came floating down from the windows in the Berlin courtyards.

With the stub of his pencil, he drew a map of the place where he had concealed the metal box. He drew it not so much to provide directions back to that exact location but to keep this day from disappearing. No matter what happened, no matter where they might go or be taken, this slow afternoon in the country would be preserved in a simple map. It was drawn without any recognizable geographical markings, to be deciphered only by insiders, by those who knew how much they loved each other. He stood with his shoulder against the doorway of the barn to get the angles right. The lines remained faithful to that afternoon, down to the slope of sunlight. He included only those features that were relevant to them—the sundial, the twin rope lines of the swing, the barns, the farmhouse, the religious shrine, the forest, the oak tree with the bench underneath. An arrow pointing to the next village, left unnamed. It was a day like no other, in a place like no other, from which they stepped out of sight and left no trace of themselves but a suggestion of the swing moving.

| 46 |

THE ROPES CONTINUED CREAKING. IT WAS EARLY AUTUMN, almost a hundred years later, and the afternoon held a stiffness in the air, like the coming sting of cold weather reaching the nostrils. There was no movement in the fields. The crops had been harvested. The ground was bare apart from the stubble of barley and some crows pecking over the remains. The barns were abandoned.

Lena looked up and said—why is that pillar leaning?

She was referring to the sundial on a granite plinth. Her intuition must have taught her that a sinking stone monument, like the graves in a cemetery, meant the ground underneath had begun to settle with time. She walked toward the sundial and began to move the granite pillar aside. Armin hopped off the swing to help her. Underneath they discovered a stone slab, which they lifted with their fingers to find a dozen or two crawling things racing to get back to darkness. Without a word, Armin walked back into the barn and began searching around, then came back out with a small, half-length potato fork that had become rusted with age. Lena stood aside as he started digging. She took over a while later and continued until the fork hit the sound of metal. The sound echoed around the farm buildings like a piece of luck foretold.

She began clearing away the soil with her hands. Once she had lifted the metal box out of the ground, Armin helped to clean off the dirt with a clump of hay quickly pulled up behind him. They kneeled on the grass and looked at the box in silence.

A breeze blew across the fields, lifting loose straws of barley and making them dance like upright figures across the soil. A crow sat on the roof watching them. The swing in the doorway of the barn was still moving back and forth in tiny, imperceptibly reducing degrees.

The lock was easy to break.

Inside, Lena found a leather pouch. The leather had gone white and dusty with mold. She opened it up and found a single item inside. It was a blue fountain pen. The metal parts were rusted. She unscrewed the cap and saw that the ink around the nib had coagulated and dried. The nib was broken. There was a tag attached by a thin string to the clip intended to hold the pen upright in a jacket pocket. The tag bore the name of a repair shop and had a comment written in pencil, hard to read with age but still legible. She handed the pen to Armin and he made out the tiny lettering in German—*Feiner Bruch in der Hülle*. He translated the words—hairline fracture in the casing.

Here they were, finders of the unexpected. They had unearthed something of no material value. They remained stalled in this moment of disillusion, too late by a century, holding the rusted evidence of some extraordinary event between two people in the past. Proof of their existence long after the people themselves had disappeared. A crucial artifact which had lain hidden from the world, waiting to be reimagined.

The landscape around them had become deaf. One of those instances in which the trees hold their breath, everything comes to a stop, a deer looks up, the crow watches. The only motion was the swing.

Holding this broken pen in her hand, Lena wondered whether they should put it back.

It seemed like an absurd question.

Now that this item had been extracted from the earth, it was impossible to put it back. It was like unremembering the people who had placed it there. Like returning all the ore of the world back to where it was found. Like dis-excavation, like reversing time, like undiscovering continents. Here was the pen used by Angela Kaufmann to write her letters to David Glückstein. The pen that leaked ink onto her fingers and made her laugh the night they first met at the theater, when she left a blue thumbprint on the program notes. The pen she used to begin writing her novel, even though there would be no publisher left in Germany to print it by the time she finished. Here it was, that defective writing implement she held so often in her hand and which left a deep blue stain in the lining of his jacket the day he carried it back with him to Berlin to get it repaired. He could have bought her a thousand new pens to replace it. He had the means to buy up several nib-making factories right across Germany, and yet he was more interested in preserving this faulty belonging of hers, the one she had used to write herself into the world. The son of a paper industrialist in love with a woman who was going to fill every blank page she could find. This was the only trace they left behind, the time between them kept safe in material form. Their story turned into archaeology. An artifact beyond use. An ending beyond ending. A cheap blue fountain pen with a tag from the repair desk to say it had served its purpose and could not be fixed.

An item so precious because it was so worthless.

Sounds that belonged to the world a hundred years back were coming from the landscape in delayed echoes. A locomotive shuffling along the edge of the fields. The clip of a carriage being pulled by a horse along those straight avenues lined with trees. Somebody whistling. A shout across the farmyard and a call coming back from one of the barns in an accent that had gone out of use.

And the illusion of a barrel organ.

Lena placed the broken pen back into the leather pouch. There was no time left for them to talk about what they had found and what should be done with it, because the sound of the living world had come back into being with a shock. The man who had been following them finally appeared in the open. His footsteps were coming along the earth. The snap of a twig.

It became clear how utterly powerless literature can be in a situation like this. How can a book give a warning? Where was the forest jay when you needed him? Even the screaming of a thousand pigs inside their enclosures was useless. It was the white noise of the fields that spoke loudest.

Out from behind the wooden barns he came walking across a stretch of open ground. He appeared at first to have come from the pig farm, like an employee sent to find out what was going on, why people were digging up the soil around here. The weight of his feet hitting the soft earth was warning enough.

Once he came close enough to be identified, it turned out not to be Mike after all. It was Bogdanov. He must have followed them all the way, by train, by taxi, right along their trail through the forest. He had waited in hiding long enough for them to unearth the past. As he strode toward them, he shouted a single word that sounded more like a handclap in the afternoon sunshine.

Fresser.

It's a hard word to translate. Armin would need a moment to explain that it meant literally—somebody who eats like an animal. Somebody who stuffs his face. A hungry person who devours everything available, like all you can eat, with no concern for manners. A term the Nazis applied to people who were unwanted, an unnecessary burden on food supplies.

There was no time to speak. Lena looked around at Bogdanov as though it was her nature to face the attacker, perhaps to negotiate, but then she changed her mind and decided to go for safety. She picked up the leather pouch and threw everything into her bag, then she pulled Armin away by the elbow, running through the open door of the barn, past the swing, back along the empty water troughs.

Distances traveled in urgency can seem longer than those traveled at leisure. From an aerial point of view, the fleeing persons appear to make no ground because they move at the same speed as their pursuer. In theory that ratio might never change, unless Bogdanov was more athletic or had some other way of reducing the gap.

He ran into the barn without taking account of the swing hanging from the framework. Perhaps he hadn't seen it with the angle of the sunlight. The two lines of rope merged in some hurried illusion with the lines of architecture. He ran straight into the swing as though he had every intention of using it, like a child trying it out on his belly. As he continued moving forward, the wooden seat of the swing rose up to meet his jaw with a slap. An insult to his intelligence. He shoved the ropes aside like a cobweb.

The delay allowed Lena and Armin to get out through a door on the far side of the barn. They ran into the central yard, where the disused tractor stood at a slight angle, parked on the edge of a dip where the pond had once been kept filled with water in case of a barn fire. Where the geese and ducks once splashed around. All dried out now. That sheltered space at the heart of the farm where the families had summer parties around a wood fire.

Where David and Angela Glückstein held their wedding reception, with tables and chairs brought out from the house and linen tablecloths pinned down in case there was a breeze. This is where they gave their wedding speeches and it seemed as though the barns were full of people clapping. A quartet of musicians positioned on the lawn playing Bach and the sound of the cello rising from under the earth. The guests sat until late in the evening with chilled wine and somebody stood up to sing a song about the Volga. Lanterns hung around the barns and they danced on a platform of boards laid out along the ground under the stars.

And the late wedding guests.

Cars arrived at the farmhouse with small clouds of summer dust swirling in the headlights. Men in uniform got out and left the engines running. They came walking straight into the inner yard as though they had been invited, ignoring the barking dog. The guests looked up. The music stopped and those who were dancing froze in their steps as the commanding officer stood by and said—don't let me disturb you. Please, continue. He gestured toward the quartet of musicians and told them to strike up again. He had no intention of bringing the festivities to an end, he was just there to congratulate the wedding couple. Keep the dance going, he said, it's such a beautiful night—look at the stars. The musicians were forced to resume playing against their will. The people on the wooden dance floor carried on their agonizing movements with the stiffness of life-size puppets, dancing to the most melancholy score.

Professor Glückstein was led away to one of the barns nearby, where they sat him down on a wooden milking stool. They took his bride, Angela, to another barn on the far side. They were questioned through the night by the light of the lanterns. The quartet carried on playing for an hour or so into exhaustion, while the remaining officers searched through the farmhouse and the barns. It sounded as though a fox had got in with the chickens. Some of the animals were allowed to wander, the cows standing in the yard as though they had come out to listen to the music. The men were wasting their time. His wealth, his knowledge, her work, her ideas, their conversations, their happiness, the day they'd stood by the sundial and buried her broken blue fountain pen, even the elusive map he'd drawn at the back of a book—everything had been placed beyond reach. By morning, the farm had been turned upside down, but nothing was found. The guests were still awake, standing in a silent group at the steps of the house as the professor and his bride were taken away, sleepless and defiant, never to see one another again. The wedding became their final night together. They were driven away in separate cars. A cavalcade of limousines moving slowly along the avenue of trees until they were gone out of sight.

47

THIS HAS BROUGHT MY TRAVELING TO AN END. AT THE center of a large exhibition space in Berlin, I now find myself lying on a small table. Next to it is a single chair. Every fifteen minutes, an actor comes to sit down at the table to read a random passage, lasting about a minute. Some well-known names from the theater world have been taking part. Voices familiar from TV and cinema as well as some people from the music industry have freely given their time, building up quite a crowd around the table.

According to the exhibition notes, visitors are encouraged to sit down and read a passage for themselves. They are free to touch, feel, hold, read, examine the exhibits as they wish. One of them will occasionally pick up the blue fountain pen with the tag from the repair shop which lies on a separate table, next to the leather pouch and the metal box in which it lay hidden for so many years. Another visitor will go so far as to study the map at the back of the book and place a little finger into the small hole where the bullet entered. A circular wound at the tail end of the title, partially obscuring the final letter in the word—*Rebellion*. Held up to the light, they can see clean through to the exit wound at the back. As they leaf through the pages, they can follow the course taken by the bullet like the burrowing of a worm through the text. The aperture is quite small, nine-millimeter caliber, shot from a Glock handgun.

Another table has been set up with a white bowl containing human ash. Some of the media have referred to the exhibition as a funeral in art. A critic at the *Morgenpost* felt it was honoring the deceased by scattering the ashes in a metaphorical sense. Others have been critical of such a public display of human remains. A visitor can occasionally be seen picking up one of the three shrapnel fragments in the bowl, which is fine—the idea of placing an exhibit like this under glass or asking people not to touch the objects would make it meaningless. It is the artist's intention to bring the viewer as close as possible to that invisible border crossing between life and death.

One of the walls carries a display of images, or screen grabs, taken from a piece of newsreel footage. The footage was shot by an Austrian television crew at the height of the Second Chechen War. It shows two children, a boy and a girl, at a hospital in the aftermath of a bombing which killed their parents. The girl is frightened. She cannot understand the sight of the wide stump of bandages where her leg has gone missing. Her expression is frozen in a prolonged state of shock, afraid to cry, looking around for her mother, waiting for somebody to explain the situation to her. She is being comforted by the nursing staff as best they can. Some of them are running along the corridor and there is a sense of panic in their faces because the bombing outside continues. They have no idea what part of the hospital might still be safe for them to take the children.

Visitors can find these scenes distressing to look at until they come to another set of photographic images showing the children in their adult years. Pictures of the brother and sister both laughing as he puts his arm around her and she shows off her prosthetic leg. Another image shows her wearing a swimsuit, standing in a lake north of Berlin on a summer evening with the sun behind her and the water reaching just above her knees. Her missing leg is concealed as though the lake from which she is emerging has found a way of undoing the bomb blast of her childhood in Chechnya, keeping the story of her life hidden underneath the surface.

The central piece in the collection displays a recent diagnostic image of the boy as a grown man, still carrying the injuries from that event in the war. The X-ray clearly shows three shrapnel fragments inside the body of a living person, which can then be contrasted to the fragments inside the body of the same person in the form of ash.

Going by medical evidence entered at the murder trial, the bullet hit Armin close to the heart. His lungs filled up with blood. He died of asphyxiation. The bullet could not be added as part of the exhibition for obvious reasons, because it became a key piece of evidence for the prosecution. It was described by ballistics experts in court as a high-quality round, enhanced with a toughened steel casing around the lead core. It had been reshaped, or misshaped, by contact with various obstacles on its way. It passed through the story of the man with the barrel organ without encountering any resistance, through the hand-drawn map at the back, roughly corresponding with the location near the oak tree where the body of the deceased man was ultimately recovered.

They had done their best to escape, running into the central yard past the pump with the cast-iron handle, past the derelict barn where the horses were once kept, out along the path where they were hoping to disappear into the forest, into that silent maze where trees duplicate themselves into infinity. Armin was carrying Lena's bag and holding her hand as they ran. Then he let go and sank to the ground. Lena kneeled down by his side and tried to keep him alive, lifting his head and asking him questions to stop him from losing consciousness. Did he still remember standing on the bridge with her, and the bar with the table made from a scrapped bumper car, and could he recall the fridge magnets, what was the one nearest to his heart, was it the bottle of Russian vodka? He did not respond to these questions, other than making a choking sound at the back of his throat. She continued speaking to him, even though it was clear that he could not hear her. She was saying his name, telling him that she would stay with him, she was going to call for help.

On the opening night the curator of the exhibition, Julia Fernreich, addressed the gathering of visitors and introduced Armin's sister, inviting her to say a few words. Madina spoke about how she and her brother had come to Germany as children with the help of an aunt who employed traffickers. They had been brought up by a wonderful family in Frankfurt, she said with a wave—their adoptive mother was in the audience. Madina recalled how, as a boy, Armin used to tickle her missing foot. It was funny, she said, that whenever he tried to tickle the existing foot, the living foot, it never bothered her. He could go at it with feathers, forks, a toothbrush, the bow of a violin, the dried claw of a turkey their parents kept over the door in the hall—nothing would make her budge. She could have lain there with her arms folded for a thousand years, she said, and he would not even have made her laugh. It was only when he began to tickle the amputated foot that she was forced to screech. She would pull the missing leg away and hide it under the pillows, begging him to stop—no, Armin, not my gone foot, please.

She then picked up the accordion and sang an acoustic version of her song—"No Time for Bones."

When Lena was asked to say a few words, she said that anything she had in mind was inadequate for the emotions she was feeling. She decided instead to read out a piece of text from one of the exhibits along the wall—a passage by Joseph Roth, in his tiny handwriting.

. . . it was not yet a matter of indifference whether a person lived or died. When somebody disappeared from among the living, that person was not immediately replaced, a gap remained, and those who knew, or even half-knew, the dead person went silent whenever they came across that gap. When a fire destroyed a house in a terrace of houses, the ruin was left empty for a long time. Builders worked slowly and thoughtfully, and those who passed by continued to remember the shape of the missing house. That's how it was back then! Everything that grew needed a lot of time to grow; and everything that came to an end took a long time to be erased. Everything that existed once left its trace, and people lived by their memory, just as they now live in a rush to forget.

48

THE ASSASSIN STOOD OVER HIS VICTIM AND PICKED UP Lena's bag. He pulled her away by the arm and she called on every self-defense move she had learned as a girl in Philadelphia until he raised his gun to her head. She thought of something else, calling out a random name to distract the attacker long enough that she could speed-dial for help on her phone.

Julia, she shouted.

Bogdanov didn't buy it. He said she could scream as much as she liked, nobody would hear her above the noise of the pig farm next door. He took her phone and forced her to walk back to one of the outhouses. Not the barn with the swing but the stable where the horses had once been kept. The roof had partially fallen in and the doors were off the hinges. He pushed her inside, into a corner where she collided with a metal hoop once used to tie horses.

He emptied the contents of her bag on the ground and the mutilated page fell open, showing the swastika. This made him laugh out loud. He opened the leather pouch and found the blue pen inside. It was a great disappointment. He had expected a better reward for his supremacy, some treasure, perhaps, instead of this broken and worthless personal artifact. He threw the pen on the ground with disdain and turned toward Lena as though she represented more immediate value to him than the contents of the pouch.

It was initially unclear who intervened at that point. Could it be possible, I wondered, that Armin had found the strength to stand up and run to her defense? It came as a double surprise to discover that it was Mike after all who stood there holding the half-length potato fork in his hand, an apparition in answer to her call.

How did he know Lena was there?

What made him come looking for her? Was it love? Devotion, jealousy, control, obsession, possession, that single-minded male attachment, whatever it is that makes a person think they own another person and not wish to let them out of sight even for a minute? He loved her so badly that he engaged his considerable IT expertise to find out that she was not going to join him on his planned Operation Happiness to Transylvania, that his marriage was in doubt and things might be falling apart. He tracked her to this location with the intention of confronting her. He was behind her all the way, following her footsteps in the form of a dot on-screen. Guiding himself to the farm with the assistance of a digital copy of the hand-drawn map she had once sent to his phone.

If only he had been there to discover the item hidden under the sundial with her. He had forfeited the chance of being the finder of this inheritance from the past and was now making up for it by stepping in to rescue her at the most crucial time. He heard the single gunshot echoing through the forest, wrapping itself in high frequency around the trees. He heard her voice calling. He heard the sound of a metal ring clanging. It took him a while to navigate his way around the empty farm buildings, but he eventually came across the half-length fork and ran with it back through the open barn door, managing to avoid the swing on his way. He stood for an agonizing moment in the central yard like a contestant in a live reality show, facing a multitude of options, spinning around to guess which direction to take. He almost ran the wrong way and turned back at the last minute on a hunch, arriving at the entrance to the derelict stables with only seconds left to spare. Without a further thought, he swung the fork through the air and struck Bogdanov across the side of the face, releasing a sustained musical note that rang out like the opening strain at a concert. Bogdanov turned with an expression of rage and made a counterattacking movement, but the fork struck a second note, followed by a soundless stab that drove him back against a disused horse trough.

Everything paused.

Lena stood without moving and looked into Mike's eyes as though she was more shocked by his sudden presence than by everything that had just taken place. He rushed forward and threw his arms around her.

Are you okay?

Behind them, Bogdanov was attempting to sit up and fight another day. Staring with incomprehension at the sight of blood leaking from his shoulder. He clutched at the source of the pain and sank back against the trough, too exhausted to do any more than sleep.

Mike gathered up the pen and the leather pouch and placed them in Lena's bag. He even had the presence of mind to pick me up, finally realizing how much I meant to her. He saw the trajectory of the bullet going through the text. The wounded book in his hands made him aware of how close he had come to being the ultimate recipient of that bullet. The pagination of holes aligned themselves into a high-velocity tunnel that left behind the shape of hatred. It was part of my life story now. The death of a reader. The murder of a man who had once entered my pages and made me human.

A sense of relief must have brought a million conflicting questions as Lena felt Mike's arm around her shoulders. She heard the security in his voice as he led her out into the open, and maybe she began to wonder about his unexpected appearance in this remote place, his technological omniscience, that extraordinary skill of surveillance with which he had managed to turn up so late and so punctual, placing her into that helpless role of a rescued person.

She broke free and ran back to the oak tree where Armin lay at the edge of the path, unprotected, one arm stretched into the weeds. She kneeled by his side and held his hand. He was no longer alive, but she continued speaking to him as though he were. She cried and said she was sorry—it was her fault for bringing him out to this place where he was so exposed. She spoke about the different ways in which she would remember him. She would stay close to his sister. They would remain best friends.

Armin, she said. Are you cold?

She took her jacket off and laid it across his chest. She rubbed his hand. She held his face.

Standing beside her and holding her bag, Mike began phoning the emergency services. He thought of the practicalities, giving the precise coordinates. He told them not to take the road to the pig farm but the next one after that. There was no sign, the entrance to the farm was obscured by some laurel trees, he told them, but they would see the apple orchard and the red-brick gateposts. Once they got to the yard, they needed to keep going all the way to the stables with the sunken roof, there was a man injured and another man dead by the oak tree. He would be standing on the path to guide them.

Lena flattened some of the weeds and cleared a space for herself to sit down. She took Armin's head onto her lap and began rocking back and forth, humming and saying his name over and over again. His body temperature was gradually dropping to match the earth beneath him, but he seemed still to be listening while Lena was singing.

Mike stood watching as though part of himself lay dead there under the oak tree with a bullet in his back. He became a spectator looking at himself lying motionless in the grass, staring at the sky. He turned into the person he saw before him, the dead man, the murdered man, the man slipping into the past tense, the person in her heart he had once been. The man with whom she sat dreaming under a stone wall one afternoon in the west of Ireland as they sheltered from the rain and the wind in a hollow scratched out by sheep. The man who stood with her in front of a painting by Georg Baselitz at the Tate Gallery in London and said—you can do that. The man with whom she spoke about having a family and who now stood listening as she was calling a child into life with a wordless lullaby.

She raised her head and stared away across the flat landscape. She stopped singing and spoke quietly to the line of trees on the horizon, not so much adding a child to the world but replacing one.

He was born in Grozny, she said. He told me that he could remember his mother once going out to buy bread. She hid the loaf under her coat, but another woman followed them and tried to steal it from her. There was a fight over the bread in the street and his mother had to let go. After he became an orphan and was brought to Germany and grew up with a family in Frankfurt, he used to ask his adoptive mother every morning—are we going to eat tonight? She would smile and say—yes, of course. Then he went off to school happy.

A new breeze came across the fields. The forest began to sway and the wind inhaled through the trees with all its strength. The oak leaves made the sound of tinfoil as they rolled along the path. The crow sounded bigger unseen. Three solid calls in a row. Followed by one more separate caw. Then a big silence. Then two more.

Author's Note

The idea of the book rescued from the Nazi book burning in 1933 comes from a true story related to me by Henning Horn in Magdeburg. His account of the banned book kept hidden by his family through the years of the Third Reich brought to mind the famous connection drawn between books and human beings by the German Jewish writer Heinrich Heine—wherever they burn books, they will end up burning human beings. Those words are written on a plaque at the site of the book burning on Bebelplatz in Berlin, where people once stood around to watch the outlawed books being incinerated and where they now stand looking down through a glass floor showing an underground room full of empty white bookshelves to remember that event. The words continue to resonate a century later, not only because they warn us about censorship and human rights abuses, but also because they can be turned around by a single act of courage to be read as—wherever they save a book from burning, they will end up saving human beings.

The lives of Joseph Roth and his wife, Friederike Roth, have been drawn from various biographies and essay collections,

AUTHOR'S NOTE

including the work of David Bronsen, Wilhelm von Sternburg, Michael Bienert, Soma Morgenstern, Géza von Cziffra, Irmgard Keun, Volker Weidermann, Michael Hofmann, and Claudio Magris, among others. Details on Friederike's illness are taken from the case notes of psychiatric hospitals at Rekawinkel and Steinhof, now housed in the public archives of the city of Vienna. Translations from Roth's work and other documents are my own. Details on the Second Chechen War are taken from the work of the murdered Russian journalist Anna Politkovskaya. The concept of the wounded book in this novel was inspired by the German artist Christiane Wartenberg and taken from an exhibition of her work which was shown by the Haus der Brandenburgisch-Preussischen Geschichte in Potsdam in May 2019.

I would like to thank Tessa Hadley, Roddy Doyle, Sebastian Barry, Colum McCann, John Banville, Eimear McBride, Neil Jordan, and Sinéad Gleeson for their generous words of encouragement. I thank my editor, Nicholas Pearson at 4th Estate, HarperCollins, for his great support since the publication of *The Speckled People*. Thanks to my German editors, Grusche Juncker and Regina Kammerer at Luchterhand, Random House, for giving life to this book in my mother's language. In particular, I want to thank my agents, Peter Straus in London and Petra Eggers in Berlin. Also to Stephen Edwards and Cathy King. And warmest gratitude to Reagan Arthur at Knopf. Thanks to Hans-Christian Oeser for his wise comments at an early stage and also to Joe Joyce, Terence Heron, and Tim Norton for their valuable insight on certain questions that came up during the writing. Many thanks to Silvia Crompton, Marigold Atkey, and all the team at 4th Estate. I appreciate the support of the Arts Council of Ireland—*mo mhíle buíochas*.

Mostly it's all thanks to Mary Rose Doorly.

I keep in mind the struggle of Joseph Roth in the 1930s, when he was cut off from his reading public after his books were banned in Nazi Germany. I think of the publishers in exile who kept faith with him when he was fighting for his life as a writer. I think of the great friendship of his fellow writer Stefan Zweig, who kept him on his feet when he became destitute. Writing was his only way of being alive, Roth said of himself. It was his survival, his refuge, his identity, his only true sense of belonging in a world from which he had been expelled. I like to imagine that Joseph Roth would be happy to hold this book in his hands today and that we could raise a glass together in his favorite restaurant in Paris, where the waitress kept his manuscripts safe from the Nazis. His work and his life stand as a witness to history. Even if the rescue of one book was never enough to save the life of Friederike Roth from the fire, I hope that she has now been given a safe place in our memory.

I am also aware that a hundred years ago, as a star reporter for the *Frankfurter Zeitung*, Joseph Roth went on a journey through the industrial heartland of the Ruhr Valley and described the cities being joined together by smoke. And perhaps this is the ultimate proof of optimism and change, that a century later an abandoned steel-making plant covering a vast area of land near the city of Duisburg has become one of Europe's greatest rewilding projects. With the help of volunteers, nature has been steadily reclaiming the spaces between those rusted towers and elevators and iron-ore silos with trees and wildflowers and insect life. People come at weekends to walk and cycle for many kilometers through this strange parkland. The derelict shapes cast abstract shadows. The sun going down turns the metal parts bright orange. The wind can sometimes produce the most haunting range of musical notes. Yes—like a barrel organ.

A NOTE ABOUT THE AUTHOR

Hugo Hamilton is the author of the memoirs *The Speckled People* (a *New York Times* Notable Book, hailed as a "masterpiece" by Colm Tóibín, translated into fifteen languages, and the winner of prizes in France and Italy) and *The Harbor Boys,* both about his extraordinary upbringing in a German-Irish household in which the English language was forbidden. Also the author of five novels, one collection of short stories, and an original play, he has been awarded the Order of Merit of the Federal Republic of Germany for his unique contribution to literature and cross-cultural understanding. He lives in Dublin.

A NOTE ON THE TYPE

This book was set in Hoefler Text, a family of fonts designed by Jonathan Hoefler, who was born in 1970. First designed in 1991, Hoefler Text was intended as an advancement on existing desktop computer typography, including as it does an exponentially larger number of glyphs than previous fonts. In form, Hoefler Text looks to the old-style fonts of the seventeenth century, but it is wholly of its time, employing a precision and sophistication only available to the late twentieth century.

Composed by North Market Street Graphics,
Lancaster, Pennsylvania

Printed and bound by Berryville Graphics,
Berryville, Virginia

Designed by Soonyoung Kwon